If Onions Could Spring Leeks

Paige Shelton
Cover credit: Spbookcovers

i

By Paige Shelton

Farmers' Market Mysteries

FARM FRESH MURDER

FRUIT OF ALL EVIL

CROPS AND ROBBERS

A KILLER MAIZE

MERRY MARKET MURDER

BUSHEL FULL OF MURDER

Country Cooking School Mysteries

IF FRIED CHICKEN COULD FLY

IF MASHED POTATOES COULD DANCE

IF BREAD COULD RISE TO THE OCCASION

IF CATFISH HAD NINE LIVES

IF ONIONS COULD SPRING LEEKS

Specials

RED HOT DEADLY PEPPERS

Dangerous Type Mysteries

TO HELVETICA AND BACK

BOOKMAN DEAD STYLE

COMIC SANS MURDER

Scottish Bookshop Mysteries

THE CRACKED SPINE

OF BOOKS AND BAGPIPES

A CHRISTMAS TARTAN

LOST BOOKS AND OLD BONES

THE LOCH NESS PAPERS

ii

For the Level 1 Trauma Team at the University of Missouri hospital. Thank you for the miracles you so skillfully performed.

The last couple of years have been a whirlwind of changes and challenges. Thanks to those who have kept me on track and who forgave me when I forgot something. Extra thanks to my agent, Jessica Faust and my editor, Michelle Vega.

There's a group of very special people out there. I don't know them all, but I do know some. An extra-extra special thank you to book bloggers and anyone who takes the time to spread the word about the books they enjoy. You truly make all the difference.

As always, thanks to my guys, Charlie and Tyler. I don't know what I'd do without your nerdy senses of humor. And Charlie, my willing and helpful research partner. If he hadn't turned the car around to go back to the building I thought I saw deep in the Missouri woods, I'm not sure what this story would have been. Thanks for not letting me fall through the floors.

Chapter One

At first the mournful whistle sounded far away and lonely. I was asleep and I liked the noise, as though it were part of a sad but hopeful dream. But then it became less a part of the dream and more the thing that was waking me up.

I sat up in bed and tried to gather my weary senses. I was home. Cliff wasn't with me. Why? I remembered - he was in St. Louis picking up some equipment. He should be back tomorrow, or was that later today?

The train whistle sounded again, its volume much louder and its pitch high enough that it would surely hurt my ears if I were standing close to it.

I didn't live anywhere near train tracks.

"Oh. Not true," I said aloud with a sleep-cragged voice.

Clumsily, I rolled out of bed. I pulled a shirt and some shorts out of my dresser and threw them on over my nightshirt. I grabbed my phone, noticing that it was 3.04 in the morning, and hurried through and then out of the house, stopping short when I got to my small front porch.

My house was located on a dead-end street, the dead-end part, the spot where now there was just an open field of neglected grass, was once home to the Broken Rope train station. In its heyday and before Route 66 was *the* Route 66, this spot of Missouri saw lots of train traffic, and the area where my house was now located had been a thoroughfare, busy with travelers coming and going. I wasn't old enough to have any memories of the station, of course, but my best friend and the town historian, Jake, had shown me pictures. Black and white renditions of women in tight-waisted long dresses and hats that made my neck ache just by looking at them, and men in heavy suits and ties posing in front of oily black engines that spat out white clouds of steam. There weren't many smiles in those pictures. I liked to tease Jake that it was because those posing for the pictures were so miserable in their heavy, tight, and itchy clothing. He insisted that it was because back then everyone had such lousy teeth.

The field was five houses away, and currently no longer a field. Well, it probably still was a field, but I was seeing it differently. I was seeing it as it was back during the late 1800s when those long skirts and thick suits were all the rage, and back when people dressed up when they traveled.

I was both concerned and fascinated, but more intrigued than anything else. I knew what was going on and it wasn't an unusual occurrence—for me, as well as for my gram, Missouri Anna Winston. I'd become used to seeing and communicating with ghosts from Broken Rope's past, so I knew the scene being played out at the end of the street was something that would contain at least one specter searching for attention from someone still alive. Mostly, my and my grandmother's ghosts were pretty harmless, but there were moments when the danger they brought with them was real and present-day, and potentially deadly.

I stepped slowly and carefully down the porch steps, pausing again at the bottom. The train I'd heard approaching the station came into view nose-first, its squeaky brakes and loud whistle announcing that it was about to stop completely. I sniffed deeply and found a scent—flowers, a big, assorted bouquet of flowers. Or was that a neighbor's garden? I couldn't be totally sure, but the scent was so strong, so pure, that I thought that it was most likely attached to a visiting ghost.

The station platform was on the other side of the slowing train, so my view of whatever was going on there was about to be blocked. I looked around, confirmed that no one was watching me or peering through their windows, and then hurried down the street. I stepped in front of the now stationary locomotive and over the seemingly very real train tracks. Those few steps transported me almost fully into the past. Different than some time I'd spent in an old bakery, I could still see my house and neighborhood in their present-day state, though all the houses, streetlights, and cars were dim and murky and much less real than the feel of the wood planks shifting with my weight as I moved onto the platform.

The station was a long, wide, one-story building that ran along the back of the platform, made of what looked like the same pinewood planks under my feet. There were two doors in its middle, both currently open wide. To the right of the doors was a small window where I assumed long-ago tickets had been purchased. I stepped toward the doors and peered inside. There were two more ticket booths along one wall. The rest of the space was filled with rows of benches, also made of the same pinewood. The handiwork on the benches was much more utilitarian than I might have pictured it to be. Perhaps it was the movies of my time that made me think of curved, ornate arms and slanted backs, but these benches were simple, straight-backed seats that must have offered respite to only the weariest of travelers. The row of windows along the back wall seemed odd in a couple of ways. Daylight streamed through them, and they were made of glass and what looked like fancy wrought-iron frames. They looked almost elegant against the light pine everywhere. The contrast of the thick Missouri woods bathed in bright sunlight on the other side of the windows made me wonder why and when all the trees had been razed to make way for the present-day vacant grass field that now extended at least a hundred yards back.

As I turned toward the train, more images began to appear. With faded beginnings, people quickly formed and solidified, becoming dimensional and bathed in the same long-ago sunlight that lit the trees.

"But, Papa, I'm so very hungry," a small girl with black curls and big green eyes said to a man with matching features who held her hand tightly.

"I know, Mary, but we'll spoil our dinner if we eat the peanuts right now. Save them. Grandmama will have dinner on the table when we get there. Don't ask me again."

"All right," she said with a sigh of disappointment.

With her bottom lip stuck out, she looked up at me. I smiled and waved, but she didn't respond, didn't even blink. Did she not see me?

An older gentleman who was still spry enough to be moving at a quick clip had his eyes on the pocket watch he held as he beelined directly toward me. I stepped to the side, but not quickly enough to avoid him completely. His left arm went right through me. I felt nothing, but it was one of those weird ghost things that I would probably never get used to.

It seemed that none of these ghosts saw me, which was a first. Usually, if there was a ghost in the general vicinity, they could see and communicate with both me and Gram. It was what I thought "this" was all about—we could see and talk to them because they could see and talk to us. But the ghost rules had already proved to be fluid, changing at least a little bit with each new ghostly guest.

I wondered what was going on, but didn't sense any danger. I decided I could either go home and go back to bed or stay and wait for whatever happened next, discover if anyone would "see" me eventually.

So many ghosts materialized that the platform became crowded. Even though I could not feel anyone's touch or any sort of breeze their movements stirred up, I became uncomfortable and a little claustrophobic. No one was dodging me, and it was impossible for me to dodge everyone else, so I wove my way to a spot close to the building's doors and out of the main streams of traffic. I heard their voices as they hurried to purchase tickets and sped toward the train or from it and toward whoever was greeting them. I saw their faces and expressions clearly, but still no one saw me.

My fascination with this step back into another time wore thinner with each passing moment. It was late and I did have to get up early the next morning. Perhaps I could ignore all the noise that I was almost a hundred percent sure I'd still hear from my house and catch a few more hours' sleep. But just as I made that decision, something changed.

The scent of flowers grew stronger, filling my nose so fully that a small twinge of sinus pain shot through my head. It mellowed quickly, becoming lighter and pleasant.

A ghost came through the doors, stepping from the inside of the station to the outside platform. She was stunning; the kind of beautiful that made it almost impossible to look away from her. I wanted to study her, see the specifics of her appeal. Since I didn't think she could see me, I figured I could stare all I wanted.

She was tall and small-waisted—probably from a tight corset—she was curvy enough not to be called skinny, but thin enough not to be called chubby. Her neck was long and swanlike. Her dark skin was smooth and flawless and she had high, delicate cheeks. Her nose was button, but for some reason it fit well with her grown-up features. The sadness in her brown eyes was so palpable that when they pooled with tears my heart ached sympathetically.

"I'm so sorry," I said quietly.

She looked at me, blinked back the tears and then opened her eyes wide. "Oh my, dear, where are your clothes? Here, let me give you my coat." She made a move to unbutton the thin outer layer that looked like it was part of her dress.

"Oh," I said as I looked at myself. "No, I'm fine, thank you anyway. You can hear me? See me?"

"Of course, silly thing, but what are you doing without so much as some good underpinnings on?"

As she continued to unbutton, the scene changed again. Suddenly, it was just she and I on the platform. The steam engine remained and puttered in the background. All the other ghosts disappeared.

She looked up and around and then at me. "Gracious, this is odd. Where did everyone go?" She stopped unbuttoning and took a large step toward the locomotive. Her fingers moved to a simple chain around her neck.

"Uh . . . I'm Betts, Isabelle Winston," I said as I stepped next to her.

"This is all strange because it's not part of what is happening in present time. My grandmother is Missouri Anna Winston. Perhaps you know her?"

She looked at me and blinked. "I do not know your grandmother and I don't quite understand what you mean. At all."

Since the ghosts' memories were sometimes scrambled when they first arrived, it could take time for them to acclimate, but if this was this ghost's first visit it would also be my first visit without Gram to help me through the introductions. I thought about one of our previous experiences.

"May I ask your name?" I said.

"Grace," she said absently as she searched the platform.

"Well, Grace, this is bound to be strange, but you are currently visiting the twenty-first century. This scene," I waved my arm, "is something from the past." I swallowed hard before I said the next part because it seemed so cruel, but Gram had told me that there was no need to be delicate. The ghosts' realization that they were no longer a part of the living world couldn't possibly harm them, and the sooner they knew the truth the better it was for them, and for her and me.

"Can you tell me what you think the date is?" I said.

"Of course. It's August 16, 1888."

"Actually, it isn't. You died long ago, Grace. You're just back visiting Broken Rope, a long time after you lived. I and my Gram are the only ones you will be able to communicate with."

"I don't understand. I'm in Broken Rope?"

I was surprised that this was the most curious part of what I'd just told her, but I said, "Yes."

"I made it then, I made it," she said as she stepped back, turned and looked around. "Is he here?"

"Who?"

"Robert. Is he here?" She continued to search.

"I don't see anyone else around," I said. "There were other people here a few minutes ago, but I don't know who Robert is."

"Oh, oh no. This isn't right," she said.

"What isn't right?"

"This is not the Broken Rope station," she said.

I felt words of protest rise in my throat—how could this be another station? We were in Broken Rope. But then I realized she might be right. I stepped away from the building and looked around. I thought about the pictures Jake had shown me, and though the people in their interesting clothing and the oily black locomotive were parts of what I had seen, the station building I was currently looking at was not. In the pictures, the building had been diminished, a part of the backdrop, but I knew it had not been an uninteresting one-story made of simple, boring pine planks. In fact, I remembered that at one time Jake had gone on and on about the station building and how it had been an attraction in itself, how it was something he wished could be rebuilt for the tourists to see and experience. I tried hard to remember the building details, but I just hadn't found it as interesting as the people and the trains.

"Where are we?" I asked Grace as I peered out toward my house. It was still there in the murky distance. I was relieved.

"I'm not sure," she said. "But . . ."

I looked at the building, searching for a name, a town, a signpost of some sort. There was nothing. In fact, there were no words anywhere.

"Grace," I said, "who is Robert?"

She blinked and then turned her confused attention toward me. "Robert Findlay was the man I was supposed to marry. I was to meet him in Broken Rope, and we were going to run away together."

"Run away?" I said. "Why did you need to run away?"

"We had to find a place we would be accepted. I'm from

Mississippi, Robert was from Broken Rope. We were going to go north, perhaps as far north as we could go."

"Accepted?" I said, but then I thought I understood what she was getting at.

"Yes. Of course, a white man marrying a negro woman is not welcome in many parts."

I cringed at the word *negro*, but I had to remember that in 1888 that word wasn't unsettling or racist, and an interracial marriage most definitely wouldn't have been welcomed back then, or, sadly, for some time afterward.

"Do you think you didn't make it to Broken Rope?" I said.

Grace fell into thought and I was once again taken aback by her beauty. She was not pretty in a youthful way, but in a wise and strong but slightly sad way. It would be easy to see how men, and women too, of all different colors would have found their eyes drawn to her.

"I don't know. Wait, I do think I made it to Broken Rope." She glanced at the building, her eyebrows coming together. "I don't know what or where this station is, though."

"Your station, from Mississippi maybe? Was this the beginning of your trip?"

"No, I really don't think so. I don't remember the station from Mississippi, but something tells me this isn't it." She paused, stared blankly at the planks of the platform, and then looked back at me. "Something terrible happened to me, I'm almost sure. Do you know what that was?"

"I don't. Try to remember some specifics," I said.

A long few beats later, she said, "I was killed, murdered, I think."

"Grace," I said as I stepped closer to her. I reached for her hand, glad it was solid. "Listen to me, you can't die twice. You're probably getting a bunch of jumbled memories coming at you at once, and that's normal, I promise. But you don't need to be sad or worried or afraid. You died a long time ago. Whatever you remember can't hurt you anymore, and things will become clearer—if you give it time and allow yourself the memories. You will know."

Grace looked at me briefly, but her anxious eyes were still focused on the past. It was long ago, but I still didn't understand how the passing of time worked for the ghosts.

"I was killed, murdered, that I'm sure of, though I don't understand *how* I'm so sure. I would never have abandoned Robert. Never." She looked at the station. "But perhaps I never did make it to Broken Rope.

Oh, dear. He must have thought I didn't want to join him. I don't understand. Is there any chance you can help me understand?"

I sighed inwardly, but I tried not to let it show too much. There was a time not long ago that I would have said there was probably nothing I could do to help her. I wouldn't have been cruel enough to tell her that the answers just didn't matter anyway. The past was the past and dead was dead. But my perspective had changed. I had been able to "do things." I had been able to help—maybe just a little, and while the historical facts hadn't been altered, little changes had been made, little changes that somehow helped the ghosts deal with their tragic situations, though I didn't totally understand what that meant. It didn't matter that I never knew the end results. I was glad to be of some small assistance.

I looked at her, squeezed her hand as I smiled, and said, "Maybe."

15

Chapter Two

I made it back to bed at around 4:00 A.M., able to easily fall back to sleep and catch a couple more hours' rest. That was something else that had changed. My visits with the ghosts didn't keep me up all night. I didn't spend as much time worrying about them or trying to figure out exactly what I could do for them. I wanted to help if I could, but I was beginning to take them more in stride. But as I swung my legs off my bed again, happy that I wasn't too worn out, I recognized my own casual attitude and a chill zipped up my back.

"These are ghosts we're talking about," I said aloud to myself. "They are beings that aren't supposed to exist. I should never, ever consider them just another part of my day or night, or as something not to worry about."

My words were greeted by silence. I looked at the doorway and took a big sniff just to see if, perhaps, someone might have appeared. No unusual or strong smells. No scent of wood smoke. No cowboy-hat-clad silhouette filling the space. No Jerome.

My first ghost, Jerome Cowbender, and I had formed a complicated relationship. I had a crush on the old dead cowboy; I was pretty sure he had a crush on me. Of course, as a *real* relationship, it could never work; ghosts and live people should probably not develop crushes on each other. The heart does what the heart does, though, no matter how much you will it not to.

I thought I'd gotten better. During Jerome's last visit, I hadn't kissed him on the lips—this was a good start. I told him we needed to quit flirting. He'd agreed.

Fortunately my live boyfriend, Cliff, and I had continued to expand our relationship. Things had only gotten better and better between the two of us. We'd been high school sweethearts, but a decade or so later, after a few career changes, post his marriage and divorce and his return to Broken Rope, we had what I thought was a bright new outlook on the kind of couple we could be. Things were going great.

Except for one thing. Okay, well, maybe two.

The first one was that Cliff was a smart guy and he had sensed that something wasn't quite right. I'd tried not to let my weird and probably morally corrupt feelings for the dead ghost (whom he could neither see nor communicate with) show. I'd tried to make those feelings disappear, actually. But Cliff had picked up on the fact that there was something "in between" us, something keeping me from jumping all the way into what Cliff and I could be. I told him that the "something" wasn't his imagination, but it also wasn't something he needed to be concerned about. There was a very weird component in my life that might make me seem distracted, but it didn't change how I felt about him. I even offered to tell him what it was if he really, truly wanted to know. But he needed to be more than one hundred percent sure he wanted to know because— and I said this a million times—it was unquestionably weird. Before he left for the weekend, he mentioned that he decided he wanted to know the full story, and he wanted to hear it this week when he got back. My mind was working double-time to try to figure out the best way to tell him the truth. I was ready and willing, but still working on the right combination of words and the best approach.

The second thing was simply this: No matter how much I loved Cliff, how often I saw us having a future together, how much stronger we had become, how I told him that he didn't need to be concerned about my feelings for him—and I believed that statement, mostly—I still could not stop thinking about Jerome. I tried. I beat myself up over it. But it didn't work. This was not good, of course, and Cliff deserved better. Unfortunately, I was just selfish enough that I wanted him to accept the messed-up me. I wanted my live man and my ghost, too.

I glanced at the doorway one more time.

No Jerome.

As I got ready, I decided I would find Jake later and discuss Grace and her situation with him. Though he couldn't see or communicate with them either, he knew all about the ghosts and was typically more than willing to lend a hand in uncovering their histories. For now, I forced the majority of my thoughts away from the ghosts and toward present-day activities.

Summer in Broken Rope was our busy tourist season. All of Gram's and my most recent crop of full-time cooking students had recently completed their nine-month training and were off beginning or continuing their food-centered careers. The school year had been unusual and punctuated by murder and danger, but then ultimately successful, turning out some stunning cooks and bakers. We were as proud as we could be and hoped next fall's students would be even better.

As the classes wound down and we kicked off the part-time evening classes with Vegetables and Why Cheese Makes Them All Taste Better, I had been recruited to assist with a new Broken Rope summer tourist attraction. One of our part-time night students (we called them "nighters"), Roy Acres, presented a proposition to the vegetable class: Did anyone want to help him with his one of his inventions? It seemed that Jake had originally approached Roy with the idea of motorized wagons. Big Old West wagons, not small red ones.

Roy was not only a country boy with a heart as big as all of Missouri, he'd also been trained as a mechanical engineer. Through the fine art of what he called "tinkering" he'd created more farm machinery around Broken Rope than you could shake a tractor at.

His experiments and inventions could be found in barns and on farms all around Missouri. Perhaps there were even some in Kansas. Most were successful and useful, but not all. Jake had attached one of Roy's fertilizing implements to his riding mower. Unfortunately, things weren't balanced correctly and the getup didn't move quite right. After narrowly escaping the mower's lethal blade when it tipped over and landed precariously close to Jake's leg, the attachment was removed and discarded. Roy abandoned that particular idea. However, he still had lots of successful inventions; one of them being his motorized wagons. He'd made three, all of them fondly named Trigger, followed by the numbers one, two, or three. They were exactly what they sounded like: wagons with motors and steering wheels. Roy had created them because of growing concern about the horses—well, both the horses and the tourists that filled the town's Main Street during the summer. Broken Rope's popularity had continued to grow. We had more tourists than ever visiting our little town. In years past, we'd used horse-drawn wagons to escort people down Main Street, pointing out and talking up the highlights. The horses never seemed to mind and the crowd was controllable enough to stay on the boardwalks. Not so much anymore. Neither the horses nor the tourists were having as much fun lately. There was just too much activity. So Roy created the wagons, and they'd become one of our more popular attractions. Everyone loved to ride the funny-looking things that seemed like a cross between a wagon and a jalopy. The tourists were happier, so were the horses.

Not only were they easier to control, the Triggers' top speed was less than ten miles per hour and the side boards were padded for comfort, at least more comfort than the original wagons offered. Safety first with the added bonus of more comfort were always good things.

My summer volunteer job was to drive a Trigger one day a week, every Monday. The task was much less wearing than some of the other jobs I'd had in the past; things like acting (which I was not good at) and clean-up duty (which I was okay at but didn't enjoy). This was the first year I got to do something that allowed me to spend more time talking to and getting to know our visitors and I enjoyed my new semi-ambassadorish role.

The invitation to participate had been almost an accident, a convergence of unexpected events. Gram and I had both been surprised by Roy's interest in our night classes. Anyone who knew Roy would find his desire to cook vegetables, or anything, curious.

But the mystery was solved when we learned that he had met someone on an Internet dating site. Roy and the "fiery woman from Iowa's" plans were to meet in person at the end of the summer and Roy wanted to be able to cook for her since she "was searching for someone who could handle themselves in the kitchen" because, apparently, she couldn't. Roy told Gram he would be participating in all our nighttime classes throughout the summer.

One night a few weeks earlier, as the vegetable class was discussing the questionable need in the world for Brussels sprouts, Roy asked everyone in attendance if they'd be willing to be his drivers. Except for Gram, we all agreed enthusiastically. I was glad to have a task already in place when the cleaning crew came looking for volunteers, and I'd had a few great Mondays so far. I was looking forward to the rest of the summer behind a Trigger's wheel.

Not only was Monday my drive day, it was also the drive crew meeting day. I wanted to be early to the meeting, which was being held at the cooking school, so I hurried to get ready. As I bounded down the front porch stairs toward my old Nova, I glanced down the street to the spot where I'd met Grace. I slowed as I thought I saw something else coming into view.

It was faint at first, an outline and then some faded colors that became a little stronger, a little deeper. Not much stronger or deeper, though, because it was daytime and the ghost world wasn't solid in the sunlight.

As far as I could tell, the building I saw was tall, two stories with a wide front porch, its ceiling held up by four columns across the front. The top floor, with three large windows, stuck out all the way over the porch. The walls were bright red and the windows were framed by white shutters.

The last two things that came into view were the sign across the front that said BROKEN ROPE and the figure of a man sitting on a bench on the wide platform. No other people appeared, just the man who had leaned forward and rested his elbows on his knees. There was no train, but I knew I was seeing the *real* Broken Rope station, the one from the past.

"That's more like it," I said aloud, now better remembering the building from Jake's pictures. They'd been black and white so my mind hadn't preserved them exactly like what was coming into view, but the image was close enough.

"And I bet I know who you are."

I looked at the time on my phone. I would probably be a little late, but I needed to talk to the man on the bench.

I hurried down the street, feeling less secure about my activities in the daylight. I didn't think anyone had observed my actions last night but if anyone was watching now, they'd wonder what I was doing in the otherwise vacant grass field.

Nevertheless, I couldn't miss the opportunity.

I scurried, furtively looking in all directions, probably being way too obvious.

When I reached the tracks, I slowed. They were like the ones last night—in good condition. There were present-day tracks in that spot, but unusable and overgrown. I glanced to the right and to the left. Though I didn't see a train, I was hesitant to cross. I'd seen the train last night, watched it stop. Ghost trains could appear out of nowhere, and though a ghost train probably couldn't hurt me, I didn't want to test the theory.

Finally, I stepped over quickly and then up to the platform. I felt sturdy planks beneath my feet and a new scent filled the air. It was earthy, perhaps musky. I couldn't place its organic form but it reminded me of a subtle men's cologne, perhaps something my dad had once worn when I was a little girl.

"Mr. Findlay?" I said when the man sitting on the bench didn't look up right away.

He brought his head up slowly and then squinted in my direction. It was difficult to distinguish his features, but he had a pleasant face, though it didn't seem happy to see me.

"Help you?" he said.

"Well . . ." I began.

He sat up straighter and squinted harder. "Who are you, young lady? You're wearing more men's clothes than women's. Why is that?"

"Do you know where you are, Mr. Findlay?"

"Of course. I'm at the Broken Rope, Missouri, train depot." He looked around and his eyebrows came together.

"You are," I said with a smile. "Sort of."

"You're not making sense," he said, but I heard the doubt in his tone. He suspected something was wonky.

I recalled my spiel with Grace. Though it wasn't easy to tell someone they were dead, my limited experience had taught me that the ghosts never fought the truth too much. Once they were told they were dead, they seemed to move quickly past that one unchangeable hitch in their bizarre existence. When I told him that he'd died a long time ago he didn't seem to want to argue the point.

"I'm part of what would be your time's future. My name is Betts Winston. My grandmother, Missouri Anna Winston, and I are able to talk to ghosts from Broken Rope's past. Do you know my grandmother? She's known as Miz."

"I don't believe I do," he muttered.

"Other than this trip, can you recall ever coming back to Broken Rope after you died?"

"No. It doesn't seem possible," he said.

"Seems to be possible around here. Broken Rope's wild and crazy past must have made quite the impression on time. I look at it as if something got stuck or hung up—pardon the bad pun—somewhere."

"I see." He blinked, looked around again and then back at me. "Young lady, if when I was alive I had seen someone who was dead, a ghost, I would be concerned and scared. You seem fine with the whole idea."

"You're not my first ghost. I've met a few, but I was most definitely concerned and scared when I met the very first one."

"I imagine so. I guess I wonder what I'm doing here. Why am I here? And what are you doing here in your pants and unladylike shirt?"

"I don't know exactly, but I suspect it has something to do with Grace," I said.

"How do you know about Grace?" He stood. "Is she here?"

"No, I don't think so," I said.

He stepped forward and then to his right and his left, stopping at the doorway of the station.

"Do you see anyone else?" I asked, because I saw no ghost other than Robert.

"No," he said as he remained in the doorway. An instant later, he turned and looked at me. "I suppose me being dead has something to do with that."

"Maybe. There aren't a lot of clear rules to this stuff. And when they become a little clear, they change. But for now, all I see is you and me. And . . . well, last night I saw Grace."

"You did? Here?"

"Not here, exactly, but at another station, though that station was here in the same spot as this station." I sighed. "I'm sure that doesn't make sense."

"Doesn't matter that it doesn't make sense. Tell me about Grace. How was she?"

"She was sad," I said. "She hoped to make her way to you, but I was under the impression that that never happened."

"No, I don't think it did," Robert said. "I . . . I waited. I came back day after day for a very long time, but Grace never joined me in Broken Rope. That was our plan, you know. She was going to meet me here and we were going to run away together."

"She told me."

"I don't know what happened to her."

"I have a little more news," I said, "but you won't like it."

Robert frowned and then squinted again. I hadn't noticed that he'd been holding a hat, but he started to rub his finger over the brim as he inspected me this time. "How could it possibly matter that I won't like it? I'm dead. I'm assuming Grace is, too."

"Yes." I cleared my throat. "Grace said she was killed, that she was trying to get to you, but she was killed—not accidently, but murdered"

As transparent as Robert was, it was a surprise to see his face become paler. He returned to the bench and sat. "Murdered?"

"Yes."

"Someone must have realized what she was doing, coming to me, a white man. Of course you know how difficult it is for people of different skin colors to be in love."

"Things have changed a little over time, Robert, but not completely yet. Prejudice still exists, but there are many biracial couples now living happy lives together without the need to run away or hide."

He looked up and blinked at me. "How wonderful. How incredible." He moved his eyes back to the platform. "We were born in the wrong time, I suppose, Grace and I."

"I'm sorry," I said.

"No matter." The set of his jaw was now straigntened with determination. "I guess the only thing that matters now is Grace. I would like to know who murdered her. I realize it's too late to truly acquire justice, but isn't knowing the truth always a good thing, and somehow its own form of justice? And, perhaps there's a hope that she and I might be together now. Oh, wouldn't that be the most amazing thing?"

"I think it would be," I said.

"What shall we do, Betts Winston? How shall we proceed?"

"I'm not sure, yet, Robert, but I promise I'll try to figure it out."

Chapter Three

"Anyone else having starter problems?" Roy asked.

Everyone except April and Todd shook their heads.

"Good," Roy said. "April, Todd, I'll get that taken care of before your next shifts. What are you two—Tuesday and Friday?"

"I'm Tuesday," April said.

"I'm Friday," Todd added.

"Not a problem. It will be done," Roy said.

We were sitting around one of the large center butcher blocks in the cooking school. Gram had come in early to make us breakfast, effectively turning the meeting into one of the more delicious get-togethers we'd had. It was unlike Gram to spend much time in the school, other than the night classes, during the month of June. This was usually her time off. I'd been surprised to find her Volvo out front and then her inside along with the scents and sounds of cooking bacon, eggs, biscuits, and gravy.

"Making some grub for the Trigger crew, Betts. After the meeting, I need to talk to you, okay?" she'd said.

I'd said that would be no problem, but I became immediately concerned regarding the subject matter of our conversation. Gram was acting strangely. Though she loved any form of cooking and baking, there was something forced in her breakfast preparation, in her voice. Unfortunately, I didn't have time to ask her any more questions because the rest of the Trigger drivers started arriving, and it was obvious that Gram didn't want our conversation overheard by anyone else. She disappeared toward the back of the school the second she had the food dished onto serving platters.

Roy Acres led the meetings. They were about his Triggers, after all. After we ate and chatted about some of our adventures with the tourists, Roy got to the business at hand and wanted to know if we were having any problems, questions, or concerns. In the few weeks we'd been driving the vehicles, the problems had been few and far between and never anything serious.

The Triggers were stored in an old, big barn right behind Bunny's Restaurant on the edge of town. As far as I could tell, Roy never slept or ate, but drank lots of coffee and was always tinkering with the machines. We all joked with him that he'd upgrade and improve them so much by the end of the summer that there would probably be flames painted down their sides and they'd hover instead of move with wheels.

Roy was in his mid-fifties, and along with a constant cup of coffee in his reach, he always wore plain white T-shirts, except on him they rarely remained plain or white for very long. Grease and dirt spots decorated the shirts and I frequently tried to interpret the resulting shapes. Just the other day, I saw a monkey hanging from a tire swing. Even though it was early, there were already a couple spots showing, though I couldn't make them into pictures yet.

Roy also always wore tan work pants, the type you'd see on construction workers in the winter. I never understood why he wore the thick, heavy pants, particularly during our hot and humid summers.

He kept his dark hair short and I was certain that behind his thick glasses were pretty blue eyes, but he was so far-sighted that the lenses enlarged his eyes to buglike, alarming proportions.

He was a true gentleman and a sweetheart, and I'd always been sad that he had never married, never even really dated anyone. When he told us about his interest in cooking classes because of a potential new romance, I'd been thrilled, almost to the point of pitching him some wardrobe ideas, but I hadn't wanted to offend him.

"I just thought of something, Roy," Lynn said. "There's a tear on the back seat cushion on Trigger Two. Did you notice that, Derek?"

"No, but I don't think I checked back there last time I drove her," Derek said.

The group of Trigger drivers/nighters was eclectic. Lynn and Derek Rowlett, the drivers of Trigger Two that operated on Thursdays and Saturdays, were family. Derek and Roy knew each other from way back. Derek was also in his mid-fifties. He was a handyman by trade and he'd been married a number of times, though I'd lost track of how many exactly. Derek was not an attractive man; in fact, Gram had said more than once, "that poor man sure got a lot of bad cards dealt his way." Looks are easily forgotten, though, if someone is pleasant to be around, but adding to his unattractiveness, he also wasn't all that pleasant—he was rude and petty like his mother. He could also be quiet and sullen and usually seemed to blend into the background. His wives, the Mrs. Rowletts, must have seen something in him that Gram and I didn't because they'd all apparently become smitten enough to answer his proposal in the affirmative. I didn't think any of the marriages had lasted long, but I'd never spent much time looking into the matter. Since he'd started taking the class, I'd shallowly wondered a time or two if the attraction had something to do with money he might have inherited from a rich relative, but Gram was certain he wasn't rich.

And the mere idea of his mother, Lynn, as your mother-in-law was not appealing. Lynn Rowlett was known far and wide as one of the most bothersome women in all of Missouri. Well, maybe her reputation was only cemented in Broken Rope, but *everyone* in town knew about it. Her modus operandi consisted mainly of filing complaints. Wherever she went, whatever she did, she would find something to complain about. She'd put her complaints in writing and send a letter to the editor of our local newspaper, the *Noose*, or she'd share her complaints with anyone who would listen. Fortunately, no one really listened to her very much anymore. Gram and I, and Roy for that matter, had yet to fall victim to one of her tirades, but we all suspected one was forthcoming. Gram and I had paid extra attention to the *Letters to the Editor* section of the paper since the night vegetable class had begun.

At the moment, I inspected her as she told Roy about the tear in the seat. Was this the beginning of a new rant?

"I'll look at that today, too," Roy said.

Lynn pursed her lips and nodded in a manner that was so agreeable I had to stifle a gasp of disbelief.

As I looked away from her, I caught a conspiratorial wink from my Trigger driving partner, Paul Stadler. It seemed Gram and I weren't the only ones watching and waiting for Lynn's next outburst.

Normally, I would smile and perhaps wink back in response to the friendly gesture, but this time I just smiled at Paul and looked back at Roy.

Paul Stadler had been a friend for a long time. In high school he'd been an acquaintance, but after high school and during the following decade or so, he'd worked with Jake on some Broken Rope historical books. As a result, Paul and Jake had become even better friends, thus, Paul and I had also become better friends.

Lately, I'd had a sense that he hoped for something more than friendship, which was both odd and uncomfortable. He knew Cliff and I were together, and that nothing was going to sever that relationship again. Unless it was a long-dead cowboy ghost, of course, but he didn't know that.

Typically, I would think I was jumping to an incorrect conclusion, that I was being overly sensitive or even egotistical, but Jake had noticed it, too; so much so that he'd thought he should talk to Paul, tell him he was behaving inappropriately. I'd asked him not to, but I suspected there was an uncomfortable conversation in Paul's and my future. I wasn't looking forward to that moment and I'd started doing little things like not winking back playfully with the hope that I could avoid any awkward talks.

Paul had never been married, but he'd always had a girlfriend. He'd always been attracted to girls with some sort of troubled background. Drugs, alcohol, abuse; there had been some ugly moments between Paul and his girlfriends as he tried to reform and "fix" them.

I thought I wasn't the type of woman he'd be romantically interested in, but Jake thought maybe he was trying to change his ways, even if he wasn't quite on the right track yet.

I hoped the friendship wouldn't have to end, but time would tell.

And, anyway, all romantic notions in our little group should have been spent on April and Todd. April was an early-twenties-something blonde with big green eyes and the sweetest smile I'd ever seen. Her family had moved to town a couple months earlier. She'd just finished her freshman year at Mizzou and was spending the summer in Broken Rope. Having no idea what to do with all her time, she visited one of Jake's poetry readings and asked him if there was anything she could to do to get more involved with the town. He'd sent her to Gram's classes, which had introduced her to Roy. She now shared her Trigger Three driving duties with Todd.

Todd was mid-twenties, back in town for the summer from dental school in Nebraska. He'd run into Gram at the post office and they'd talked a little about the recent passing of his grandmother, who had also been a good friend of Gram's. She mentioned the classes and told him they'd be much easier than dental school. Little had Todd known he would meet April and fall head over heels for the pretty girl from Chicago. We all hoped he would work up the courage to ask her out, but he wasn't there yet. Poor guy was so tongue-tied and clumsy around her that everyone else had to frequently bite the insides of their cheeks to keep from smiling sympathetically at his self-conscious behavior. I wasn't sure if she noticed or just thought the tall, good-looking guy with the crooked smile was simply unable to control his long limbs and didn't quite have a grasp on the English language.

"Oh!" April said. "I almost forgot. I think one of the spokes in the front right wagon wheel might be cracked. I'm not sure if that's important, but I saw it last week and just now remembered to mention it."

"Good to know, April. I will check that out for sure," Roy said.

Todd nodded as though he agreed with April's assessment. He sat up a little straighter and opened his mouth as though he was going to say something, but then must have thought he might not be able to handle the task. He closed his mouth as his shoulders fell.

"Todd?" Roy said. "You notice anything else?"

Todd shook his head. I was afraid he'd become so embarrassed about his speaking ability around April that he might never talk again.

"Okay, then, well, it looks like it's Monday again, Betts. You ready to get out there and drive?" Roy asked.

"Absolutely," I said. *After I talk to Gram for a minute.*

I would make sure I wasn't late for my shift, but I might cut it a little close.

"Good. If anyone needs anything today, I'll be at the barn. Stop by if you need to," Roy said.

Everyone scooted their stools back from the butcher-block table.

"Thanks to Miz for the breakfast spread," Roy said. "Is she still around? I'd like to chat with her for a minute."

"Yes, she's in the back," I said. "I can give her the message. I need to talk to her for a minute, too."

"No, I'd like to tell her myself," Roy said as took off toward the part of the building that housed our infrequently used sit-down classroom and my and Gram's offices. Lynn and Derek walked toward the front swinging doors of the kitchen. I saw Todd steel himself as April walked by him. I suspected he was telling himself that he was going to talk to her. Now. Unfortunately, as he scooted the stool back a little farther, it went down, and so did he.

Paul, April, Lynn, Derek, and I hurried to his fallen body.

He was already trying to get up, his face as red as a ripe tomato.

"You okay, Todd?" April was the first to crouch down beside him.

"Fine, fine," he said, though he sounded exasperated, irritated, and annoyed. Almost anything but fine.

"Here," Paul said as he extended his hand.

"I'm fine," Todd said adamantly as he ignored the friendly gesture and propelled himself to his feet.

We'd gathered around him quickly, and then tried to step back casually, all of us feeling his pain and discomfort, with the possible exception of April. She hadn't known Todd before joining the cooking class and the Trigger driving crew so she hadn't seen what a genuinely sweet guy he was. He was also smart and clever, but those traits had gone into hibernation, too, perhaps waiting for him back at dental school.

"Miss April," said a voice from the back of the kitchen.

We all turned to see Roy and Gram, her hands on her hips and her face pinched with impatience. She wore a University of Washington T-shirt, and the purple in it brought out the blue in her eyes.

"Yes, ma'am," April said.

"Do you have a minute?" Gram said.

"Of course," she said. She sent Todd a quick and friendly smile that was more "you poor thing" than "I'm sorry for what you're going through" before she stepped around the rest of us and walked with Gram toward what I assumed was her office.

"Thanks for the minute, Miz," Roy said. "You on your way, Betts?"

"I'll be there in a few. I won't be late," I said, but I was looking at Todd. I debated asking him to stay and talk, but it was clear that he wasn't in the mood. I caught his eye a moment and we both nodded before he took off out through the front swinging doors.

"See you there." Roy gathered the few folders he'd brought with him as well as a toolbox I hadn't noticed he'd placed under the butcher block. It was an old rusted box pocked with dents. I'd seen it at the barn many times. As he lifted the box, the lid opened and two long wrenches fell to the ground, causing enough metallic clunking and clanging to make everyone jump.

"Sorry, folks. Sometimes the latch works, sometimes it doesn't. I really should get another one," Roy said as he crouched to clean up the tools.

"Why in the world did you even bring it to our breakfast meeting, Roy? The noise was so loud I thought we were being attacked," Lynn said.

The noise hadn't been quite that loud, but it had been startling.

"Sorry, Lynn," Roy said distractedly. He was looking in the toolbox as if for something specific.

I was about to ask him what it was, but he suddenly closed the box, picked it up, and stuffed the whole thing under one arm before he hurried out of the kitchen.

Lynn watched him go as if she was expecting him to say something else to her, probably hoping for another apology. When he didn't offer anything else, she looked at me.

"Betts, what are we preparing tomorrow night?" she asked.

"I think we're frying some green beans. It's a simple but really good recipe," I said.

"Frying green beans? No cheese? I thought all our dishes would include cheese. I can't imagine a more contradictory food item—frying something healthy like green beans. That makes no sense. Hopefully you and Miz will come up with something that will finally taste good enough to eat."

"I hope so," I said. I wasn't going to once again explain to Lynn that the name for the class was just for fun, but that not all vegetables truly needed cheese to taste good. Besides, doesn't frying anything make it taste better? But I refrained from going there.

Lynn tsked and then turned to leave. "Come along, Derek."

Derek didn't ever apologize for his mother—either vocally or with shoulder shrugs or help-me glances. He just nodded and obediently followed behind her.

A moment later, the only ones left were Paul and me.

I quickly started picking up dishes and moving them to the sinks.

"Let me help," Paul said as he reached for the same plate I was reaching for.

His hand lingered a little too long on mine.

"Sorry." He smiled, pulled his hand away, and then reached for another dish.

I smiled briefly and continued to gather. Before long, we were at side-by-side sinks, rinsing and placing dishes into a dishwasher.

"Boy, that Lynn is something," Paul said. "She's just never happy about anything."

I gave a little shrug but didn't say anything, though not because I thought he was flirting. It wasn't wise to speak badly about any student, particularly with other students. Under the cover of darkness when Gram and I could confirm without a doubt that we were alone, we might have a bad word or two to say, but rarely.

After a pause that wasn't too uncomfortable, Paul said, "I hear Cliff was out of town this weekend."

"Yes," I said and then I wondered why I hadn't heard from him yet this morning.

I wasn't surprised that Paul knew that Cliff was out of town. If he'd seen Jake at all over the weekend it could have come up. It was kind of a big deal. The equipment Cliff was picking up was for Broken Rope's newest addition—its very own crime lab. Of course, the crime lab was going to be housed in a backroom space next to the ME's small office, a space that had just last week been used to store a bunch of nooses long ago packaged to sell to tourists. Apparently, the nooses had been far too real so tourists hadn't found them appealing. So, the "crime lab" was remedial at best, but it was a fresh start that was long overdue.

"He's really done well, Betts," Paul said.

I stopped rinsing and loading and looked at him. He sounded genuine. "Yes, he has."

"He's a good guy," Paul said.

"Yes, very," I said, now wondering where this was going.

"You know, I thought that once the two of you spent a little time together again, you'd get married quick, kid on the way, all that stuff."

I was torn between wanting to defend my relationship with Cliff and wanting to tell Paul that he was beginning to dip his toe into that end of the pool that was none of his business. I was also tired of the strain that had come between Paul and me. It was ridiculous. We were all grown-ups.

"What's your point, Paul?" I said, getting to my own.

"I'm sorry," he said. "I'm just . . . well, Betts, let me just put my cards on the table." He cringed, probably realizing how silly the cliché sounded. "Look, I've always admired your relationship with Cliff. It's really terrific. Or . . . well, or it used to be. I'm not seeing what looks like a big commitment and I'm not sure if it's you or Cliff, but if you feel like you don't belong together, I guess I'd just like to put my name up for consideration." He blanched before he took another breath. "Oh man, that sounded absolutely awful. I'm sorry. Betts, I like you. I always have. It's pretty simple—I'd like to ask you out. If you're available to go out, that is." Paul's shoulders slumped. "Holy cow, I sound like such a fool. Maybe we could just forget this conversation." He smiled both sheepishly and hopefully at the same time.

"No, we can't forget it, Paul, but probably not for the reason you might think."

Paul's clumsy declaration didn't embarrass me or make me feel uncomfortable about his feelings. In fact, I was glad to have the words spoken aloud, floating out there in the universe instead of being bottled up and causing discomfort. But, I had questions. I was about to ask him to explain what he thought he'd seen. Why in the world had he interpreted things the way he had? For a moment of gut-wrenching frustration, I wanted to be on the outside looking in. I wanted to be able to objectively observe myself and whatever it was that I was doing to cause people to think I wasn't head-over-heels crazy in love with Cliff. How in the world could everyone not see what I so strongly thought I felt?

But my questions were interrupted by Gram and April reentering the kitchen. And then the scent of wood smoke.

Gram and April were laughing together lightly. Whatever their conversation had been about, it had at least ended cordially.

As the smell of smoke filled the air, I abruptly pulled my attention away from Paul, Gram, and April, and twisted my neck back and forth in search of the ghost that went with the smoke. But there was no Jerome.

Gram noticed the smoke, too. She stopped laughing, sniffed, and then looked around the room. It was obvious that she didn't see him either.

"Hello, Miz, Isabelle," Paul said.

But it wasn't Paul's voice. Well it was, but it wasn't spoken with the same tones and inflections.

"April, dear, it's been great to have this little talk," Gram said as she grabbed April's arm and led her though the kitchen and out the front swinging doors. I knew she'd make sure April's car was well out of sight before she came back in.

I swallowed hard and whispered, "Jerome?"

Paul blinked and shook his head. "I'm sorry, Betts, what did you say?"

"Oh. You know, Paul," I said, searching for the best way to continue as normally as possible. "I really appreciate your honestly. I've felt like there was something you wanted to tell me. It's good to know I wasn't imagining things. But, I have to add that Cliff and I aren't on the verge of breaking up. Perhaps what you've seen is just the fact that we're all older than we were in high school. Relationships should be different after thirty than they were when we were seventeen, shouldn't they?"

Paul nodded and then squinted, confusion pulling at his features. "Sure, but, Betts, I'm not sure that's what it is. Never mind, though; I've stated my case. Now you know. Broken Rope is just too small to avoid anyone, so I'm not going to. I'm sure that later when I replay this conversation in my mind, I'll be mortified, but I'm not going to avoid you or be weird about it."

He was trying to convince himself that he was going to accept what he'd done. I stepped toward him and gave him a friendly hug. "Paul, we've been friends for a long time. There's no way I would let this get in the way of that. I promise."

"Thanks, Betts," he said with an embarrassed smile. Then he sniffed. "I smell smoke."

"You do?" I said as I stepped back just as Gram came and rejoined us.

"I do." Paul sniffed deeply. "Do you think something's burning?" He looked around the kitchen once again, searching for the source of the smell. "It's right here, I think. It's staying with me. But there's nothing here that could be burning. It's not an electrical smell so I don't think it's wiring in the walls. It's woodsy, like something from a campfire."

"Maybe something from outside?" Gram offered.

"It's pretty warm out there," Paul said. "But maybe. How strange."

"Hmm. I don't know," I said.

"You don't smell anything?" he asked.

"Not like what you're smelling. I might have caught a scent of something earlier, but nothing right now." I didn't want Paul to think he was completely crazy. Perhaps my casual suggestion would make him think the smell was dissipating and didn't need further exploration.

"Strange," Paul said again. He looked at me a long moment, and I thought I saw a slight and brief shift in the focus of his eyes and the way he held his mouth. It was so fleeting that I couldn't quite register it before he normalized again.

"Paul?" I said.

"Paul?" Gram said.

"I'm sorry. I need to go. I don't feel quite right."

"You want me to take you home?" Gram said.

"No, I'll be fine. I just need to go."

We followed Paul out to his car. He seemed less wobbly with the fresh air and sunshine, and by the time he pulled out of the parking lot, Gram and I both thought he'd be fine. We hoped so. Once we were alone, we silently and in tandem walked over to Jerome's tombstone and looked at it.

"What do you think that was?" I said.

"I have no idea," Gram said. "No idea at all."

"What did you say to April?"

"I'll tell you later. Right now, I need to talk to you about some other things. You still have time?"

"Of course," I said, even though I was going to cut it very close. Roy would understand.

Gram looked around and then said a moment later, "Let's get inside."

I followed her, but glanced back at the cemetery before I went through the front doors. I saw nothing but a cemetery, but a tingling under my skin told me I might not be seeing everything that was truly there.

Chapter Four

"Betts, have you ever experienced anything like that?" Gram said after she finished giving me the gruesome details of the nightmares she'd been having.

"No, Gram, I've had bad dreams but nothing like those. I might have a theory about what's behind them though. It might be a stretch, but maybe."

"I'm listening," Gram said.

"I met two ghosts; haven't had a second to let you know. Anyway, one last night, one this morning. Grace and then Robert Findlay. They were in love with each other back in 1888. Ever met them?"

"I don't think so," Gram said.

"That's what they said, but I wasn't sure."

I relayed the details that I'd gleaned from the two ghosts, but I did it backward. First I told Robert's side of the story and then I told Grace's, explaining how I thought Gram's nightmares about being the victim of a murder seemed like they could be similar to what Grace might have experienced. Gram said her nightmares were unusually loud, as if there were train whistles blowing right in her ears. She also mentioned that the brutality she experienced as she slept was uncomfortably close to the real thing. All of it: the fear, the pain, the horror.

"I suppose that could be it, Betts. In the crazy ghost messiness, it makes sense that I've been dreaming about Grace a week or so before her visit to Broken Rope even if I've never had such dreams before. And, last night, it was all much worse. If I'm . . . experiencing even a little of what she, or anyone for that matter, went through, it was awful. I'm sorry for her," Gram said.

The shiny panic I'd seen in Gram's eyes had dimmed a little. Of course, we couldn't be sure that we'd figured out the reason for the dreams, but it was a distinct possibility, and that was better than nothing.

"You told me the details of the . . . well, the murder, I suppose. What did the killer or killers look like?" I asked.

"There were two of them, but what good is knowing what they looked like, particularly if they're from 1888? They aren't still living, and it's not like we can find anyone from back then based upon descriptions."

"It might lead somewhere," I said hopefully. "Maybe we can

describe them to Grace and Robert so they'll at least know."

"Of course. That makes sense." She bit her bottom lip a second. "I have an idea. Call Cliff. I think he has a sketch artist now."

"He does?" I said.

"Yes, part of the new crime lab. We'll start there and with Jake. Maybe he has pictures of all the old train stations. Maybe we can at least narrow down where Grace was—and confirm that Robert was at the Broken Rope station," Gram said, her senses realigning again, coming back to normal after being frantic from the telling of her nightmares.

"How are we going to explain to Cliff why we need the sketch artist?"

"Good point. I'm not sure yet, but I'll think about. Okay, let's start with Jake. You'll talk to him today?"

"Yep, right after my Trigger shift." I didn't look at the clock on my phone because I didn't want Gram to think I was anxious to get out of there, but I felt the pull to do so.

"Of course. I don't suppose missing the shift would be a fair thing to do to Roy. Okay, okay, this afternoon then. How's that?"

"Definitely."

Gram nodded and bit her bottom lip again, but with much less ferocity this time.

"Before you go, should we talk more about Paul and how it seemed like something Jerome-ish was happening to him?" she said.

I shrugged. "I don't know what else there is to say. It was very weird, but Paul seemed okay by the time he left. Have you ever seen anything like that?"

"Never."

"I haven't seen Jerome since the poetry convention. Have you?"

"Heavens, Betts, I would have told you. No, I would have called you immediately and told you to come get him. These ghosts." She shook her head and sighed heavily. "You're right. Paul seemed okay. We'll go with that until something changes."

"Gotta go," I said. I hopped off the stool and gave her a quick hug and a kiss on her cheek. She was better, much better, but still a little off. She'd bounce back.

I grabbed my bag from a shelf by the front swinging doors and hurried out of the school.

Without one backward glance I fired up the Nova and sped a little too quickly out of the parking lot.

Gram was suffering from ghost overload. I was sure there was such a thing, but finding a cure would be difficult.

Since I was also suffering from a little overload, or frustration, or just a sense of feeling late and rushed, I didn't notice that another smell had filled the air outside the school and cemetery.

It would register later that at some point during that day I had smelled something tangy, something akin to an onion but not quite as strong. It was certainly heady, but not enough to make eyes water. I just wouldn't be able to place exactly where I'd smelled it, and I would unconsciously file it away to the back of my mind.

Downtown was busy. It was still morning, but the tourists and the actors were out in force. Since the barn was behind Bunny's Restaurant, she'd allowed the Trigger drivers to park their cars in her small but conveniently located parking lot. I had to circle it three times before a space opened up.

"Hi, Betts," a voice called from the front of the lot as I was running toward the back of it and a walking path that would take me to the barn.

I stutter stepped and turned to wave. Opie. My new "best friend," and my brother's reignited love acquaintance. I couldn't bring myself to use a stronger word than "acquaintance." Opie and I had been enemies since we were kids. And when Cliff broke up with her in high school and then started dating me a less-than-polite time span later, she and I had really not liked each other.

But since she'd started dating Teddy—well, they'd had a brief breakup—but since they'd gotten back together, and Gram and I had been the ones to tell her that one of her ancestors was a semi-famous historical figure from Broken Rope, she had been doing everything in her power to be nice and friendly to me. Surely something heinous was being plotted, but she'd yet to follow through on any mean intentions.

"Hi!" I waved and smiled and then moved along quickly. She seemed okay with the fly-by greeting.

The barn was old, and had once housed real horses and real buggies that some of the town's residents had owned, sharing the space and the responsibilities for caring for the animals and the equipment. Jake had explained to me that it had been a unique operation and, according to some records that he'd found, had worked well for about a decade, after which some less-than-enthusiastic participants let things slip too much, so everyone had to go back to caring for only their own horses. The barn had been reinforced over the years and used to store different items. Just when it was about to be torn down for good, Roy jumped in and said he'd fix whatever needed fixing so he could use it for the Triggers.

The town council had approved, and since it was technically on Bunny's property she gave her okay, too. Roy had reinforced the structure of the building, and it looked okay, from a distance at least. It was still pretty old.

The front double doors of the barn could be opened wide, wide enough to allow the Triggers to travel through. The doors were typically swung open because the barn had also become a tourist attraction, bringing a few curious people around Bunny's as well as down the paths in between the boardwalk buildings to see the goings-on inside. Roy had been a welcoming figure and he'd found a new small bit of fame with his summer role this year.

But at the moment the doors were closed. A couple reasons for this occurred to me. Maybe Roy had gotten hung up somewhere and hadn't made it to the barn yet, or maybe he was working on some top-secret addition for the Triggers and he didn't want to be bothered by curious tourists.

I pulled on the right door. No, *pull* was too delicate a word; I *heaved* the heavy right door open, using both hands and stepping backwards as I moved.

"Roy?" I called as I walked inside.

The barn was jam-packed. The three Trigger wagons fit snuggly next to one another, and there were pieces of equipment and worktables everywhere else. A number of coiled ropes hung from long nails that had been pounded into the wood-planked walls. The ropes had been there when Roy took over the barn. I asked him why he hadn't removed them, but he said there was some Broken Rope superstition about removing those particular ropes from their resting places. I'd never heard the superstition, but I was all for not messing with juju.

"Roy?" I called again.

Still no answer. Evidently, he hadn't arrived yet. But I'd seen him ready the Triggers enough times to know what I needed to do.

I stepped carefully around the machine at the end, which was Trigger One and the one I drove, and threw my bag into the space below the driver's side of the bench seat. The machines had brakes, but Roy always placed bricks on each side of the wheels when they were parked. I had a faint memory of him working on some brakes recently, but I couldn't remember which Trigger had been involved or why. Everything looked fine so I picked up the first two bricks and carried them to a small table against the wall. I did the same with the next two bricks, but when I went back toward Trigger One to pull the bricks from another wheel, I stopped in my tracks. I was frozen solid, just like I'd heard happened to people when they came upon something that wasn't quite right. The scene before me was not only not right, it was horrifying and sickening.

After I unfroze myself, I hurried to the body on the ground. I had no thoughts of protecting evidence. I was merely trying to help the person who I quickly determined was beyond help.

"Derek!" I said as I tried without much success to roll his big body over.

"Derek!" I said again, but he still didn't answer.

There was no mistaking the vacant look in his eyes. He was dead. The side, top, and back of his head were covered in blood, but I couldn't see any specific wound through all the mess.

I was about to exclaim his name again, though I understood that he wasn't going to answer, when stars suddenly circled in front of my own eyes. A second later I realized there was pain to go with the stars. Someone had hit me on the back of my head. Before I passed out, thinking I was headed toward my own death, I managed to do two things: I eliminated Derek from the list of people who might have hit me, and I wondered if I'd maybe see Jerome after I died.

Chapter Five

"Isabelle, wake up," the voice said. It was Jerome's voice, I was pretty sure.

"So death's not all that terrible, then," I muttered as I tried to lift my eyelids. "Did someone tape these?" I said as I put my fingers on the immovable lids.

"You're not dead," Jerome's voice said quietly in one ear.

"Hey, Betts, you're not dead," another voice said in the other ear. I was pretty sure this one belonged to Cliff. "You were hit on the head, but you're going to be okay. Your eyelids are heavy, but they'll open."

I gritted my teeth and willed my eyes to open. It took a second to focus away the fuzzies, but another few seconds later I saw Cliff looking down at me. Only Cliff. The backdrop behind him was made up of ugly fluorescent lights and a white panel ceiling.

"Oh, hi," I said as I now blinked double-time.

"Hi," he said with a worried but relieved smile.

"I was hit on the head?" I said as I reached for it and tried to sit up. I was on an exam table, but the back had been raised so that I wasn't all the way flat. "Oh my, that hurts." I melted back down.

"Rest, Betts. You're going to be fine. No concussion even. You'll be good as new in no time at all, but you need to take it easy for a day or two," Cliff said.

"Where am I?" I said as I looked around the room, quickly realizing I'd been in it before, or at least one very similar to it.

"You're in Dr. Callahan's office. We were going to transport you to a hospital in either Springfield or St. Louis, but you were awake earlier. Doc did a CT scan and your noggin looks okay."

"I don't remember being awake earlier. What day is it? When did this happen? How long have I been out?"

"It happened just this morning, only about an hour and a half ago. You were conscious when Roy found you, but you were woozy. You were given a sedative when you got here so that might have messed with your memory. Dr. Callahan made sure there was no bleeding in there, no fractures either."

Either the sedative was dissipating, or I was recovering rapidly now. The moments before I'd been hit came back to me in a giant wave of memory.

"Derek—I found Derek. Cliff, Derek!" I sat up again even though the movement didn't seem much easier.

Cliff nodded. "I know. Roy found him, too. He was in lots worse shape."

"He was dead?"

"Yes, Betts. Hit over the head with a blunt instrument, more than once, and he didn't fare as well as you did. He was dead."

"Oh no, that's terrible. Did you or Roy catch whoever did this to him—and probably the same person who did this to me?"

"No, Betts. Roy found only you and Derek," Cliff said. He swallowed hard.

I sat up even straighter, hopefully indicating that I was going to be all right.

"That's terrible, Cliff. Poor Derek, and poor Lynn. I'm sure she's a mess," I said. One of my eyes wanted to close from the surges of pain with every beat of my pulse, but I willed it to stay open just so Cliff was assured that they wouldn't just close forever.

I did not see Jerome in the room. I didn't smell him. But I was certain I heard his voice in my head.

"Isabelle, you're trying too hard. You're only going to give yourself a whopper of a headache. Just rest. You're going to be fine by tomorrow. Cliff knows that. I'm trying to get to you. I'll be there when I can."

This was new. Or maybe it wasn't. Maybe the bump on the head was causing auditory hallucinations. I didn't acknowledge Jerome's voice, but his words didn't quite fit. If Cliff knew I was going to be okay, why did his face say differently?

I inspected Cliff closer just to see if it was maybe my vision, maybe the eye that so desperately wanted to close was not seeing correctly. But no, something else wasn't right.

"Cliff, what is it? Am I worse off than you want to tell me?"

"No, not at all, Betts. You're going to be fine." Cliff forced a semi-comforting smile.

"Darlin', you've been muttering my name. That might be what's bothering him. I have to go. I'll get there, Isabelle, or I'll die again trying." Jerome's voice faded.

"Derek was killed, murdered?" I repeated. Of course, I couldn't respond to Jerome's disembodied comment.

"Yes," Cliff said, turning on his professional side again. "Any chance you saw anything or anyone? Can you remember going into the barn?"

"Yes, now I can. Clearly, in fact. But I didn't really see anything. I was surprised that Roy wasn't there yet, but I thought I could get the Trigger ready without him." I paused as the scene played in my mind. "My bag. I remember putting it in the front of the Trigger."

"No," Cliff said, "actually, it was on the ground beside you. It's right here. Your cell phone was in your pants' pocket." He reached to a chair behind him against the wall, grabbing my backpack and phone and then handing them to me. "Can you look in your backpack right now? Is there any chance something was taken? If so, that might help us understand motive. Theft, maybe? It's not much, but it might be something."

I ignored the pain in my head. I left the phone on the exam table beside my leg and opened the bag. I didn't carry all that much with me, so it was easy to take a quick inventory. Brush, elastics for my hair when it had enough of battling the humidity, ChapStick, grocery list for Gram, sunglasses, and my wallet. The twenty-three dollars I remembered having was still there along with a small assortment of change. I had two credit cards and one debit card; all were present and accounted for. My driver's license—check. Same with my library card.

There was only one more thing to find. The coin, the one from

Jerome's hidden treasure that I'd been carrying around with me. I'd been keeping it in a pants' pocket until a couple months earlier when I thought that tucking it away in my wallet was a better idea. I'd put it into a slot that would normally hold a credit card.

It was there, but I tried not to look too relieved.

"Nothing is missing," I said.

"That's good," Cliff said. "You definitely remember putting the bag into the Trigger?"

"Yes."

"Do you mind if I take it? There's a chance there's some evidence on it. It's been touched by a few people since then, but it's worth a look."

"No problem." I handed him the bag. "No one else is hurt? How's Roy?"

"Shook up. Worried about you. Jim's shut down the Trigger operation until we get things figured out." Jim was Broken Rope's police chief.

"That makes sense. I'll let Roy know I'm okay. He wasn't there when I got there. I thought he would be." It didn't occur to me that I might be shining the light of suspicion on Roy with that statement, but not surprisingly, Cliff was ahead of me.

"Right. He had to run some errands. We're looking into it."

"Roy couldn't hurt anyone."

"Let's hope not. What else can I get for you?" Cliff asked.

"I'd like to go home," I said. "I just have a headache. I'm fine."

As if on cue, the door swung open and a small woman in bright blue scrubs entered. She pulled a small boxy machine on wheels along with her.

"You're awake," she said.

It didn't sound like a question, but I said, "Yes, I'm feeling okay."

"Good. I'm here to check your vitals. Dr. C. should be in shortly."

She rolled the machine around Cliff, who then moved to the corner of the small space. I didn't know her, but I thought I'd seen her around Broken Rope. She must have been somewhere in her mid-to-late forties, petite, with a curly, short brown ponytail and small brown eyes that matched her hair color. Her mouth was pinched tightly, which made me think she was concentrating hard on checking my blood pressure. But at second glance, there was something else. She seemed upset.

"I'm Betts," I said, surprisingly curious as to why the nurse had red-rimmed eyes.

"I know," she looked at me briefly but didn't smile.

"What's your name? I know I've seen you around Broken Rope."

"I'm Ridley." The monitor beeped. She looked at the display on the front and then wrote something, presumably the numbers, on a small pad of paper she carried in her pocket. "Your vitals are perfect. I expect you'll get to go soon."

"That's good," I said as the exhaustion I wanted to fight seemed to dig in against me. I was suddenly tired enough not to care about pursuing the reason the nurse was upset. I slunked down and relaxed my head back on the exam table. If my vitals were fine I didn't think I needed to fake feeling a hundred percent better anymore.

"Betts Winston," Dr. Callahan said as he came into the room, making way in the doorway for the nurse and the machine to exit.

"Hi, Dr. Callahan," I said.

"How are you feeling?"

"Like I was hit in the head, I suppose."

"Imagine that."

It was always a little surprising to find him dressed in an official white doctor's coat. He was more known for his emergency after hours' attire, a plaid robe. He'd been seen in it so many times, tending to the sick or injured when his office was supposed to be closed and he was supposed to be at home, that it had become somewhat legendary.

"I'll be okay," I said.

"Yes, you will. In fact, you don't even have a concussion. I thought you must but you got really lucky."

"That's good."

"Very good."

Dr. Callahan went over what I needed to do to heal and feel better. I thought his idea about getting rest was the best idea ever in the history of all ideas. I was tired.

As he was wrapping up his instructions, someone peered through the partially open doorway.

"Hi, Jake," I said.

"You're awake? You're alive? How are you?" Jake said as he came into the room, too. It was getting very crowded.

"I'm fine."

Jake stepped around Dr. Callahan, acknowledging neither him nor Cliff, and put his hand to my forehead. "No fever."

"No, no fever."

"Holy smokes, what in the world happened?"

I stayed out of the conversation as Cliff and Dr. Callahan relayed the story to Jake, and when Dr. Callahan told me I could go whenever I wanted, I just nodded. Jake told Cliff that he would see that I got home okay. Cliff didn't want to leave me, but he knew I was in good hands with Jake and I wanted him to hurry and test my bag for evidence. The flurry of activity finally settled, and Jake and I were the only ones left in the room.

I'd swung my legs around so that they were dangling over the side of the exam table. I was sitting fully upright and I wasn't woozy. I did have strange, multi-directional shooting pains in my head and I was still tired, but had continued to feel better with each passing minute.

Jake held onto my arm as I stood.

I remembered that I was planning on finding Jake after my Trigger shift. Now seemed as good a time as any to talk to him. "Hey, I was going to come find you this afternoon. Gram and I have something we're dealing with."

"Ghostly?"

"Yes, two of them."

"Tell me."

"Do you know about a Broken Rope resident named Robert Findlay?"

Jake smiled. "The man who spent every day of the last ten years of his life at the Broken Rope train station waiting for the woman he had loved to arrive? Yes, I might have heard of him."

"I met him. And the woman he was waiting for."

Jake's face lit with a huge smile. "They found each other in death?"

"No, not quite."

We left the doctor's office and Jake deposited me into the passenger seat of his VW Bug. As we headed toward my small neighborhood, I told him about meeting the two ghosts, about their respective stories and the different stations, and about Gram's nightmares. He listened with the same focused interest that he gave all the ghost stories.

"It's so tragic," Jake said. "The passed-down story doesn't mention who Robert's love was. Over time, she lost her identity, or it had taken on so many versions that she became a footnote to the story, perhaps even a figment of Robert's imagination. He lost his mind, of course, or at least that's the story. Grief, frustration, just not knowing what happened to her must have been awful."

"I didn't get the impression that he'd lost his mind, but maybe that's not the version *of him* I met. I also didn't know he'd spent so much time waiting for her. Ten years? Wow, that's a long time." I squinted and wished for the sunglasses in my bag. Jake noticed and handed me some from the side pocket in his door. They provided immediate relief. "I think we have two places to start. We need to figure out where Grace was, which station. That might tell us a lot, maybe where she was killed. Gram's convinced she could describe the killers—well somebody's killers—at this point. It's worth a shot."

"You sound good. You must be feeling okay?"

"The sunglasses helped."

"Keep them."

"Thanks."

"Right down there?" He nodded toward the field as we pulled onto my street.

"Yep, that's where I saw them."

"Makes sense," he said as he parked next to the curb in front of my house. "Come on."

"I'm fine, Jake." It suddenly registered that he was wearing his costume. As the fake sheriff in town, he dressed up and performed a new piece of his original cowboy poetry each year. He was one of our bigger draws. "Oh, no, you're missing a reading, or more than one. Go. I'll be fine."

"Betts, please." He looked at me. "Priorities, my dear."

"I'm just going to sleep. You don't need to be there to watch me do that. I don't have a concussion. Get back to work, and then look for stuff that will help us. Seriously."

Jake walked me in but didn't stay. It might not have mattered who'd been there, ghostly or alive. I was going to sleep until my body didn't want me to sleep anymore. Trains could have whistled right in my ears and it wouldn't have fazed me in the least.

I didn't rest without dreams, though they were mild, not violent like Gram's. They weren't about any of the ghosts, unless of course Derek could now be considered a ghost. In my dreams, I saw him as I'd seen him over the years—quiet, withdrawn, not friendly. But I also saw something else. In life Derek had been haunted by . . . something. I'd never noticed it when he was alive, and unfortunately, it never became clear in my dreams. I was curious enough, though, to tell myself as I slept that when I woke I should look at Derek's life a little closer; whoever or whatever haunted him might have also killed him. It wouldn't hurt to dig a little.

Chapter Six

It turned out that I lost the entire rest of the day and then the night, too. I slept, apparently, pretty hard. I was surprised not to find Cliff in bed next to me when I woke up, but my bag was on my dresser with a note that said he didn't need it any longer, that he'd call later, and that I should sleep as much as I could. I didn't like the sense that I'd lost so many hours. I had to check calendars and clocks to understand where and when I'd landed. When I realized the amount of time that had passed, I mostly wondered what I'd missed. I thought I'd better begin to find out by asking the person who signed my paychecks.

"Betts, are you okay?" Gram said as she answered her phone.

"I'm fine," I said. "I slept through the night and I'm trying to get my bearings. I'm sorry if I missed something I'd committed to do, but at the moment I can't think of what it would be. How was your night? Bad dreams?"

"You didn't miss anything important from me. My dreams are still there, but Jake's got a sketch artist coming over this morning so I can get on paper what these people looked like. My goodness, young lady, thanks for talking to him even in the midst of being hurt. How are you? You need more rest."

I remembered talking to Jake but not about a sketch artist. He must have had the idea himself or Gram had mentioned it. I appreciated the attention to the matter.

"I'm too antsy to rest. Have you seen Jerome?"

"No."

"Have you met Grace or Robert yet?"

"No, not yet."

I wasn't sure what to do next, but I'd think of something. "I'll call you later, Gram."

"Okay, sweetheart, but I really hope you're all right. Try to get more rest."

At the moment, that was the last thing I wanted to do. "I will if I need it."

"Good girl. And call your parents. They're wondering about you. I told them you found Derek's body, but I didn't tell anyone you were hurt. They'll have my hide, of course, when they find out I knew. It's okay, I can take it."

"Thanks for that, Gram." I was sure I would have had the whole family in Dr. Callahan's office and hovering over me at home if they'd heard I was hit on the head. It was better for everyone that they hadn't known.

When I disconnected from Gram, I noticed that Mom, Dad, and Teddy had all called and texted me a number of times. I hadn't turned the volume on my phone down—boy, I really had slept hard.

I brewed a full pot of coffee, drank lots of it, filled a travel mug with the rest, left a message for Cliff, and then revved up the Nova. It knew the route to my parents' house almost on its own. I thought it would be good to show them in person that they didn't need to be worried about me, and I hadn't seen them in a couple weeks anyway. Good parent-bonding time was in order. And just by looking at me they'd never know I was hurt.

As I pulled into the driveway, however, I regretted not calling before stopping by. Teddy's big red truck was there, which meant that not only was he there (which wouldn't be a bad thing), but Opie might be with him, and I didn't want to talk to Opie. But if I pulled back out of the driveway, someone might see me and I'd have to explain. I didn't want to come up with a good lie even more than I didn't want to see Opie.

"Isabelle Winston, as I live and breathe," my dad said as he came out of the house carrying a large mirror and wearing two pairs of glasses on the top of his head. "Is it really you? I was beginning to think my daughter had moved far away. Two weeks, I think it's been, and we reside in the same small town." His face became serious over the top of the mirror frame. "Hey, I heard you found Derek, poor guy. I'm sorry for him and I'm sorry you had to see that."

"I'm fine. Sorry I've been busy, Dad," I said as I kissed his cheek and pulled off one of the pairs of glasses. I folded them and put them in the pocket on his shirt. He always wore a shirt with a pocket. High School math teacher habits were hard to break even if he had been promoted to principal almost two decades earlier. "What are you doing?"

"Your mother wants me to re-glaze this mirror. Do you even know what that means? I don't know what it means, and I have no idea how I'm going to do it, but she thinks that Google can tell me all I need to know. I'm moving it out to the garage because I think that anything called 're-glazing' will be a decidedly messy process."

"I don't know what it means either, but Google *can* find anything, I'm sure of it."

"Hope so."

"Teddy inside?"

"Yes, he and Opie stopped by for brunch. Your mother invited you and Cliff, too. It's our annual school's-out so-we-can-get-together-during-the-week event."

"I got some texts but I didn't take the time to read all of them. I woke up late. Cliff's swamped, though, I know that." At least I thought that was why I hadn't seen him since Dr. Callahan's office.

"You okay, Red?"

Dad had called me Red when I was a little girl and only in times of crisis as I'd gotten older. My hair was more auburn than red. It was good to hear the nickname, but only when he said it.

"I'm fine. I wish Derek hadn't been killed, of course, but I'm fine." I reached up to the tender spot on the back of my head and realized it was still sore, but I pulled my hand away before Dad noticed what I was doing.

"Cliff and the other police have any leads?" Since Cliff and I had become a couple again, Dad had decided the police force was made up of Cliff and "the others." Dad and the police chief, Jim, were very good friends, but family was number one in Dad's mind, and Cliff was family. Even Opie had become family.

"I don't think he has anything yet."

"He'll figure it out."

"I hope so."

Despite the fact that my mom was the auto mechanic teacher at the high school, my parents' attached garage wasn't filled with tools and doo-dads. They frequently used the two bikes that were against one wall, and one old toolbox sat on a bottom shelf of a rack of four. The other three shelves were filled with things like WD-40, paint, cat litter for ice storms, etc. There was also one large table in the back corner. Oddly, even though the garage didn't look like much happened inside it other than parking cars and bikes, Dad seemed to always have a small project going on the table. I followed him into the garage as he set the mirror on top of it.

"Re-glaze. Why in the world can't I just buy a new mirror?" he said.

"I don't know, but the frame is pretty on this one," I said, running my finger over the thick and ornate silver frame that curved in and out as it bordered the glass.

"Yeah, Miss Winny gave it to us when we got married," Dad said. Miss Winny was what he sometimes called his mom, Miz, aka Gram, and Missouri. She and I both had our fair share of nicknames.

"Really? Why don't I remember seeing it around the house?"

"Well, that's my fault, I suppose," Dad said as he rubbed a finger under his nose. "I got spooked by it and I hid it."

"You? You don't get spooked by anything. What happened?"

"You can't tell your mother. I hid it all those years ago and she found it just recently. I'll tell you the story, but don't tell anyone else, especially your mother. Promise?" he said.

"Of course." The last time Dad told me not to tell Mom something was when we'd made a secret trip to St. Louis to replace a bowl from her best china that I'd broken with a poorly aimed basketball, something I wasn't supposed to have in the house in the first place. To this day I didn't think she knew how many times she'd served mashed potatoes in the replacement bowl. Dad and I had years of shared conspiratorial glances over holiday dinner tables.

"Well, I thought I saw something in it. No, someone. Someone over my shoulder."

Goose bumps sprung up on my arms. "Really? That's creepy."

"It was, but the figure wasn't a creepy figure. He was just a cowboy. You know, from the olden days. Old hat, old-fashioned mustache. Know what I mean?"

"I think I do."

"I saw him in the mirror. He tipped his hat to me. When I turned around, he was gone. Not there. I never saw him again and I hid the damn mirror. I blamed it on the mirror, not any sort of mental condition I might have. My diagnosis has thus far been proven correct, because I haven't seen any surprise visitors in any other mirrors."

"Huh. What if you see him again while you're re-glazing?" I asked.

"I'll break it. Surely, accidents happen during re-glazing." Dad smiled. He was all dad when he wasn't all high school principal. The gray patches at his temples had gotten a little grayer but mostly he had a full head of thick, dark auburn hair. His green eyes were friendly, intelligent, and constantly somewhat suspicious. This probably happened to all high school principals. Whenever he smiled, he looked somewhat baby-faced. I thought he was an adorable man. He was also a great dad, even if terribly mechanically uninclined, unlike my mother. Mom could mop a floor with precision, turn around and fix a carburetor without breaking a sweat or a nail, and look amazing doing it all.

"I'll help you break it if you want," I said.

"Oh, good. That sounds like fun. We'll have to do it when we're in bad moods about something. Take out our aggressions on an innocent mirror. To hell with superstitions. I suppose, though, if I see that cowboy again, it won't be so innocent."

At this point in his life, it would be, at best, confusing, at worst completely discombobulating to tell Dad that he probably had inherited some of his mother's skills of seeing and communicating with ghosts. Besides, since the ghost rules kept changing anyway, I didn't want him thrown into the mix just when we weren't sure what might happen next.

If I ever saw him in person again, I'd try to remember to ask Jerome to stay out of Dad's mirror if he could help it.

"It was probably just a trick of light or something," I said.

"Maybe," Dad said doubtfully.

I put my arm around his shoulders and hugged him. He put his hand over mine.

"You really okay, sweetheart?"

"I'm okay," I said.

"Well, let me know if you need anything from me. I suggest running inside for some of your mother's breakfast casserole. I'm sure it is delicious enough to help ease all ills and worries, but, fair warning, as I said, Opie is in there."

"I'm trying to be nicer to her. I think she and Teddy actually like each other. It baffles me."

Dad shrugged. "Love is weird and blind, and sometimes plain old stupid. She's trying—well, she's doing the best she can do with the personality quirks she's been dealt. Oh, that sounded a little mean. I don't want to be mean. Don't tell your mother about that either."

I laughed. Dad was far from mean. He was just trying to be supportive. I appreciated the effort and kissed his cheek again.

"I'll go say hi and have some casserole," I said.

"Good girl."

As I made my way into the house, I thought briefly about how much fun it would be to have Dad in on the ghostly encounters. But there was no need to bother him with it at this point. If his ability hadn't been strong enough to see and communicate clearly with Jerome outside a mirror back then, then maybe his abilities just weren't all that important. I hadn't had much choice but to talk to the ghost who seemed so real to me from the first moment I'd met him. I wondered if Dad had—or has since— smelled the wood smoke, but there was no way to ask that question without causing him to have a million more.

"Betts!" Mom said as I came through the front door. The kitchen was a straight shot to the back of the house. She could see me when I came in as she stood at the sink washing something. "You're here—I'm so glad. Come join us and have something to eat. There's still some left."

I heard laughter, but I couldn't see Teddy and Opie until I reached the kitchen.

"Smells great in here," I said, my stomach waking up voraciously.

"Have a seat," Mom said as she nodded at the table at the far end of the room. Mom was tall, thin, blond, and very pretty. She was one of those women whose features got better as she got older. Even though she'd always been thin, her face had been pleasantly round when she was younger. As she'd hit her mid-fifties, her facial features had sharpened, giving her a regal look. She'd gone from cute to beautiful. I looked nothing like her so I didn't plan on such an outcome for my middle age. I looked like Gram, but though she wasn't beautiful in the ways my mom was, I liked the way she'd aged, too. I got some lucky genes.

And so had Teddy. He looked more like Mom than Dad, but his male version had caused more heartbreak and heartache than one small town and a big sister in Missouri should have to suffer.

He'd never had a serious girlfriend. Until Opie—Ophelia Buford. Opie was older than Teddy. She was my age. The relationship between she and Teddy had caught everyone off guard. There had never been any indication that the two of them were attracted to each other, but one day they were together. Happily. Sappily. Awfully. Together.

For a short time, I'd thought it was disloyal of my brother to date the woman who'd made my life so miserable during our growing-up years. But then I'd watched them together and even I couldn't deny that they were a good couple. However, their "coupling" still got under my skin.

"Betts, how ya doin', sis'?" Teddy said as he stood and gave me a hug.

"I'm fine. That's quite a greeting." I hugged back with almost as much enthusiasm as he'd put into it.

"It's good to see you," he said. "I heard about Derek and I'm sorry."

I looked into his eyes. Nope, he didn't know I'd been hit over the head either. So far, so good on keeping that secret.

"Thanks. I'm sorry, too. Not a good way to go."

"Hi, Betts," Opie said from the table. I would have thought it phony and suspicious if she'd gotten up to hug me. She knew that.

"Opie, how are you?"

"Well. You? Sorry about what you went through yesterday." Opie looked good. She was a pretty woman anyway; curvy and blond. She typically wore a thick coat of makeup, but lately that had been mellower. She looked very happy and so did Teddy.

Who was I to judge who my brother dated?

"Thanks. I'm fine."

"Come sit and have some of your mother's wonderful casserole," Opie said, sincerity lining her words. I pushed away the encroaching suspicion.

I pulled up a chair and hurriedly scooped out some of the casserole and plopped it onto a plate.

"I bet it was one of Derek's wives," Opie said after I'd had a bite or two. I was sitting right next to her, but she leaned a little closer to me.

"Which one?" I said around the egg, ham, and potato concoction that was one of mom's few recipes. She wasn't the best cook, but she tried. And Dad hadn't gotten his mother's cooking abilities, so Teddy and I had always enjoyed going to Gram's house for meals, which is where I first learned my cooking skills and deep appreciation for her food and cooking methods.

"How many have there been?" Mom asked.

Teddy fell into thought and started ticking off his fingers. "I think he was married five times."

"Five?" Mom said. "I knew he'd been married a lot, but how is five even possible?"

"Gram was married a couple," Teddy said, as if that was an equal amount.

"But she quit doing all that silliness after two," Mom said.

I wanted to say, *"How in the world did Derek find five women who wanted to marry him?"* That would have been extremely rude and uncalled for, but I still wondered.

I knew he'd been married more than once, but five times? He was not a nice enough man to participate in a decent conversation from all I could tell. How did five women get past that?

"Do you know who they all were?" I asked Teddy.

"Sure, I dated one after they divorced. She was lots older than me." He cringed the second after he said it.

"It's fine, Teds, I know you've dated almost everyone who has spent any time being single, even older women. Quit worrying about that stuff," Opie said.

I was struck silent with my mouth slightly agape. It was a good thing I'd already swallowed the bite of casserole. There was nothing phony in Opie's voice. She meant exactly what she said. Where was jealous, overly-involved Opie?

"Yeah, but I've never been as happy with anyone as I am with you,"

Teddy said.

I put the fork on my plate. If they kissed, I was going to have to go out to the garage and help my dad learn how to re-glaze the haunted mirror.

"So true," Opie said with satisfaction.

"Anyway," I said. "Who were the wives?"

"I know their first names and where they work, I think," Teddy said. "Let's see, Wendy from the nail shop; Gina from the post office; Ridley, Doc's nurse; Bonnie, the attorney; and Rachel, who works at the bank."

"Ridley, the nurse?" I said. "Petite, brown curly hair?"

"That's the one. She's the one I went out on a date with. You know her?"

"I think I remember her from when I was in there for a cold or something. When were they married?" Just in time I stopped myself from telling them that I'd seen Ridley the day before, when I'd been looked at for a head injury. I thought I remembered her being upset. If she'd been married to Derek and even if their divorced had been less than amicable, she might have been upset about his murder.

"She was his third wife."

"Do you remember when they were together?" I said.

"Mid-two-thousands some time, 2004, 2005 maybe."

"What was she like on the date?" I said.

Teddy shrugged. "Oddly, she spent most of it talking about Derek and his mother and what a bizarre relationship they had."

That comment garnered everyone's attention.

"I know that Lynn is a complainer and I know that Derek always kowtowed to her, but is there more?" Mom asked.

Teddy bit at the inside of his cheek as he fell into thought again. "Ridley said that Derek answered his phone every time his mother called. No matter when or what it was, if she needed him, he'd go help her. This happened at all hours for all things."

"I don't understand, Teddy," I said. "If Lynn was like that with Derek, who didn't seem all that personable anyway, why were so many women interested in marrying him?"

"It baffles the mind, doesn't it?" Opie said. "But I might have some insight into that."

Opie liked the spotlight and she'd just said the right words to get it to shine in her direction.

"Go ahead."

"Derek dated lots of girls, me included." Opie smiled at Teddy.

"Of course he did," Teddy said. "Who wouldn't want to date you?"

Please.

Opie laughed a little. "Well, we only went out on one date. There was no spark. At all. But the date was nice. He was nice. Well, he wasn't *not* nice, you know. Anyway, he was normally so quiet and withdrawn, but when you were with him one-on-one, without his mom, it was like he was *almost* clever and funny. It was like he was saving that part of his personality just for that date and it just never quite blossomed. Perhaps all those silly women thought they could change him."

I looked at Opie and then at my previously love-'em-and-leave-'em brother and then back at Opie. I sensed that even my mom was thinking pot/kettle/black, but neither of us commented.

"Did his mother call during the date?" I asked.

"No, but he did check his phone a couple times. Not rudely, but casually. I didn't know anything about his attention to his mom until just now, but I bet he was looking for her call. Though, I can't know anything for sure."

My appetite had returned so I took another bite and thought as I chewed. There had to be more. Good dates don't always make for good marriages. And if he dated any of them long enough and Lynn really was that demanding, there was no way he could have hidden it through an entire courtship.

Would Ridley talk to me? Girl to girl. She and I didn't know each other but perhaps we'd bonded over my good vitals. It might be worth a shot.

Of course, Derek's murder might not have one thing to do with the fact that he'd been married to five women. I didn't know all that he did with his days. I knew he worked as a handyman, but surely there was nothing in the handyman business what could get someone killed. But anything was possible.

When Dad came in from the garage without the mirror, our conversation turned to things other than Derek Rowlett and his murder. It was much more interesting to talk about Mom's latest muscle car and how she restored the engine in two days flat; a new record.

I left not too much later. It didn't occur to me at the time that Opie and I had spent over an hour together and neither of us had insulted the other one. If I thought about it, I wasn't sure if that was a good thing or a bad thing.

Chapter Seven

All summer long, Jake had had them right where he wanted them. His performances captured his audiences. They loved him. He was such an appealing character, both in real life and in his actor/poet's persona. He was short, but handsome in ways that reminded people of dashing heroes from classic movies. His deep voice and the poems he wrote along with his fake sheriff character mesmerized our tourists every year. He was one of the bigger draws in town, and his stellar reputation only continued to grow.

He had most recently dated a woman he'd met when the town hosted a cowboy poetry convention in April. He and Esther were still seeing each other, but Jake was never one to discuss his dating life all that much, even with me. I liked Esther and I liked how happy she seemed to make Jake, but she lived in Kansas City. The trip between Broken Rope and Kansas City wasn't terrible, but I knew the almost four-hour drive each way wasn't always a welcome adventure.

Despite his mostly quiet personal life, every year Jake gained a faithful following of women of all ages who thought he was too adorable not to flirt with. It was mostly harmless, but there were always a few who were more than serious about wanting to get to know him better. I thought he handled those moments so well—friendly, but clear that he wasn't interested in any future rendezvous with transitory visitors.

He was in the middle of one of the more harmless moments when I entered his fake sheriff's office. The show was over, the crowd had cleared, but a small group of female tourists was hanging around, hoping to get Jake to join them for coffee.

"Thank you, ladies, but my appointment is here. Hello, Betts," he said with a smile.

"Jake, good to see you," I said. "Thanks for fitting me into your schedule."

Each in the group of females gave me a once-over and then tried to get Jake to commit to something later.

"Too busy, but I sure appreciate the invitation," he said. "Hope you all enjoy your time in Broken Rope. You'll find a great reenactment of a gun battle just down the way. I think it starts in about ten minutes. I've heard we've got a particularly large crop of handsome cowboys in the gun battles this year," he said.

He'd mentioned the right thing. The young women left, ignoring me and smiling once more at Jake as they exited.

"Having fun?" I said when it was just the two of us.

"Always," he said waving off the moment. "How are you feeling?"

"Almost as good as new. I slept so much that I'm a little tired, but I'll recover soon enough."

"Good. You look great." He inspected my eyes and put his hand to my forehead. "Yep, you're fine. I found some pictures of train stations, or depots as some of them are called. You up for looking at them?"

"Definitely."

"Come on back and we'll see if we can figure out what's going on."

Jake led the way to his back archive room. The room with tall ceilings and shelf-filled walls was fitted with temperature and humidity controls that kept all his archived materials safe from environmental harm. The shelves were stacked with folders full of items pertinent to Broken Rope history. The folders were made of a special plastic created for document archives. Regular old plastic wasn't good enough. I wasn't sure how much money Jake had spent on his room, but he could afford it, whatever it was. He was rich; a self-made millionaire who'd dropped out of college and made his fortune via the stock market. He had a gift. He often told me he'd invest my money for me and make me rich, too, but I didn't think money and friendship mixed well. Besides, I'd invested in a few stocks on my own and had never once made a cent; I didn't want to jinx his good run.

A big table filled the middle of the room. It was illuminated by an old Broken Rope saloon chandelier, once lit with candles, now wired for electricity. One corner of the table currently held a couple of small stacks of what I guessed were pictures of old train stations.

"You do know that our station was one of the more amazing stops through the middle of the country," he said after he closed the door behind us.

"You've mentioned that before," I said.

"It was grand," he continued as he walked around to the far corner of the table. "It was a two-story building, with the ticket counter and some sort of food vending on the bottom level. There was a barbershop and a beauty salon on the top floor. Shoe shining—you know, all the good stuff from back in the day."

"Was a train station an odd place for such things at that time?"

Jake shrugged. "Usually, train stations around here, in the country, were just train stations, but the mayor of Broken Rope wanted to do something spectacular, something that would make Broken Rope stand out for much more than all the criminal activity."

"Did it work?"

"I'm not sure." Jake shrugged. "I haven't had a chance to really dig deep. I haven't found any articles regarding the popularity of the station or its appeal. But of the station pictures I've found so far, Broken Rope's architecture, the building, was definitely the most interesting."

"We should have kept it around," I said. "It would have made a good tourist stop."

"The town's layout changed when passenger train travel stopped being so popular. At the time, no one knew that the town would become what it has become, and trains don't travel through here anymore. It might someday be a good idea to re-create all that, though probably not at the end of your street. We'd need a new location." Jake pulled the first few pictures off the pile. "Here, look at these."

The pictures were all black and white, or perhaps sepia would be a better description. The building in the first one was definitely the one I'd seen during Robert's visit.

"That's it, the Broken Rope station. I think this was all red," I said as

I pointed to the darker tones.

"Really? Oh, that's great to know. What else do you remember?"

"The shutters were white. Not off-white, but bright white. The building that I visited was clean, almost as if it was brand new."

"What year was it?"

"I can tell you the exact day Grace thought it was. August 16, 1888."

"Good to know." Jake wrote the date on a piece of scratch paper.

"Something's different, though." I inspected one of the pictures.

"What?" Jake inspected it, too.

"I'm not sure. It's like it's *almost* the building, but it's a little off."

"Could that just be you? Your memory or the fact that it was part of a ghost visit?"

"Probably," I said. "No, this is the one. Must be. It's too close not to be."

"All right. Take a look at these. One of them might be the other station."

Jake pulled out three more pictures, one at a time. "This one is from Vicksburg, Mississippi. I don't know if she was from anywhere near Vicksburg, but it's the only Mississippi station picture I've found so far." He pointed to the next one. "This one is from Little Rock; she would have gone through there to get to Broken Rope from Mississippi. And, this one is from Frankland, Missouri, right down the road from us—well, by a couple hours; she might have gone through there, too. These are the only pictures I've been able to find so far, but I'm still working on it."

The three stations were all very different. The Vicksburg station was impressive, wider than the Broken Rope station, two stories with a round balcony coming out from the middle of the top floor.

"Not this one," I said as I pointed at the Vicksburg station. "It's beautiful."

The Little Rock station was also impressive. It wasn't wide, but it stood two stories tall with a long platform and what looked like loading docks extending backwards away from the main building.

"No, this isn't it," I pointed at the Little Rock picture.

The Frankland station might have been the one, but it was difficult to tell from the picture. It was a side view with the building barely visible. I could see it was one story and fairly simple, but not much more than that.

"I don't know, Jake, this might be it. It's the closest of these three, that's for sure, but I just don't know. Any other angles?"

"Not yet, but I'll keep looking. That's interesting to note, though,"

Jake said. "If this is the station and if Grace was killed here, that means she might not have made it to Broken Rope. On her route, Frankland would have been before Broken Rope."

I picked up the picture and looked even closer. Finally, I shrugged.

"I just can't be sure. I should have paid better attention to the buildings. Sorry."

"I can keep looking. I'll find some more shots of the Frankland station."

"Thank you."

The air in the room suddenly changed, and became scented—to me at least.

"Uh-oh, I think we have a visitor," I said as I looked around for Grace. Her soft floral aroma was unmistakable even after only one previous sniff.

"Let me grab my camera," Jake said as he hurried to his desk. "It might not be fixed, but I want to give it a try."

The floral scent suddenly mixed with the musky scent of Robert Findlay. The smells were good together and I wished Jake could smell them, too.

"I think we're getting two," I said.

Across the room and on the other side of the table, Robert and Grace did appear, both of them in the almost transparent forms that went along with so much light. They were briefly disoriented, but soon they noticed me and Jake, and then they noticed each other.

"This is going to be interesting," I said to Jake. "Let me listen to them, and I'll interpret later if your camera isn't working."

"Deal," Jake said as he started the camera and pointed it at the space I was watching.

"Grace, Grace, is that really you?" Robert said as he looked at her, his eyes wide, unbelieving and surprised. I wondered if a long-dead man could go into shock.

"Robert! Yes, my love, it is me, it is." She looked around, at me with knitted eyebrows, and then back at Robert. "I don't know where we are, but I have met that woman. Do you know where we are?"

"You're both dead," I said, offering a quick summary of our previous conversations. They'd catch up. "You're the ghosts of your former selves and you're back in Broken Rope. My name is Betts, this is Jake. He can't see you or hear you but I can. We're all in the back of his building."

"Yes, I remember now," Grace said. "But Robert is here, too."

"I am, dear, sweet Grace."

They moved closer together and then reached for each other.

"Uh, that might not turn out like you expect," I said. "You might not actually be able to feel each other. I'm not really sure."

They both hesitated and then glanced down at their own hands. They looked up at each other in tandem and smiled.

"Grace."

"Robert."

They reached and they touched but it would be impossible to understand what they were or weren't feeling.

"Okay?" I said.

They didn't waste another moment before their ghostly forms came together in a kiss. Typically, I wasn't all that interested in watching people kiss each other, but I was fascinated by Grace and Robert and their almost transparent lips touching.

"They're kissing," I said to Jake.

"Nice."

"It's lovely," I said as I looked at him. I looked back at the couple, "but a little different. Ghost kissing."

"Oh, I see. Well, when you're kissing Jerome, there's only one ghost involved. I have pictures and it didn't seem all that different to me."

"Right."

"Grace, I waited for you. I waited forever," Robert said when they disengaged.

"And I came to you," Grace said. "At least I was on my way. But something happened, Robert."

"Betts says you were murdered. Who killed you, Grace?"

"I don't know." Grace surprised me with a nervous laugh. "What good would it do to know at this point, Robert? We're here, we're together. Even if we don't stay together, we have this moment."

"Well," I interrupted, "it would maybe offer you a little peace. I don't know how unsettled you feel, but it might not hurt to find out more details, if it's even possible. It will be pretty hard to get answers at this point. It's been a long time." I didn't bring up Gram's dreams or the sketch artist. Not yet.

"Where in the world would we begin?" Grace asked.

I shrugged. "How about right now and with a few questions? Answer whatever you can. Just do your best."

"All right," Grace said. Robert nodded when she looked at him.

But there was something in that nod. I barely caught it, but I was sure I saw some hesitation, something that made Robert less than thrilled about answering questions. So, naturally, I started with him.

"Robert, do you have a last memory of Grace?" I asked.

He blinked. "Yes, I do. A letter. Grace, you sent me a letter to tell me that you would be coming to Broken Rope, and in the letter you wrote the date you would arrive."

"Yes."

And then I saw some hesitation in Grace. Suddenly, I had a huge realization. Neither of these ghosts was being completely truthful, or at least, that's what I sensed.

"Do you remember something different, Grace?" I asked as I stepped around the corner of the table and a little closer to the ghosts. I needed to see them better. "Jake, can we dim or turn off the light?"

"Sure." He put down the camera and hurried to the switch. He turned the lights down enough that I didn't feel like I had to squint to see the ghosts better.

Grace looked at me. "I don't know . . ."

"What? You're remembering something. I can tell," I said.

"Well." Grace looked at Robert. "I did tell you a date I would arrive, my love, but I was late."

"No, you weren't late. You never even made it," Robert corrected.

"I don't know exactly. It's confusing. I do think something happened to me, but I also know I was late leaving Mississippi, but only by two days. I meant to send a letter or a telegram to let you know, but I was just so anxious to get to you that I didn't take the time."

"Why were you late?" Robert asked.

"I had to take care of something before I left."

"What?" Robert and I asked.

"Oh, dear," Grace said as she wrung her hands. "I suppose none of it matters now, but it's something I should have told you about then. I just couldn't."

"Grace, what? You know you can tell me anything," Robert said.

I knew that that statement usually preceded something that one shouldn't ever tell anyone. I held my breath.

"Robert, I was married. When you and I met, I was married."

Given the passing of time, that might not have been too huge a hurdle to overcome emotionally. Placed in context back in 1888, the fact that Grace was married and that she was running off to be with another man, not even taking their skin colors into account, was a big deal. Divorce was almost unheard of. Grace probably hadn't even bothered with trying to obtain one.

"Back up just a little. Where did the two of you meet?" I said.

"I was in Vicksburg, Mississippi for business. We met there," Robert said. I'd have to let Jake know later that he'd managed to find the correct Mississippi station. "I went back three times and we saw each other each time."

"It was love at first sight," Grace said.

"Got that, but, Robert, you never knew Grace was married?" I asked.

"No."

"I didn't tell him."

"Grace, I don't understand. You fell in love with Robert but were married to someone else?" I said.

"Yes. I didn't want him to know. And I . . . well, I couldn't get away from my husband at first. That's why I was delayed. I escaped when I could."

"You escaped? Was your husband a bad man?" I said.

"Yes, he was a horrible man." She looked away from Robert and down at the ground. Her hands came together and her index fingers met worriedly. "He hurt me frequently."

My reaction began with a hollow pit in my stomach. Anger at

Grace's husband and at the prevailing attitudes of the time buzzed inside me. The shame she felt was wrong. I wanted to take her by her shoulders and explain at least that part of feminism to her, but it wouldn't have helped at this point. I might tell her about it, but not right now.

I knew Robert's reaction wouldn't be the same as mine. He was a product of Grace's time, too.

"You belonged to another?" he said.

I cringed. I'd been correct. No sympathy there.

"I did," Grace said, bowing her head even more deeply.

It was too much.

"Grace, Robert, the times have changed," I interjected. "People can easily—well, for the most part—leave their spouse and obtain a divorce with little hassle. Robert, if a woman is being brutalized, nowadays we cheer her on when she escapes. And, I believe *escape* is the exact word that Grace just used."

"But we were going to be married. Along with whatever else was wrong with what we were doing, we would have been committing bigamy," Robert said.

"Robert," Grace began, "I would have risked it. And if I'd ever been caught, I would have made sure the authorities knew that you'd been kept in the dark about my past. You wouldn't have been in trouble."

Robert seemed to suddenly better understand what was important here. He stepped closer to Grace and studied her. He ran the tips of his finger over her jaw and chin. I could see the decades of history shift. He hadn't lived through the changes that had occurred over time, but that didn't matter. What mattered was his love for Grace. He would have gotten there eventually on his own, but I was glad to have helped. I held back a fist pump.

"Grace, there's something I need to tell you, too," Robert said.

"Uh-oh," I said again.

"More kissing?" Jake asked.

"Nope. Keep filming. Hopefully we can look at it later."

"Anything, Robert," she said.

"Grace, I was late to the station, too. I mean, when you didn't show when you were supposed to, I left and then didn't return for at least three days. If only I'd gone there those days and you'd made it to Broken Rope, I might have found you."

I leaned over and said quietly to Jake, "In their own ways, they were both late."

"That could cause some problems," he said.

"Were you angry at me for not being there that day?" Grace said.

"No. I became ill," Robert said. "Very ill. I didn't even make it home that first day. I was put up in the back of the saloon by the barkeep himself

"I collapsed inside the bar. He thought I was drunk, but when he found I was ill, he put me in a bed and let me get well. I'd planned to go back to the station, but I became so sick. I didn't return for days." Robert paused as his eyebrows came together. "I'm trying to remember the time in between coming to the station the first time and then days later, when I started going every day. Some things are suddenly becoming so clear, but others aren't. I'm missing some memories." He looked at me. "Betts, I think something important must have happened, but it's as if I have a giant hole in my memories."

"That's normal. All the ghosts' memories are a little vague for a while," I said, but I didn't think that's really what he was saying. His memories seemed pretty darn clear, except for the blank spot. The normal ghost Swiss-cheese memory was spotty, not distinctly broken in only one spot. At least, that's not how it had worked up until now.

"I'm sorry you were ill, Robert. That's terrible," Grace said.

"Excuse me," I interrupted. I turned to Jake. "Is the legend that

Robert went to the train station every day for the rest of his life because he was hoping Grace would still arrive?"

"Yes."

"Does that help at all?" I said to Robert.

"No," he said firmly. "I knew she wasn't coming." He blinked. "Oh, dear. Until this very moment I didn't remember that. I knew Grace wasn't coming. That's part of my missing memory. How did I know that?" Confusion pulled at Robert's handsome face. "I went to the station every day to punish myself."

"Why? Why would you punish yourself?" I asked.

"I don't know."

I bit my lip as I looked at the ghosts and then at Jake. I didn't know if there was any way Jake could figure out the facts from that long ago. The legend was apparently incorrect. He knew his Broken Rope history, but I suspected the only people who would really have the answers were Grace and Robert. "The legend was wrong," I said to Jake.

"What? I don't understand," Jake said.

"It wasn't about sadness, it was about guilt." I looked at each of the ghosts. "Something tells me Robert knows much more than he's remembering about what happened to Grace."

"You think Robert killed Grace?" Jake asked, his words sending the ghosts into genuine surprise and confusion.

"I don't know exactly. But we're missing something," I said. "Robert's missing a chunk of memory."

"We all are, apparently," Jake said.

"I would like to know what happened," Robert said, but, of course, Jake didn't hear that part.

"Keep filming," I said. I literally pushed up my sleeves. "Let's see what I can get out of them."

"All right."

But the ghosts' confusion caused them to want to retreat to wherever they retreat when they're visiting Broken Rope. They were polite but distant as they told me they needed to go, despite my pleas for them to stay just a little longer. They even stepped away from each other before they disappeared. Their sudden strange behavior and departure made me wonder if their time here was shortened, as if their batteries were running out. But I did not sense that they were gone for good. I hoped not.

"Never mind, Jake. They're gone."

The best we could do was hope for another chance.

Chapter Eight

We played back the recording from Jake's camera but all we got was fuzzy nothingness. It was disappointing for us both.

I relayed as best I could everything that Robert and Grace had said. Jake said he'd try to pursue new avenues of research even if he couldn't quite figure out how to readily find those avenues. I left as he was cussing the camera and searching for either a sledgehammer to destroy it or a screwdriver to attempt to fix it.

As I walked to the Nova I called Gram to tell her I was on the way over but she didn't answer her phone. I'd forgotten to thank Jake for rounding up a sketch artist and I hoped they'd still be there when I arrived. My rush to get to her, however, was diverted when I noticed a few women making their way into the nail salon.

The salon was located in a bad spot, at the end of the block and around the corner from the main tourist attractions. A nail salon didn't fit with the Old West theme of Main Street. *Unless it was a horseshoe nail salon*—I remembered the town councilmember's joke during the meeting in which the nail salon's location was discussed.

No one had laughed much.

But despite the poor location, Broken Nails? nail salon did a booming business. They were the only nail game in town, unless of course you did consider the horseshoeing activity done in the livery. Locals and tourists alike enjoyed a good manicure or pedicure. I'd indulged a couple of times, but I was far from a regular.

Teddy had mentioned that one of Derek's ex-wives, Wendy, worked at the salon. I thought I knew who Wendy was, but I wasn't sure. I was overly curious about Derek and his numerous wives. Maybe it wasn't all that complicated but it still seemed odd, him being married so many times. On impulse, I decided it wouldn't hurt to take a few more minutes and introduce myself to Wendy, maybe see where the conversation went from there.

"Help you?" a bright eyed and friendly teenager greeted me at the tall, narrow front counter. She had to speak up because the hum of conversation, foot whirlpools, and battery-powered nail implements kept the noise level high. As was usual, Broken Nails? was doing a brisk business.

"Is Wendy here and available?" I asked.

The teenager looked over her shoulder. "Wendy! You available?"

"Mani or pedi or both?" Wendy, I presumed, said from the second manicure table in. I couldn't see what she was doing, but the woman across from her had her hands on the table.

The teenager looked at me with lifted eyebrows.

"Actually, neither, I just want to talk to her," I said. I should have agreed to a nail treatment, but I didn't want to take the time. I pulled out a five-dollar bill—that was all I had in my pocket. "Just for a second or two."

The teenager fought a laugh, and her eyebrows rose higher.

"Just a question, Wendy," she said over her shoulder.

"Sure, give me a minute," Wendy said.

I realized I'd probably just made a service industry faux pas but I was in too deep to back out now.

"Have a seat," the teenager said.

The black plastic chairs weren't inviting, but I sat nonetheless and then picked up a gossip magazine, perusing it only for show.

"Can I help you?" Wendy said a moment later. She was clearly over fifty, but was still petite and cute, in a wholesome way. Her short brown hair and makeup-free ivory skin made it difficult to determine exactly how far past fifty she was.

"I'm Betts Winston." I stood and extended my hand.

Wendy laughed. "Everyone knows who you and Missouri are, Betts. I'm Wendy Miller. Nice to meet you."

"Thanks," I said. I looked around. "I know you're busy, but any chance you'd like to go for a cup of coffee?"

Wendy looked back toward the salon's depths. "Oh gosh, I don't have time and I don't have a break for another couple hours. I have about five minutes while my client dries. Do you want to step outside? We've got a bench."

"That'd be great," I said. I followed Wendy as she pushed through the door and took a seat on the bench that was to the side of the front window.

"You found Derek's body?" she said before I sat down all the way.

"I did. I'm sorry for your loss," I said.

"I appreciate that. Did you come here just for condolences?" She didn't seem sad.

"No. I was curious and I hoped I could ask you a couple questions." I cringed inwardly but hoped I kept my face neutral. This wasn't exactly the right way to handle things, but, again, I was now in too deep.

"You're dating Officer Sebastian, right?"

"Yes, but this . . . this isn't police business."

"Are you asking because you were interested in dating Derek?"

"Oh. No, not at all," I said.

"Okay, then I'll do what I can to answer," she said.

"What wife were you? I mean, what number?" I cleared my throat. "When were you two married?"

"Why do you want to know that?" she said, her tone suddenly becoming less friendly.

I turned a few mental summersaults, thinking I should have been better prepared for this conversation, thinking maybe I shouldn't have even started it in the first place.

"Wendy, I'm curious about Derek. He was married five times. I don't know anyone else who's so prolific, marriage-wise—and divorce-wise, too. Though Derek and I weren't dating, I got to know him a little better because he and his mother participated in one of our night cooking classes. He was great with green beans. Anyway, I wonder how in the world anyone can go through marriage and divorce five times. It seems like most people would quit trying at about two or three."

Wendy's mouth made a straight, tight line.

"You mean, how could five people be so attracted to someone who isn't attractive?" she said.

"Actually, the sheer number of times would be unusual for anyone. And, I was mostly thinking he wasn't all that outgoing, and a . . . shy person would have an even more difficult time. Anyway, I hope I don't sound mean. Perhaps he and I just never connected."

Wendy scratched a spot under her ear as she looked at the sidewalk. Since this area of town wasn't part of our main attractions, it received the luxury of cement sidewalks instead of wooden boardwalks. She looked back at me. "Derek wasn't the best-looking person, but he was a nice guy. Nobody's a supermodel, Betts."

I wondered what I'd said to make her think I was talking about his looks. But then I realized that her response was practiced, a script she'd read from before. I must not have been the only one curious enough about the attraction to ask. My other fleeting thought was that this was just her defensive way to make someone sorry they brought up the subject in the first place and end any chance to delve deeper into the conversation. "I'm sorry. I didn't mean to offend you," I said.

"Right." Wendy stood up and marched to the door. "Next time you'd like to give condolences, just say you're sorry. You don't need to know so much."

"Of course," I said.

Wendy opened the door with much more force than necessary and went inside.

I glanced around at the pockets of tourists making their way to Main Street.

"That didn't go quite as planned," I said aloud to myself.

I hoped things would go better with Gram at the cooking school, but my hopes deflated when I saw not only Gram's Volvo in the parking lot, but an old Honda, too. It was Paul's car. There were no other vehicles, so I assumed that the sketch artist has already come and gone. Why would Paul be there? I had all but forgotten that we had a vegetable class scheduled for that evening. Considering the circumstances, I guess I thought it must have been canceled, but maybe Gram hadn't thought the same, or she'd forgotten to make the phone calls.

I didn't get a chance to ask, though, because the next surprise was even bigger than the first. Paul was the sketch artist.

"Betts, come see what Paul has done," Gram said enthusiastically as I came through the front swinging doors.

"You're an artist?" I said as I approached.

"Yeah, sort of," Paul said.

"There's no sort of about it," Gram said. "He's really, really good."

Both Paul and Gram were sitting on stools. Large pieces of paper were spread across the center butcher block. Paul balanced a large sketchpad on his thighs and held a charcoal pencil.

"Thanks, Miz," Paul said.

I glanced over the sketches on the table and then moved to a spot behind Paul and looked over his shoulder.

"Wow, I had no idea," I said. "You really are good."

"Thanks," he said as humbly as possible.

The fact that he seemed to have moved beyond our recent uncomfortable moments helped me do the same.

"Uh-oh," I said as I looked closely at a couple of the pictures.

From the pieces of paper spread on the table, it was clear that he had been working to create the likenesses of two different men; a couple of the sketches were complete or close to it.

"What?" Gram and Paul both said.

"This is Robert. This is the man Grace was supposed to meet." I looked at Gram.

Paul had captured Robert's features, though they weren't the same gentle though somewhat grumpy features I'd seen. Instead of questioning eyes, these eyes were squinted in anger. The mouth was a mix between a frown and a grimace. The Robert I'd met had short, neatly groomed hair. In the pictures, a tuft had come loose and fallen over his forehead.

"Oh. That's not good," Gram said.

"I don't understand. You know this man—Robert? Who is he and who is Grace?" Paul asked.

I didn't know what Jake and Gram had told Paul to get him to sketch the pictures. I looked at Gram again. Did Paul think this was about nightmares?

"Interestingly," Gram began, "this man is a person from Broken Rope's past. Betts has recently learned his story. He was in love with a woman but they were never able to be together. I wonder if Betts's recent education has contributed to the nightmares I've been having. Perhaps that's why I've been 'seeing' this man." Gram lifted her eyebrows and sent me a tiny shrug.

"That *is* interesting," Paul said. "Your nightmares are showing you someone from Broken Rope's past. Actually, it's more than interesting. It's pretty amazing."

"That might be it," I interjected, hoping Paul didn't spend too much time thinking about it. "Tell me more about the nightmares."

"It's all very brutal and not pleasant to think or talk about," Gram said. "No one needs the details except to know that these men, in my nightmares, are vicious killers."

"Do you see their victim?" I asked.

"No, never." Gram paused. "Instead, I feel like I'm their victim."

"Oh, Gram, I'm so sorry," I said.

"It's okay. We're going to understand it all better and they will go away. That's what will happen, I'm sure," she said, not sounding sure at all.

"How about this man?" I picked up the rendition of the other killer.

He was also a white man, not old, but it was difficult to tell his age because he had a round face with heavy jowls. His nose was sharp, contrasting with his fleshy cheeks. Despite how the individual features shouldn't fit together, he wasn't an unpleasant man to look at.

"The two of them are different from each other. That man is silent and focused, but not as frightening. The other one, the one who looks like

Robert, is loud. He's in a rage and he's yelling. I can hear his yells, but I can't understand the words."

"That's not good," I said, repeating what Gram had said a moment earlier.

The realization that Robert might have contributed to Grace's murder was more a surprise than it should have been. I had thought it was a possibility but I hadn't seriously considered it. It was also deeply bothersome. The ghost I'd come to briefly know had tricked me—and Grace and Jake. If he proved to be a killer, his potentially deep-seated betrayal would be hard to accept.

There was also the "why?" Why in the world would he have killed Grace? What had happened that had caused his love to change so drastically? If I had to guess at this point, I'd probably say that he learned of her husband. I was convinced that in his current form he had no memory of knowing when he was alive that Grace had been married. His surprise had been too genuine. Either that, or he was a great actor.

Putting aside my thoughts about Robert, I wondered who the other man was. Would Robert and Grace recognize him? Had he killed or helped Robert kill Grace?

There was a chance I was jumping to all the wrong conclusions, or that Gram's nightmares were deceiving, but it was a challenge to put the elements together any other way.

"Not good?" Paul asked.

"Well, it's good news to have the faces. You really are talented, Paul. Thank you, but no, having these men haunt Gram's dreams is not a good thing. Any nightmares are scary."

In response, he blinked funny. His eyes closed quickly and then his eyelids seemed heavy as he dragged them open. He dropped the charcoal pencil; it fell to the floor and rolled under the butcher block. The sketchpad tilted back and landed on the table as he stood.

"Isabelle," he said as he grabbed my arms and a faint scent of wood smoke made it to my nose. His voice didn't sound right.

"What is it?" I said.

"Isabelle, it's me. It's Jerome," Paul said.

"Jerome?" I said.

"I've tried to get to you. You are in danger. You were almost killed. I've tried to get here, but something, someone, is stopping me."

"I'm fine, though," I said as I looked into Paul's eyes, searching for something that made me believe Jerome was in there somewhere. I saw nothing.

"You are still in danger. I'm trying to get there." Paul's voice had changed and though it wasn't exactly like Jerome's, it was close.

"Were you in Paul's body at the school and then just a voice when I was in the doctor's office?"

"I tried to be there, but someone is holding me back. I'm using Paul and I wasn't sure you heard just my voice. But, Isabelle, you are in danger."

"Another ghost is holding you back? There are two men," I began, gesturing towards the sketches and hoping whatever Paul's ears were hearing, the information wasn't going to his brain.

"No, not them." Paul released my arms and then pointed at the mostly complete picture of the jowly man. "But this one might be dangerous."

"But the other one isn't?" I said as I pointed at the sketch of Robert.

"I don't think so, but this one"—he pointed adamantly—"this one is receptive to the other side, if you know what I mean."

"No, I have no idea what you mean."

"Do this old cowboy a favor and find Cliff or Jake and don't leave their sides. Missouri, you're fine. Your nightmares will go away soon, but you're safe. Isabelle isn't."

"Howdy, Jerome," Gram said as she stepped around so that she was looking directly at Paul. "I hear you, and I'll make sure Betts is okay."

"Good. Thank you, Miz. I'll keep trying to get there."

"I'm sure you will. Will Paul remember any of this?"

"No, ma'am." He looked at me again. "He's sweet on you, you know."

"This is only getting weirder," I said.

"I know. I'll leave him be, but if I need to come back and I can't find any other way, I'll use him again. I'll use whoever I need to."

I sighed. "You okay?"

"Right as a turkey pie."

I laughed. I'd eaten Gram's turkey potpie a number of times and it was delicious. The thought of being "right as turkey pie" conjured the image of warm, steamy food on a cold day. Comfortable and homey.

Suddenly, Paul's hands pulled me close. I did not resist as his lips came to mine. Paul was a pretty good kisser.

When he pulled away, Jerome said, "I wasn't missing my chance. Just in case, Isabelle."

I opened my mouth to say something. I'd been working on my loyalty to my live boyfriend. The last time I'd seen Jerome, I'd been careful not to be too passionate with the kissing. I'd made progress. I felt the distinct step or two backward with the kiss with Paul. I couldn't find the right words. I closed my mouth.

"Betts? Paul?" Cliff said from an area by the front swinging doors.

Suddenly, Paul became Paul again and the look in his eyes made it unquestionably clear that he had no idea why he was holding onto my arms. I really hoped he didn't remember the kiss.

"Oh, crap," I said.

"Yeah," Gram said. "That about sums it up."

Chapter Nine

"Cliff, I have no memory of kissing Betts. I'm... I'm... I'm so confused. And I'm terribly sorry, though I still don't remember what happened. Oh, hell, this is one of the strangest moments of my life," Paul said.

"Sit a minute," Gram said to Paul. "You too, Cliff. Betts, quit standing there looking so scared. You grab a stool, too."

Robotically and with the fear that Gram had just accused me of, I sat, too.

I had nothing. So far, since the ghosts had started communicating with me and when they'd interrupted someone or something in the living world, Gram and I had been able to come up with a story that could potentially explain the circumstances. Our explanations hadn't always been great, but they'd been good enough. People wanted to believe us, so they did.

But there was nothing I could say that would make the fact that Paul and I were kissing each other when Cliff came into the kitchen okay. We weren't rehearsing for a play. We weren't trying to get something out of each other's eyes, our lips accidentally falling together in such a way that we both thought we'd ride out the moment and enjoy it. Nothing.

It *was* wholly enjoyable, by the way, but that was the last thing I should be thinking about.

Cliff was obviously upset. He wasn't the jealous type. He never had been. But even non-jealous types couldn't help but be bothered by some things.

As far as he knew, I'd never given him a reason to suspect me of doing anything disloyal but let's face it, even if Paul hadn't enjoyed the kiss, I certainly had and I hadn't tried to get away.

"I wonder if I have some sort of brain tumor or something," Paul said.

"No, Paul, you don't have a brain tumor. And, Cliff, you can relax, too. Betts and Paul weren't in the middle of a romantic moment," Gram said.

"Okay," Cliff said doubtfully.

"Listen, gentlemen, there is some weird stuff going on around Broken Rope," Gram said. She'd used that line before, and then followed up with only a partially filled in explanation.

Was she going to tell them the truth this time?

I looked at Cliff. He wouldn't look at me. I looked at Paul. He wouldn't look at anyone.

"Cliff, I've been having some terrible nightmares and Jake sent Paul over to sketch out the people who are haunting me at night. It's bad, Cliff. Very scary. Anyway, as I mentioned, Broken Rope is strange and it has some pockets of weirdness. You two might not be totally aware of those pockets but I have no doubt that you've had moments of wonder. Perhaps you've felt, seen, or smelled something but couldn't figure out what was attached to the sensory activity. Think about it a minute."

Cliff and Paul looked at each other. I thought Paul might throw up. But a second later and as they thought about Gram's words, both he and Cliff made a small shift back toward normal.

"Like yesterday when I smelled wood smoke, but couldn't find the source?" Paul said. He sniffed. "I think I smell it a little bit right now."

"Exactly," Gram said.

"I kind of know what you mean," Cliff said, his eyes finally landing on me.

I'd already told him that I was extra aware of the Broken Rope weirdness, and that I would tell him whatever he wanted to know, if he truly did want to know. Cliff was sturdy, logical, with no patience for anything that wasn't of the real and natural world, but he deserved the truth. But only if he wanted it.

With my own eyes, I tried to let him know that, yes, this is the weird and spooky stuff I'd mentioned to him. I also tried to put some regret in my glance.

Cliff's features normalized a little more.

"Well, we've got one of those pockets right here. I think it's because of the cemetery but I can't be sure."

"Okay," Cliff said, less doubtful this time.

"Anyway, we think these sketches are of murderers from a long time ago. As they were being drawn, I felt the air in the room change. I don't know what that really means, but both Paul and Betts got weird at the same time. They both became someone else. I'm sure that's what happened."

"They were possessed?" Cliff said doubtfully.

"No, not that. Okay, maybe a little, but not dangerously so," Gram said.

Her story was weakening, but she was sticking with it.

"Neither Betts nor Paul knew what they were doing. They did not know they were kissing each other. It was other people kissing other people, I'm convinced." Gram paused and looked at Cliff. "Come on, you think I would have allowed that to happen if they'd been themselves? You think they would have done that in front of me if they'd been themselves? I don't think so."

Cliff didn't buy it completely, but Paul really wanted to. He looked at Cliff again.

"Cliff, I would never have done that. Betts would never have done that. You have to believe me." He looked at me and I knew our earlier conversation would remain a safe secret. He would not tell Cliff that he had expressed questions about the strength of our relationship.

"Cliff," I said. "I'm so sorry."

"Wasn't their faults, Cliff, I promise," Gram said.

Cliff nodded. "I don't understand, but I believe you, Miz."

"You do?" Paul said, his voice squeaking as it rose.

He cleared his throat, but Gram and Cliff both fought a small smile.

"I do, Paul. I have to," Cliff said as he looked at me, the smile quickly gone and replaced with an odd but determined expression.

I knew he didn't have to do anything. If he really wanted to know, how in the world was I ever going to explain Jerome? How could he understand what was going on and still want to stay together? Even a ghost could be the "the other man."

I tried to smile but I was still so upset that my face didn't want to cooperate.

"This is all really creepy, you know," Paul said.

"Oh, I know," Gram said as she put her hand on Paul's arm. He was still clearly shaken up.

"Right. Well, the reason I stopped by was to see Paul's work. Jake told me he was coming here to sketch some people for Miz. I wanted to see how he did. We need a sketch artist."

"Not the best way to apply for a job," Paul said without even a small trace of humor.

"He did great, Cliff. Really great," Gram said. "Come look."

"Look over them all you want. I'll leave them all here. I'm going to go home and get some rest," Paul said as he ran his hand back and forth through his hair.

"You okay to drive?" Cliff stepped around the butcher block.

"I'm fine to drive," he said. "Yeah, I'm okay. I think I just want to get away from this school, or maybe it's the cemetery."

Cliff inspected Paul's eyes and then stepped back but watched him walk out of the kitchen. Paul didn't wobble.

After the swinging door stopped swinging, Cliff turned toward me and Gram.

"Excuse me, I have something to do in the back. Betts, we haven't paid our respects to Lynn. I feel badly about that. We'll need to stop by this evening or tomorrow morning, okay?" Gram said.

"Sure," I said as she disappeared toward the back. I slid off the stool and moved to the other side of the butcher block and next to Cliff. "I don't know what else to say except that I'm deeply sorry."

One corner of Cliff's mouth pulled. It wasn't a smile, not really, but it told me that there was good reason to hope we'd be okay.

"I know, Betts. Truly, it didn't occur to me that you and Paul were having a fling and Miz was cheering you on. I knew something was weird and not normal. It was bothersome to see you kissing someone else, don't get me wrong." He squinted and bit his bottom lip. "I know this is part of what's been strange between us. After all that, I'm really not sure if I want to know what it's all about."

"Really?"

"Yeah, I can't imagine not being able to have at least a little control over almost every aspect of my life. I mean . . . I'm not explaining this well."

I nodded but remained silent as he thought.

"Betts, does someone named Jerome have something to do with all of this today, and before?"

"Yes," I said quickly, wanting so badly not to lie, to put some solid truth out in the universe. However, my throat tightened up after I spoke.

"I see. And, oh God, this sounds stupid, but does this Jerome have any connection to the old Broken Rope legend, Jerome Cowbender?"

"Yes."

Cliff smiled and nodded again. "Got it, Betts." He paused and inspected me even more closely than he'd just inspected Paul. "You do know he's dead, right?"

"Yes. He died a long time ago."

"I don't really want any more details right now. I think I kind of get what's happening, but I don't want you to confirm or deny my suspicions, because it doesn't matter. Here's the thing: If what has come between us is a long-dead person, I can't see getting upset or concerned about it. It wouldn't make sense. From my perspective, it's like when one person in a relationship has a crush on an unreachable celebrity. If a dead person or a celebrity is involved, chances of the crush going anywhere are slim to none."

"Right," I said. He was sort of wrong, but not totally and now wasn't the time to nitpick. We were working with big picture here. I got that.

"Anyway, I think more than the fact that you might or might not have a crush on a dead person—and please don't confirm or deny—what's come between you and me even more than the crush is the fact that you're beating yourself up over it. You're nervous about it."

"I don't know."

"I think I do, so here's the thing. I'd like to welcome that crush into our lives and see how that goes. I can't make any promises that I'll keep this attitude, but I'd like to see if this is better than me knowing that you feel guilty about something and wondering what could be so awful that you're mad at yourself. Quit being mad at yourself. I don't care if you have a crush on a dead person. I don't see that it matters in the least."

"Wow."

"I know. Progressive, right?"

"Very," I said with a smile, and then something happened. I was suddenly less burdened. Truthfully, I didn't feel like I deserved to *be* less burdened, but I was, nonetheless. "You might be right."

Cliff shrugged. "I might be. I might not be."

"Huh," I said.

"Betts, you are the girl for me. You have been since I dumped Opie so I could date you—I know, back then and for all this time I've denied that I dumped her for you, but now I'm telling the truth. I think it happened during math class. Your hair was in a messy ponytail and you were disgusted with how silly Lenny Warren was being when the teacher asked him a question. You didn't hide your disgust. You raised your hand, gave the right answer, and told Lenny to stop acting like such a child."

"I have no memory of that moment."

"I do. I fell head over heels right then and there, funny hair and all. I dumped Opie at lunch, waiting two whole weeks to ask you out. And, no matter what I told my ex-wife, you were a big part of the reason I wanted a divorce. I tried, but I could never feel for her the way I felt for you. That didn't seem fair to anyone."

"I guess I should apologize to her," I said, hiding the shock that zipped through me with the confessions. I'd had no idea.

"Anyway." Cliff smiled. "I'm not going to try to win your heart by fighting with a dead guy. I think you're just like me, Betts; I think you have no real doubt who you belong with even if you feel pulled in other directions sometimes. You'd come back to me. I can always wait. So, I'm welcoming Jerome into our lives, whatever that means, and remember, I don't really want to know what that means. I'm okay with thinking abstractly. I don't need real pictures in my head."

"I'm beginning to think I might not be worth all this," I said.

"I'll be the judge of that."

"Thank you, Cliff," I said.

Much to my disappointment, our moment had to end because Cliff was called back to the police staion, which turned out to be a good thing. Gram and I suddenly had to think about vegetables because, surprisingly, she had not made the calls to cancel class, and a few students started showing up.

Chapter Ten

"Isn't there just only so much someone can do with green beans?" April said.

"Oh, pish," Gram said. "Green beans can be simple and delicious or a little more complicated and still delicious. They're one of my favorite items to put with garlic. And green bean casserole? Who in the world doesn't love that?"

April, Todd, and Roy had come to class. April hadn't heard about Derek, and I suspected Todd's feelings for April caused him to stalk her house and follow her almost wherever she went. Honestly, I didn't think that was much of an exaggeration. Roy had come just because he thought he should. He hadn't heard from anyone, so he didn't want to be rude.

We'd shared the news with April, and then moved awkwardly on to the cooking. There would be no fried green beans because we hadn't had time to prepare, but we improvised with something simple: green bean casserole, with the crunchy onions on top.

"I love green bean casserole," Roy said as he twisted the crank of the can opener. "I love cream of mushroom soup no matter what, but on green beans, it's so good."

"I'm not a big fan of the soup, but as part of the casserole, I'm in," Todd said.

Actually, he'd been behaving much better than the last time I'd seen him. He'd either had a talk with himself or someone had told him to relax a little and just try to get to know the new girl in town, without accidentally killing himself along the way.

April was a little different, too. Though I hadn't asked specifically, I was under the impression that Gram had told her exactly what was causing Todd to act so strangely. April tried to make innocuous jokes with him—maybe trying to put him at ease a little. I was sure that we all hoped for the same thing, that Todd and April would actually date and we could all get over the uncomfortable parts together. Whether or not the relationship would be successful would be up to them, but their dating might, at least, put us out of our misery.

"All right, here it is, stir everything together except for two-thirds of a cup of those crunchy onions. Good, Roy. Yes, Todd, just stir. Pour the mixture into your casserole dishes and put 'em in the ovens for twenty-five minutes. We'll take them out, stir them again, and then cook for five more minutes," Gram said.

Everyone put their casserole into an oven and took their seats again. Though we weren't prepared, Gram had enough knowledge to have something to talk about while the casseroles cooked.

"While we're waiting, let's talk about onions," she said.

Everyone nodded agreeably.

"Not those crunchy onions that I love so much, but just plain old onions. They're a pretty amazing food, magical in some peoples' minds," Gram said.

Roy laughed.

"True," Gram said. "Egyptians thought onions could cure thousands of ailments. They included them with their pharaohs when they buried them in their tombs. They saw the onion as a representation of eternal life, with its circle-inside-of-circle pattern. King Ramses IV was entombed with onions in his eye sockets."

"That's weird," Todd said.

Gram shrugged. "Beyond that, they have always been a part of diets everywhere, mostly probably because of their durable qualities. Stored properly, onions can last a long time. They can also be dried and eaten later, perhaps in the winter when other fresh food is more difficult to come by, like in the days of old."

"Oh, hang on, I remember reading somewhere that Russians applied onions to open wounds during World War II," Roy said.

"Doesn't surprise me. Onions are amazing; so is garlic, but that's for another day. Basically, our stinkiest food items are known to be full of healing properties, too," Gram said.

"I have eaten a raw onion or two in my day," Roy said. "Though I've only done so when I knew I wasn't going to be around many people."

"I like onions sautéed in olive oil," Todd said. "And I add mushrooms, too."

"Delicious," Gram said.

Everyone smiled along with Gram, but then a lull suddenly hit the group.

"Roy," Todd said, bringing us out of the lull and addressing the eight hundred pound elephant that had been lurking in the room. "You found Derek and Betts?"

"I did," he said. He glanced at Miz, as though to check if it was okay to take the conversation that direction. Gram gave him one quick nod.

"I thought they were both dead," Roy continued as he scooted up and onto a stool.

I didn't like hearing that; neither did Gram. She cringed. I sent her a small smile but it didn't help.

"That sounds just awful," April said in a tone that meant *tell me more*.

"Yeah," Roy said as he pushed his glasses up his nose a little. "It happened quickly, but I think my heart stopped beating, and I stopped breathing from the second I saw them in the barn until the police got there. It was like I got detached from myself. Even my hearing stopped working, I think. Or that's what it seemed like."

"What, you just walked in and saw them there?" Todd asked.

"No." Roy shook his head. "I came in the front doors and heard something in the back."

"The back of the barn? Is there a back door?" I asked. I didn't think there was a back exit.

"Sort of. It's a skinny door that we're not supposed to use because it isn't regulation size, but I use it. It's a slat more than a door," Roy said.

"Did you see someone back there?" I asked.

"As I went through the front doors, I thought I heard a crash, metallic. Like big, heavy chains falling to the ground. I asked if there was anyone there, but no one answered. I thought I should check it out, so I walked around the perimeter of the inside of the barn to make my way. There was no one there and no chains. I stood there probably a good minute, scratching my head and looking around. And then I heard the front doors shut. From where I was I couldn't see the front anymore, so I called out again. But when no one answered this time, I cut through the middle. That's when I came upon Betts and Derek. And, here it gets a little foggy, but I think I ran to Betts and shook her shoulders. She groaned. You groaned, Betts, and there was no blood on you so I thought you were probably okay. But I could tell right away that Derek was worse off. I didn't want to touch him but not because there was blood everywhere. I was more concerned with hurting him worse if something was broken. I think I called his name and pinched his arm, of all things. He didn't respond, of course. But you sat up." He looked at me. "You said Derek was dead and that I should call the police."

"I don't remember any of that," I said.

"I wondered if you would," Roy said. "Anyway, Jim was there only a minute after I called. Jenny must have gotten ahold of him right away."

"The woman who answers the police dispatch phone?"

"Yeah, Jenny. You know Jenny," Roy said.

I didn't, but I didn't feel like now was the time to bring up my experiences with Jenny, the woman everyone but I seemed to know, and the woman who never seemed to get my messages to the police.

I hadn't noticed that Gram had moved next to me. She squeezed my arm.

"I'm so sorry about Derek, and I'm sorry for Lynn," she said. "I'm grateful my granddaughter is fine, but Derek's death is a real loss. Betts and I are going to go see Lynn tomorrow. We'll be sure and extend everyone's condolences if you'd like."

"That would be great, Miz," Roy said. "I've wanted to talk to Lynn. I wanted to come talk to Betts, but I've been in shock, I think, and I heard you were doing all right." He looked at me again.

"I didn't know either Derek or Lynn well at all," April said. "But Derek seemed like a nice enough guy even if he was really quiet."

No one had voiced their opinions of the much more vocal Lynn. Even April had had the chance to figure her out. Now, of course, wasn't the time, but you could see those thoughts in their expressions.

Gram, probably sensing everyone's discomfort, said, "You know, Lynn saved a group of Broken Rope tourists many years ago, back in the early tourist days. There was a time that she was looked upon as a town hero," Gram said.

We all turned toward her as silent disbelief filled the air.

"Yes, she was quite the spirited woman when she was younger, which was before everyone here's time. You might have been a child when it happened, Roy, but you were probably too young to pay any attention."

"I don't know a thing about it," Roy said.

"It happened right in the middle of the summer. The weather was cooperating and we weren't experiencing our typical miserable humidity, so the town was extra busy. Back then we performed more fake gunfights than we do now, and there was one that was particularly popular. It took place down the middle of Main Street—almost all of Main Street. Lynn was a young woman, maybe not eighteen yet, I'm not sure." Gram squinted back into the past. "Anyway, she was in the skit. She played the 'damsel in distress' part, and she was glorious." Gram looked at me. "You think Opie has a flair for drama, you should have seen Lynn." She turned her attention back to her students. "She was tied to a post by the bad guy and then saved by the good guy, but only after a rigorous gun battle. The participants moved up and down the street, hiding behind posts, or horse ties, or swinging saloon doors. It was all very participatory—the gunfighters would even hide behind tourists and shoot around them. Frankly, even with blanks, it wasn't all that safe and I was relieved when we stopped doing it, but that day it got really out of hand."

"Oh, don't tell me someone was killed by a gun that was shooting blanks," Roy said.

"No," Gram said. "Some horses got loose. We used to keep a number of them corralled right next to where your Trigger barn is. That was a convenient spot to keep them for the skits they participated in. No one paid attention at the time to the fact that spot might be a danger for the tourists. And for some reason, that day the horses got spooked by the gunshots and they broke down the corral posts—the posts weren't reliable anyway. The horses stampeded the street. They were frantic, tourists were frantic. Lynn freed herself from the ropes that were loosely tied around her and the post and she put herself in the middle of all the chaos. She stopped the horses, not before getting hurt first. One horse ran into her, knocked her down, almost trampled her, but didn't. When she stood and brushed herself off, she became single minded. She was going to stop those horses. Ultimately, it was almost like she hypnotized them. This was long before the term 'horse whisperer' came into fashion, but I am sure that's what she was, a horse whisperer."

"How?" April asked.

"She stood and put her hands up in the halt position. They'd run right at her, but she was so angry about being knocked over, I think, that she didn't want them to ever think they had one up on her. They'd just stop right before trampling her. It was an amazing sight."

"That must be one of those tales that's changed over the years, become a better story than it really was," I said. "That doesn't sound possible."

"I watched the whole thing."

"Wow," I said.

"However, something else happened at the same time," Gram said. "After that was when she became more like the Lynn that we all know. I'm sorry for her loss, but we all know how Lynn complains about everything. That's when it all started. We all thought maybe she got knocked around enough that it put her in constant pain, so those who know about it are more tolerant than those who don't."

"Wild story," Todd said.

"I know. Everyone was amazed, and extremely grateful to her. No one else got hurt. She was the town hero for a long time, until everyone got tired of hearing her complain about everything," Gram said.

"Didn't I hear something about Derek being married a bunch of times?" April asked.

"Yes, he was married five times," I said.

"Some people just get married a lot," Roy said as he shrugged.

I, and probably Gram too, noted his unspoken words. There were some people, like Roy, who never got married at all.

His shrug put an end to the conversation.

"Casseroles are ready to stir and then cook for a little longer," Gram said as an egg-shaped timer dinged from the top of one of the stoves.

The rest of the evening was filled with casserole sampling and food discussions—everyone was pleased with their green bean efforts.

Once everyone was gone, Gram and I cleaned up, both of us too tired to rehash the afternoon's events. We promised we'd revisit everything the next day. And I was so exhausted by the time I got home that I didn't even consider calling Cliff to ask if he'd be coming over that evening. I crashed on my bed, and though my sleep wasn't disrupted by any ghosts, a human wanted to rouse me at a ridiculously early hour.

Chapter Eleven

Whoever was pounding on my front door must have been endowed with some strong arm muscles.

"Good grief," I muttered to myself as I looked at the time on my phone. It was almost six in the morning, but not quite.

The pounding continued.

"I'm coming," I said. I sat up and made sure I was dressed appropriately enough to answer the door. I was in a T-shirt and shorts. My legs didn't have much opportunity to get sun so I might blind the person knocking, but I figured they deserved it for bothering me at that hour.

I looked out one of the small fanned windows at the top of the front door. It was a woman I thought I'd seen around town a time or two, but I didn't know who she was. She was older than me, pretty, in an "I'm ready for work and you aren't" way, and serious, if the pinched look on her face was any indication. Her blond, short ponytail was neat and her makeup conservative and in place. She wore clothes that I would regard as dressy, but were technically classified as business casual.

Keeping the chain on, I opened the door a small gap.

"Yes?" I said in a not too unfriendly manner.

"You're Betts Winston, right?"

"Yes."

"I'm Bonnie Rowlett. I kept my married name. I was married to Derek at one time. Can I come in?"

I blinked and put her in focus a little better. It was unwise to allow a stranger in, but she seemed pretty harmless. I also remembered Teddy mentioning she was an attorney. Though that didn't make her non-threatening automatically, she at least had learned the law. Hopefully she was, in turn, abiding it.

"Sure, come on in." I unlatched the chain and welcomed her inside. "Coffee?"

"No, thanks; I really can't stay long."

"Have a seat."

She took one end of the couch and I took the other.

"What's up?" I said.

"I heard you asked Wendy about Derek and Lynn and their

relationship," she said.

"Sort of. I didn't get far, and I didn't ask about Lynn at all, I don't think." If I was going to be chastised I wanted it to be for the correct things.

"You need to stop doing things like that," she said.

I couldn't squash the huffy laugh that came out. I said, "I'm sorry, Bonnie. That was a bad reaction. But, I'm not sure why I can't ask whatever I want to ask to whomever I want." I blinked. It was early and I couldn't be sure about the grammar, but I didn't want to lessen my stance by attempting to correct it.

"Because, you just need to leave well enough alone," she said.

"Well enough? Derek's dead. Well enough has left the building."

"I don't mean with Derek, but between Lynn and the rest of us. We all have a decent relationship with her and we all want to keep it that way."

"Why in the world would my questions to Wendy, you, or anyone matter to Lynn? And you divorced Derek." I looked at her a long moment. My vision was no longer morning fuzzy. "I understand wanting to keep a civil relationship with your ex-mother-in-law, but frankly, you seem kind of scared. What's that about?"

"First of all, we know you know Lynn. Everyone knows Lynn. We wouldn't want anything that we say getting back to her. Even if we say nothing bad, she finds ways to interpret things badly."

"I believe that, and just so you know, it would never occur to me to tell Lynn about any of my conversations with other people, whether they were her former daughter-in-law or not. And more importantly, what happens to you when she interprets things badly?"

"That's not important."

"Really? It certainly sounds very important."

Bonnie pursed her lips and looked down at her hands on her lap as she shook her head slightly. "I should not tell you this next part, but I will only if you promise not to tell a soul."

"I promise." I knew I might be lying because if she told me something important regarding Derek's murder and my assault, I'd be on the phone to Cliff before Bonnie got to the bottom of my front porch stairs.

"None of us should have married Derek. It was a mistake for all of us. We have all come to know each other and we all know we should have stayed away from him."

"Was he mean to you?"

"No, not mean, certainly not abusive in any way. It's just that he was more about keeping the relationship between him and his mother strong and happy than his relationship between himself and any of his wives."

"Why did you marry him, then?"

She shook her head again. "It was just a mistake, that's all. We were all kind of duped."

"Duped? By what? He wasn't dashingly good-looking, though I don't want you to think I'm about looks because looks mean nothing once you truly get to know someone." It was something I believed, but also felt the need to reinforce with Bonnie after my intentions had been so misinterpreted with Wendy. "But I didn't see a shining personality either. I'd love to know more details even if they aren't any of my business."

Bonnie smiled a sad smile and said, "Can't go there."

"I'd sure like to understand why."

"Would it help if I told you that the peace will be better kept for everyone if you don't?"

"Not really." The idea suddenly occurred to me that these five women might have killed Derek together, or plotted to. I wasn't going to make any sort of accusation to the woman sitting on the other end of my couch, but I was surprised I hadn't given serious credence to the idea earlier. Even Opie had.

"It's better that way, I promise," she said.

"Okay." I nodded.

"I appreciate that."

"Where were you the morning Derek was killed?" Dangit, I couldn't help myself.

"At home alone. Just like Wendy. Neither of us have a legitimate alibi. We've both told the police as much. Neither of us are *suspects*, but I'm sure they suspect us, at least a little. How could you not?"

"They stick with evidence more than assumptions." But she had a point. How could Derek's ex-wives not be considered?

"We'll see," she said.

"Lynn must be something else," I said, still digging.

"Lynn is one of the most interesting people I've ever known," she said as she stood. "However, I wouldn't recommend spending a lot of time with her."

"I don't have plans to." I stood, too. She didn't need to know that Gram and I were visiting Lynn that morning.

"You'll be better off that way. Don't talk to the rest of Derek's wives. Don't ask any more questions."

I didn't want to make that promise, even as a lie. "Bonnie, I don't want to hassle anyone, but I can't guarantee that I won't want to talk to any of you again. If I do, I'll make sure it's not out in the open. I'll be more private about it."

Bonnie said. "I guess we'd all appreciate that."

I stood and followed her. She stepped out the door and onto the porch, looking every direction a few times. Then she kept her eyes on the end of the street where I'd seen the train stations. She looked there so long that I wondered if she might be seeing something other than the empty field. I leaned out the door and looked, but there was nothing ghostly there.

"You okay, Bonnie?" I asked.

"I'm fine," she said before she hurried down the stairs and into her car. She'd driven off my block and out of the neighborhood only a moment later.

If I got to Gram's early, we'd have enough time to discuss some of yesterday's events and my morning company before we set out for Lynn's. I reconfirmed that there were no ghosts down the street, got ready in record time, and drove over to Gram's.

"Betts, you're early," Gram said as she opened the door.

"I had a surprise visitor this morning," I said.

"Come in and tell me all about it."

I told her about my conversations with two of Derek's ex-wives as we both enjoyed big mugs of coffee.

"That is strange," she said. "I don't like to judge, but you're probably right, there's something weird—other than the fact that it's unique—about Derek having five wives."

"And then there's Lynn."

"Yes, there's Lynn," Gram said.

"You think she's a pain, too; I know you do. Even with the story of her saving the day all those years ago."

"I wouldn't say I think she's a pain. I think she's a challenge. I'm beginning to wonder if Derek's ex-wives might be just as much of a challenge. You might not need to have any more conversations with them, Betts. Think about it."

"I will," I said, but I didn't think I was quite done talking to them.

"Hmm. Right. Let's get this over with."

Lynn's house wasn't far from Gram's. It was only slightly newer than Gram's, but Gram's was one story with an attic space that had been renovated a long time ago and had been used as my dad's bedroom. The houses in Lynn's neighborhood, including Lynn's, were all true two stories with three bedrooms and a small bathroom on the top floors. And almost all the houses had two front dormer windows extending outward.

Lynn's neighborhood was also one of the woodsier ones, with lots of old, big trees on each of the extra-large lots.

"Where did Derek live when he was killed?" I asked Gram.

"He lived here with Lynn," Gram said.

"What about when he was married the last time? Well, actually, when he was married any time. He and his wives didn't live with Lynn, did they?"

"I don't know about all of them, but I know there were times when he and a wife lived in an apartment just outside of town."

"At least he didn't always live with his mother," I said as I parked the Nova on the street in front of the house.

"Oh, something tells me that Lynn was always been in the middle of her son's life no matter where he lived. He didn't even go to college because she didn't want him to leave town."

"I know he was a handyman, but did he have any other jobs?"

"I don't know."

Gram opened the car door and stepped out and onto the curb. I glanced up at the house for a moment before I joined her. One thing I knew was that everyone was weird in their own way. I was sure people thought I was sometimes strange—and if they only knew the complete truth; weird and strange wouldn't even begin to cover it. It was clear that Lynn and Derek were at least a little weird with their mother/son relationship but that was obvious to everyone in Broken Rope. What was really going on? What was their less obvious "weird?" I would have bet that every one of Derek's wives knew exactly what it was, but they weren't going to tell me. In fact, I bet what they knew scared them and had made Bonnie seem frightened this morning. Between Gram and I surely we could figure out what it was even if we didn't ask too many questions.

Gram reached into the back seat and pulled out a platter of cookies and one of the green bean casseroles from last night's class. She handed me the cookies as she cradled the casserole.

"You knock," she said as we approached the front door.

Lynn answered quickly, as though she'd seen us coming.

"Miz, Betts, come in, come in," she said, her demeanor subdued but attentive. "Oh, thank you." She held out her arms for the food.

We handed her the items and watched her shuffle away with them, disappearing into the kitchen at the back part of the house.

"You two need to take off quickly?" she called from the kitchen.

"Actually, we have a few minutes, Lynn," Gram said, sending me a shrug. "We're awfully sorry about Derek."

Lynn came back into view. "Thank you. It's been downright terrible."

Gram and I stood still for a moment and blinked uncomfortably.

"Oh! I'm so sorry. Come in and sit down," Lynn said.

Lynn led the way into the comfortable living room that was located off to the left. Out of the corner of my eye, I spotted an old pair of men's slippers tucked under a side table. Derek's? Or did Lynn have her own love life? That idea hadn't ever occurred to me.

If they were Derek's, the slippers were a sad reminder, and I was compelled to look around the room for other things that had been left behind. The space was neither masculine nor feminine, neither messy nor extra tidy—it was lived in and filled with cushion-y furniture and framed pictures. I didn't have time to inspect each picture, but I saw a few that were of Derek and Lynn together.

Lynn sat down on a chair that faced the couch Gram and I sat on. Lynn was also facing the big window that looked out toward the front yard of the house. As she sat, she seemed to be glancing out the window, looking for something.

I couldn't ignore the urge to twist around and look, but all I saw were the large trees in the yard and the Nova in the road out front. I turned back and saw that Lynn wasn't pleased that I'd caught her searching, but she normalized her expression quickly.

"Betts, I'm so sorry for what happened to you. So sorry. You could have been killed, too," Lynn said.

I hadn't been sure if Lynn had heard the details of what had happened, but someone must have told her.

"Thanks, Lynn. I'm fine. Gram and I are so terribly sorry about Derek. What can we do to help you out—anything at all?" I said.

Lynn cocked her head and her eyes filled with tears for a moment, but she didn't allow them to fall down her cheeks.

"I'll be okay," she said. "I'll be okay in time."

I realized that Lynn was coping, but she was also in denial, which I thought might be a good way to go for a short time. Pure grief would take over soon enough.

Her bright, watery eyes glanced out the window again. This time I resisted and didn't turn around. I could tell that Gram had noticed but she kept her eyes on Lynn too.

"Has your boyfriend mentioned anything to you, Betts? Have they any clues as to who the killer is?"

"Cliff wouldn't tell me if they did," I said. "But I know the police will find . . . solve the mystery." For some reason I didn't want to say the word "killer."

"I don't know. I doubt we've got a very good police force, Betts. No offense to your boyfriend, but we are just a small Podunk town."

I bristled, but bit back the fighting words that wanted to jump out of my mouth. Lynn complained; it's what she did. I shouldn't expect her to have changed because of the tragedy.

"We are also Broken Rope," Gram said gently. "We've had so many strange things happen in this town that we have to have a good—no, a great—police force. I'm sure they'll find the killer."

Gram didn't mind using the K word.

"Well, I suppose we'll see, but I don't have much faith."

Gram nodded patiently. I tried to imitate the move but I doubted I pulled it off well.

Suddenly, the air in the room changed and began to smell like flowers. Like two dogs on point, Gram and I both sat up a little straighter and looked at each other, then around the rest of the room. Lynn looked around, too.

"Oh my gracious," Grace said when she came into view directly next to Lynn. "I was pulled to her like a magnet to metal."

Neither Gram nor I could talk to her, so I tried to communicate by opening my eyes wide.

"Oh, yes, this one doesn't know about us, about the ghosts?" Grace said.

I nodded and scratched my ear.

"That your grandmother?" She nodded toward Gram.

I blinked in the affirmative.

"I wish Derek had wanted to be a police officer," Lynn continued when neither Gram nor I bit at her pessimistic bait. "He could have shaped that place up."

"You're probably right, Lynn," Gram said, but her eyes were on Grace as she bent down and inspected Lynn. Lynn looked at the space next to her because that's where Gram was looking, but she didn't see anything.

"I know I'm right," Lynn said, turning forward again.

"This one is like someone I knew," Grace said. "She's a

manipulator. I can smell it on her."

I really wanted to say, *"You can?"* Instead, Gram and I just shared a quick look of surprise. I was sure she thought the same thing I was thinking—they can smell? Was Grace being literal or figurative?

"Of course, Lynn," Gram said.

"Oh my goodness, why are you two here talking to this one?" Grace said.

"Do you need anything?" I said to Lynn, repeating my offer. "Gram and I would like to help in any way we can."

"Thank you, but I can't think of a thing. I won't be continuing the cooking class of course, but I imagine it's too late to get a refund," Lynn said.

"Not at all," Gram said. "You will get a full refund. Please don't worry about that."

"That's nice, Miz, especially considering I won't have Derek's income to help me out anymore."

"Of course," Gram said.

"There's something else," Grace said. She suddenly froze in place with her eyes directly on Lynn's. An instant later, just as the pause in the conversation seemed to go on too long, Grace said, "You should have told me. You just should have told me."

A long few heartbeats later the ghost snapped out of whatever trance she'd gone into. She looked at me and said, "What just happened? Why am I here?"

I shrugged my shoulders, not caring if Lynn noticed.

"Betts, Missouri, you two okay?" Lynn asked.

"I have to go," Grace said distractedly before she disappeared.

Gram stood. "We need to go, Lynn. Again, let us know if you need anything."

"I will." Lynn stood too and seemed confused by our hasty exit.

She walked us to the door and bid us a thankful farewell. Gram and I didn't say anything else until we got into the Nova.

"That was Grace, I assume?" Gram said. "I hurried out because I hoped she'd join us out here, but it looks like we're out of luck."

"That *was* Grace. She's gone, I think. Hang on, Gram, I'm going to pull over up here."

I steered the Nova to a spot around a curve in the road. If Lynn looked out her front windows, she wouldn't see us unless she really craned her neck.

"Why was Grace there?" Gram said. "And that moment when she

was so still. The look on her face reminded me of Paul when he was . . .
when Jerome was there inside of him."

"I don't think that was Jerome in Grace," I said.

"I don't either," Gram said. "You thinking what I'm thinking"

"Probably. Derek?" I said.

"I can't imagine it would be anyone else."

"Me either."

"Maybe Grace, or Derek through Grace, can tell us what happened
to him, but I have to say, Betts, I'm more than a little bothered that Derek
might have been able to do that. I like that the ghosts I've met so far are
long gone, their marks on the living world faded to nothing, the people
they knew gone. This is all too . . . soon," Gram said.

"We don't know for sure. I'll work on it," I said.

"Good. Why are we still here?"

"Lynn was looking for someone or something," I said. "I want to
know what."

Gram looked around and seemed to evaluate the surety of our safe
distance from Lynn's house. Finally, she said, "Good plan."

Chapter Twelve

"No, I haven't noticed her in my nightmares," Gram said. "She doesn't look even slightly familiar. You're right, though; she's beautiful. Striking."

"As I know them, she and Robert are both likable ghosts. They both have secrets, kept things from each other, and both had bad timing when it came to the train station. Your descriptions of one of the men in your nightmares is Robert. From the little I've seen, I find it hard to believe that he was a violent man, but anything is possible."

"That's true. Oh, look, there's someone." Gram nodded toward Lynn's house.

A red Explorer stopped and parked, and a moment later a woman hopped out of the driver's side and hurried up to the front door. Once she was at the door, we couldn't see her, but I'd already gotten a good enough look.

"She's familiar," Gram said.

"Very. She works with Dr. Callahan Her name is Ridley. She checked my vitals the day . . . the day of the barn. She seemed sad. Maybe that had something to do with Derek."

It would be perfectly reasonable for me to stop by the doctor's office with some sort of medical question so soon after having been there for a bona fide emergency. Maybe I could talk to her there. No one would think there was anything strange about that, would they?

"You really think one or more of the ex-wives were involved in the murder?"

"Maybe."

"Divorce as a motive?"

"Possibly, but there's more. Bonnie said they 'shouldn't have ever married Derek.' I don't think any of them are upset over divorcing him as much as having married him in the first place, if that makes any sense at all."

Gram was silent a moment but then said, "You might be right. There might be a big, ugly, hairy secret there."

"Ugly, hairy secrets make the best motives for murder," I said.

"We going to sit here and wait for her to come back out?"

"No." I started the Nova and backed up and away from our hiding spot. "I'll take you home, and then I think I'll track down Cliff."

Gram was glad to go home. She'd slept better the night before—fewer and less violent nightmares. She wasn't ready to be relieved, yet, but she and I both hoped that the sketches might prove to be a catalyst for making the bad dreams go away. Now that the images were on paper, perhaps they could leave her head and leave her alone. Despite the better rest, a nap sounded appealing. I dropped her off and went back to town to find Cliff.

He was in his new crime lab and I suddenly understood part of why he'd been missing in action since he got back from St. Louis. He had lots of new, shiny toys to help him solve crimes.

"Betts, come on in," Cliff said when he saw me after he pulled his face away from a microscope. "Come and see this."

The room wasn't large but it wasn't cramped either, and it was much more decked out than I'd expected. In a way, the space reminded me of a modern version of Jake's archive room. But instead of old and archived, the items were new and modern. A large, lighted top steel worktable took up lots of space in middle of the room, and sturdy, metallic shelves lined the walls, some of them holding intimidating machines with buttons and displays I would never understand.

I knew what a microscope was, of course, but the one Cliff had been looking through was bigger than the ones from high school, more heavy duty, more official.

I put my eyes to the scope and peered in at what looked like a single item with a bunch of stringy branches. There were bumps along the item and its branches. The picture was clear but I had no idea what it was.

"What is it?" I asked as I pulled away.

"It's a strand of your hair."

I looked in again. "I have some bad split ends."

Cliff laughed. "Not really. This microscope is just that good."

"Where did you get the hair?"

"From the wrench that killed Derek and knocked you out."

"Oh," I said. "A wrench, huh?"

"Yes, that was the murder weapon. How's your head?"

"Fine. A little tender, but better."

I took a seat on a stool not far from the microscope. It shouldn't have been surprising that there had been some of my hair on the same item that had killed Derek, but hearing it, knowing it was real, was unsettling. "Where's the wrench?"

Cliff stepped around the worktable and to a shelf on the other side of the room. He grabbed a big baggie and brought it back around.

"It's in here. It's been processed—this is something I've not been able to say without having to send evidence to St. Louis or Springfield; *I* processed it."

"Does that make you more a crime-scene person than a policeman?" I asked.

Cliff shrugged. "I think it makes me both. I'm a police officer, but I know a little more now about crime-scene investigation and the processes and procedures. I can't do anything big—perhaps something that would involve heavy-duty chemicals or more advanced machinery. But I could figure out that on this wrench were a few things—your hair, Derek's hair and blood, Roy's fingerprints, and two other prints with unknown origins—they aren't in any criminal database."

"That's pretty cool. How will you figure out where the two mystery prints come from?"

"The old-fashioned way. I'll start with all the Trigger drivers and get their prints. However, the possibilities could be endless. Though not likely, it is feasible that a tourist or two even touched it. We'll just have to keep looking for other clues or some other real evidence."

"About that . . . ?" My tone was a giant question mark.

"You want to know what we've got, don't you?" Cliff smiled. "I guess I'm not surprised, and I bet that your curiosity is piqued since you were involved directly."

I nodded.

"Unfortunately, we don't have much at all. We have the wrench and the mystery prints, but there's nothing else on there that might give us anything. No possible DNA to match with anything. No witnesses. We're still questioning lots of people, all the Trigger drivers included, and we've got more to ask Roy."

"Roy? As in, he's a suspect?"

"He's more a person of interest, but we're looking at everyone," Cliff said.

I realized that this case was not only personal to me, but also to Cliff since I'd been hurt. He wouldn't leave any stone unturned. Heck, he'd probably turn them all over a few times before he gave up. I liked having him on my side, but I didn't think Roy was a killer. "I never saw any problems between him and Derek."

"There might be other angles there."

"Like what?"

"Like Lynn—and I should not have said that. If you tell anyone I told you, I will have to arrest you."

"If anyone is going to arrest me, I want it to be you," I said with a bad attempt at a flirtatious smile. "But Lynn?"

"Lynn talked to Jim last week about her concerns over some possible safety issues with the Triggers. Jim checked out her complaints and found nothing of substance. It appeared to Jim that Roy was upset by the way Lynn handled her concerns. He wished she would have talked to him first."

"I didn't know she'd done that. Roy hid any surprise or irritation well. And that's what Lynn does; Roy knows that."

"Sure, he does, but it's difficult to find objectivity when it's about something you're so close to, something you've invented. Roy's Triggers are like his kids, maybe."

"I don't believe objectivity is really ever possible, no matter what, so I get what you're saying. However, I do have a hard time with Roy killing Derek over something he was mad at Lynn about. Lynn and Derek were . . ."

"What?"

"I was going to say 'two different people' but though that was technically true, I saw how they were often thought of as being their own little team against the rest of the world. And I'm beginning to wonder just how much time they actually did spend apart. It seems like Lynn was in the middle of all of Derek's life, marriages included."

"That's what Rachel said."

"Rachel? One of Derek's wives? She works at the bank?" I remembered Teddy's wife list.

"That's the one."

"You talked to her?"

"Yes. Well, she came in and talked to us."

"And?"

"I can't really tell you all she told us, but, yes, Lynn was right in the middle of all of Derek's marriages. Way too much in the middle."

"I would love some details."

"I know, but I also know you'd go searching for some stuff on your own if I tell you any more, so it's for your own safety that I don't. I might later, though, once we exhaust all of our leads."

"Hmm. That's no fun."

"I know."

"Did she hint at the reason that Derek, with his sparkling personality, was able to find five women who wanted to marry him?"

Cliff smiled and raised one eyebrow. "No, she didn't go into that. We didn't ask her any questions that might give us those sorts of answers. We were just more interested in the amount of time that Lynn was 'in the middle' of the marriages. Rachel was pretty forthcoming, but I can tell you this, she asked us specifically not to tell Lynn that she spoke with us."

"Did you agree?"

"For now, yes. Jim's a firm believer that we as a police force don't bargain for much of anything, but he was willing to tell her he'd let her know if he felt compelled to tell Lynn."

I nodded, and then looked appreciatively around the room. "All right, show me what all this stuff is."

Cliff didn't hurry, but he didn't go into great detail as he described all the items and what they did. The things were interesting, but his enthusiasm was the best part. I found myself trying to imagine him as the architect that he used to be and the idea didn't fit quite right; it was as if the edges of the pictures in my mind weren't even. He'd found his true calling back home in Broken Rope.

Many times I'd tried to imagine him married to his first wife and my mind only formulated a blank screen. I hadn't known her, hadn't ever seen a picture of her, and I hadn't made it a point to memorize her name. Mostly I'd just pretended that Cliff had never been married. It wasn't that I was jealous of the other woman he'd fallen in love with, it was simple and pure denial; so much better to pretend she just didn't exist.

After the equipment tour and when I realized he didn't need me further interrupting his work, I left. Our farewell was brief and only a little romantic, but that was okay. I had no sense that he was concerned about my kiss with Paul, nor did he push for more information about Jerome. In fact, I sensed there was a new balance to our relationship since the incident in the cooking school. I really liked the hint of normalcy that came with the balance.

Normalcy—not a bad plan, and something I needed to aim for more often.

Chapter Thirteen

As I left the crime lab, my head—now being mostly but not entirely freed from worrying about Cliff's potential hurt feelings—reeled with everything else.

What had happened to Grace when we were at Lynn's? Did Derek jump into Grace's ghostly skin, or was it another ghost? If so, who? Why else would Grace have appeared at Lynn's if it wasn't Derek?

You should have told me.

Told me absolutely nothing, but I knew the phrase was vastly important. There was no way that Grace could have somehow been tied to Lynn, was there? I'd have to ask Jake to explore, but I would be surprised if there was a connection.

It was an easy walk to the doctor's office from the new crime lab and my thoughts rattled around in my head as I dodged tourists and a swarm of actors that were heading toward the other end of the street to either round up some cattle or stage a fake gunfight.

I recognized the Explorer out front as the same one I'd seen earlier in front of Lynn's house. Whatever Ridley had been up to, it hadn't taken her very long. I glanced inside the front passenger window as I meandered by. Even though it was a nurse's vehicle, I was surprised to see typical nurse items on the front passenger seat—a stethoscope, some medical tape, and some gauze. I wondered if any of the items had been used on Lynn and, if so, why. Lynn hadn't appeared injured or ill when Gram and I had been at her house. I remembered seeing Ridley exit her car; she hadn't carried anything with her.

"What time's your appointment?" the front receptionist said when I came in. There was no one else in the small waiting room and she looked perplexed by my arrival.

"No appointment. I was here a couple days ago and I wondered if there was a nurse I could talk to about my continuing headache."

"Oh, actually, I think the doctor would prefer to see you himself."

Darnit.

She continued, "But he's not here at the moment. Let me talk to Ridley and I'll have her determine if she wants to call him back in."

That worked. Sometimes you just get lucky.

"Thanks."

The receptionist reappeared a few moments later and signaled me in through the side door. She deposited me in one of the examination rooms I hadn't yet been in. It was a small room down a side hall, and it was decorated with cowboy wallpaper. In the rest of the world, it might have been considered a children's examination room, but since this was Broken Rope it was probably just something that Dr. Callahan had done to keep up with the town's theme.

Ridley entered the room only a brief instant later. The door opened almost the second the receptionist had closed it.

"Hi, Betts, how are you feeling?" she asked.

"Not terrible. I'm still a little headache-y though."

"Dizzy?"

"No."

"Any nausea?"

"No."

"Funny vision?"

"No."

"Tell me more about the headache. On a one-to-ten scale, how bad is it? What kind of pain—sharp or dull—and where is it located?"

"It's about a two is all, and it's mostly that the knot on my head is tender to the touch. I can't really get comfortable on my pillow."

"I see," she said as she reached to the knot on my head. She touched it very gently. "Right here?"

"Yes."

She stepped back. "And you're not having any other pain?"

"Not really."

"Hmm. Well, when's the last time you took some Tylenol?"

"Yesterday."

"You'd do better if you kept on a well-timed schedule of Tylenol for a few more days. You should feel as good as new very quickly."

She was probably wondering how I managed to fare in a kitchen, with knives and other sharp things, if I couldn't handle a two-on-the-pain-scale headache.

"Of course. I should have thought of that. I'm sorry. I feel kind of dumb," I said.

"Not at all. You should come see us any time you have any questions or problems. That's what we're here for. Anything else?"

"Yeah," I said, and then I hesitated awkwardly. "You know, I really want to thank you for taking care of me the other day. I'm sure it was very difficult considering what happened to Derek."

Surprise lit her eyes briefly. "It's okay. It's my job."

I slid off the examination table. "I know, but still, thank you."

"You're welcome."

"Boy, I sure have heard some odd things about Derek's mom lately," I said, ever so un-smoothly.

"Really? Like what?" She had her hand on the doorknob but removed it and crossed her arms in front of herself.

"Like she was pretty meddlesome in his marriages. That had to be hard."

She knew the door was closed because she had never opened it, but she glanced at it nonetheless as if to confirm that it was shut tight.

"I don't know what you mean," she said with such a quaver to her voice that she had to clear her throat when she was done.

"Nobody can hear us, Ridley. I'm sorry if Lynn mistreated you—or any of Derek's wives for that matter."

Ridley laughed nervously and then looked at the door again. "Look, I don't know what you've been told or what you've heard, but I promise whatever it is or was, it wasn't accurate. Rumors never are," she said.

"So, Lynn was a good mother-in-law?"

Ridley's eyes became fierce. The sudden change was shocking, but I tried to hide my reaction.

"Why do you care? Derek's dead."

"I'm sorry, Ridley. I never meant anything by it. I was just curious about Lynn, not really Derek."

"Then you should probably ask Lynn about Lynn. She's still alive."

"That's true," I agreed.

The fire in Ridley's eyes lessened to something more smoldering than volcanic. "I'm sorry. I'm sensitive and, of course, sad right now. I should not talk to a patient the way I just spoke to you."

"No problem. I'm doing fine," I said, not completely fessing up to my transparent plot.

Ridley looked at the floor and took a deep breath. She looked back at me a moment later, her hand now firmly back on the knob. "You're good to go. Let us know if you have any other issues." She left me to find my own way. I didn't blame her.

I sat on the examination table a few seconds more. Was there anything I could do to ease the strife I'd just created? Probably not; at least not anything that would make it better. There were many ways, however, I could make it worse. Leaving was the best option.

As I slid off the table, my phone buzzed. Jake texted, telling me he'd found more train stations.

I was glad for something to do that might not make someone angry at me. Since the receptionist wasn't still out front, I managed to leave the doctor's office without having to say anything more to anyone.

"Okay, though a search for 'plain, boring train stations' pulls up just about nothing, a simple search for 'historical Missouri train stations' did result in several pictures. I don't know if the one you saw was in Missouri, but I thought I would start there, and I found a few really simple stations, one that looks lots like your description."

"I'm ready," I said. I kept the Nova parked down the street but I'd grabbed Paul's sketches from it and brought them with me to Jake's. We decided to look at the station pictures before we looked at the sketches.

"Okay," Jake said as he lifted the pictures, one at a time, from the short pile he'd made. He turned them over and placed them in a line. "This is the Katy station in the Flat Branch area in Columbia." He moved back to the first picture and pointed at it.

The Katy station was fairly simple and small, but not simple enough. It wasn't a wide building either, but more like a house that extended backward.

"Nope, not the one," I said.

"This is Eldon." He pointed.

Eldon's station was also simple. It was wider than it was long, but it still wasn't simple enough. It had a couple of dormer windows on its second floor. The station I was looking for had neither dormer windows nor a second floor.

"Closer, but still no cigar," I said.

"Scruggs station," Jake said as he pointed at the third picture.

"Not even close," I said as I looked at the building made of stone with wooden pillars along the platform.

"I didn't think so, but it's so beautiful; I had to show it to you."

"It is definitely beautiful."

"This is the Russellville station. Keep in mind, I'm not just staying close to Broken Rope, in case she went farther."

"Got it, and this one is pretty similar, but still not it. This one isn't fancy, but the one I saw was even wider."

"Okay, this one is Olean."

"Wait." I picked it up and inspected the fuzzy black and white picture. "This one's even closer, Jake, but I still don't think it's the one.

This looks whitewashed and there's something different about the placement of the doors, but I'm not sure what it is."

"Well, the white-wash might not be a big deal, but if the door placement is off, then it's probably not the one. I saved the best for last."

With his typical dramatic flair, Jake turned over the last picture in the stack.

"This is a better picture of the Frankland station," he said. I heard the unspoken "ta-da" in my head.

"That's it! That's the one, I have no doubt. Why did you save it for last?" I said as I looked at the wide, simple—really simple—wood plank building.

Jake shrugged. "I thought it would be fun for you to see them all."

"Okay. It was."

"Good. Well, here it is, then. The station *was* the Frankland station, like you thought; it was a couple of stops before Broken Rope, on the route I think Grace would have taken from Mississippi."

"Do you think she was killed there?" I said.

"I would hate to speculate, but it must mean something."

I moved my thoughts back to the moments I first met Grace as I looked at the picture even more closely. There was no doubt in my mind that the station in the picture in front of me was the same one where I'd met her.

"Jake," I said. "I don't know how you would begin to do this, but is there any chance you could see if Lynn and Grace are somehow connected?"

"That sounds like a big challenge. What'd I miss?"

I told Jake about Grace's appearance at Lynn's house. He listened with his normal interest, but the note he jotted down didn't give me much hope.

Grace and Lynn????

"Wild-goose chase?" I said.

"I've been on wilder. I'll let you know. Now, I'd love to see how Paul did for Miz."

I grabbed the rolled-up sketches. "Okay, this one is, without a doubt, Robert," I said as I unrolled the first paper and spread it on the table.

"Excellent," Jake said. "Paul is really good, isn't he?"

I nodded. "I should tell you everything that happened when he was there sketching. At some point or another you'll probably hear about it from either Paul or Cliff or both."

"Uh-oh, that doesn't sound good. Tell me."

I went over the details and, again, he listened intently. His eyes widened slightly when I told him about the kiss, but he didn't add a comment.

"So, other than that moment, you haven't seen or heard from Jerome since?" he said.

"That's your first thought—where's Jerome?" I said.

"Yes, but for a good reason. He's trying to get here, which means your life must be in danger. How and why—and if something is stopping him from saving you, how strong must that ghost or thing or person be? It's worrisome."

"Gram and I are choosing to look at it differently. I think my life *might* have been in danger, but when I didn't die with Derek, I escaped the danger," I said.

"Maybe, but there's still a killer on the loose."

"Derek's killer."

"Who hit you on the head, Betts! Probably not with the intention of you getting up and back to your life so quickly. The killer might think you saw something and still want you dead."

"No, they know I didn't see anything. They came at me from behind, and I was out."

"Right, but Roy said you talked to him, so you weren't as out as you think you were."

"I promise I'll be careful."

"I hope so, and I hope Jerome gets here on time, and in his own ghostly body, if his services are needed." Jake took a deep cleansing breath. "All right, I'd like to see the other sketch."

I unrolled the second piece of paper. He looked at it a long moment and then he looked up at me, his eyes big.

"I know this man," he said.

"You do?"

"I do. Hang on."

Jake practically leapt to his computer chair and rolled it close to his desk.

"One second," he muttered as he pushed keys and different images flashed over the screen. "Hang on."

I looked over his shoulder and marveled at his command of the technology in front of him.

"Found him! And you won't believe this one," he said.

"Who is he?"

"Let it print." He stood and hurried over to the printer that was, for some reason, on the other side of the room. He smiled mischievously at me as he put one hand on his hip and one at the ready for the paper spitting out of the printer.

Not soon enough he hurried back to where I stood and plopped the two papers down on the table in front of me.

"Look. At. This," he said.

The papers had information printed on them about someone named Justice Adams—Justice being the man's first name, not his title. And there was no doubt that he was the man in the second sketch.

"Justice Adams was not a killer, Betts," Jake said. "I have no idea why Miz is seeing him that way."

"Who was he?"

"He was an amazing man—a well-respected one. He was a leader. He was the one responsible for creating the Frankland mining economy. Here, read this."

I focused in on the article that Jake pointed at. It was a short couple column inches and about a ground-breaking ceremony to be held for a new building on the mining company's land, but it was not conservative in its praise for the special man who would be landing the first shovel. He was exactly what Jake had said, and more. "He created jobs, he was the mayor. Yes, he was something."

"Yes."

"What in the world is he doing in Gram's nightmares?"

"I have no idea," Jake said. "You know, there's a small museum devoted to Justice in Frankland. Coincidentally—or not—it's attached to the building that used to be the train station. I know, could all be connected. I know the curator of the museum—well, that's a big word for the person who unlocks the doors and lets people in, but that person is a descendant of Justice's. Her name is Mariah. I think you and I should go talk to her right away."

"Right now?"

"Yes. I don't think we have time to waste, do you? Nor do we have any reason. Let's go!"

"Your shows?"

"I'm canceling them. It's okay. I'll deal with any complaints later. Betts, I don't like that your life might be in danger . . ."

"I don't think it is."

"Still. Now's a good time."

"Uhm. Okay."

"Come on, I'll drive"

Jake didn't change out of his costume. He led us authoritatively (just like any good sheriff from the Old West) out to his old VW Bug that was parked in the back. He always behaved a little differently, maybe even looked a little taller, when he was in his costume.

Despite being a millionaire, Jake still loved his old Bug though. I always wondered if we'd make it to whatever destination we had in mind when we were in it. Today was no different than any other day. Or so I thought.

Chapter Fourteen

The route to Frankland wasn't complicated. A quick twenty-minute-or-so jaunt down Highway 44. The last time I'd been to these parts was to pick up a book from the Frankland library for our own Broken Rope branch a few years earlier. I'd first stopped by our library to pick up the latest from one of my favorite authors, but it hadn't been delivered yet. The Broken Rope librarian, Sarabeth, somehow convinced me to make the drive to Frankland to pick up one of their extra copies. It had been a beautiful summer day so I'd gone without even feigning resistance. Sarabeth would have won anyway; she always does.

The highway this time of year was lined with Missouri woods made up of full, green trees and the occasional wide river. As Jake steered his Bug—going only slightly over the speed limit—I looked out the passenger window and watched the woodsy world go by, sometimes stretching my neck to see over a bridge or into a deep gully or upstream one of the rivers. Missouri didn't have mountains like those found in the western United States, but this part of the state was plenty hilly as well as dotted with tall, rocky cliffs—the Ozarks: not like the Rockies, but still stunning in their own way. I always thought it felt primitive and wild, and though I preferred the small-town life, I was still intrigued by the backwoods.

"Jake!" I said after we passed over a bridge. "What did I just see?" I turned around and tried to look out the back of the Bug but the only things in my line of vision were trees.

"I don't know."

"You have to go back," I said.

"We're on the highway, Betts," Jake said.

I remembered an exit not too far back. "Take the next exit, turn around, and then take the exit behind us. Go under the freeway to the frontage road and we can snake our way back to the building."

"Wow, Betts, what do you think you saw?" Jake asked as he peered out the front windshield, probably looking for an exit.

"I saw an old building, but it was next to a train—a locomotive that was puffing steam. And I would put money on the fact that it was the Broken Rope station. It was clear and real, though not in as good a shape as I've recently seen in the pictures. I think."

"That's not possible. The train part I mean. There might have been tracks over there, though, and maybe an old building that resembled the station."

"I saw a train. Look, there's an exit."

Jake veered the Bug off and then back onto the freeway, taking us back the other direction. From the other side of the freeway it was impossible to look down and into the lower area where I'd seen what I'd seen, but it wasn't too long before we found the other exit.

"One step up from a dirt road, at least," Jake said cheerfully.

The road was pocked but paved, and it seemed no one had intended for it to move in a straight line or be wide enough to allow more than one vehicle. Fortunately, there wasn't a lot of traffic and we were left alone to snake our way back around to the other side toward the old building.

"This is reminding me a lot of *Deliverance*. You saw that movie?"

"Of course." I laughed, but he did have a good point. The freeway wasn't far away, but we were below it, and unless at least one of us could jump up about a hundred feet, getting to civilization wouldn't be quick or easy.

"There it is," I said as we came around a curve.

"I see the building, Betts, but I'm not seeing a train," Jake said.

"There's no train anymore," I said.

"You can see the tracks next to the building but they're old, overgrown, and unusable. Trains used to run here," Jake said as he steered the Bug off the road and onto a dirt road that led directly to the front of the building. He slowed substantially but the Bug was jolted every direction as it rode over the uneven ground.

"That was the old Route 66, wasn't it?" I said as I nodded back toward the road.

"Yep. The one and only. Though I can't see ghosts, I think Route 66 must be one of the more haunted places anywhere. It saw lots and lots of people."

I looked at the building. "Jake, this is the station building that I met Robert at, the Broken Rope station. Or at least it's very close to it. This one's older, in worse shape, but still the same place. Maybe this was just the style of buildings they used for train stations."

"It's obviously not the Broken Rope station because it's not in Broken Rope." Jake stopped the Bug, its engine putter the only sound until he turned the key.

"It's beautiful," I said. "Even if it is in bad shape.

"Shall we explore?" he said.

"Absolutely."

We both stepped out and into a patch of low weeds. We high-stepped our way closer to the building.

"Oh, look," I said as we veered to our left and I looked toward where the tracks extended into the distance.

"That really is beautiful." Jake pulled out his phone and snapped a couple pictures.

About a hundred feet back, the tracks moved over a bridge, the bridge presumably over a river, but we couldn't tell from where we were. The bridge was train tracks only, and had steel beam arches on each side of it, which made it seem more modern than it probably was.

"Should we go and check it out?" I said.

Jake looked at his cell phone. "I've got no reception out here. You?"

"No," I said as I looked at mine.

"Everything looks pretty sturdy, but I'd hate to find out something wasn't. It's just you and me, and we didn't tell anyone where we were going. Even if we had, no one would look over here. Let's think about it. Maybe after we explore the building."

"Deal."

A closer inspection of the building showed that though the outside was in rough shape, it wasn't dilapidated. Both stories had been trimmed in gold paint. The gold was still there, though flecked in places on the decorative bumpy trim. In my mind, I saw the pictures, the ones with the people wearing the uncomfortable looking clothes. The men were smoking pipes and the women fanning themselves with real fans.

An old brass bell lay on its side on the porch, but nothing else was there.

The double front doors hung a little funny from their loosened hinges, and neither of them had knobs or handles.

The other outside paint, some red, some white, was in decent condition, though. It was as if someone a few years ago thought a new coat of paint or two might hide the other blemishes.

Jake cautiously stepped onto the porch and put his face up to the window.

"Oh. My," he said, his voice deep with awe.

"What?" I said as I carelessly hurried up next to him. The boards under my feet moved too much to be totally safe, but they held us both.

"Wow," I said.

The inside of the building was stunning. I'd never seen anything like it. The ticket counter on the right wall had a glass window at the top of it that was still totally intact, and from where we stood seemed only a little dusty. The sign above the window that said TICKETS must have been made of carved wood. There were a number of benches throughout the rest of the lobby/waiting area. They were the ornate variety, with curlicue armrests and sloping backs that curled under at the tops.

"The benches are even in their right spots," I said. "How can that be? You would think that someone would have broken in and moved things around or stolen them altogether. The doors aren't on the hinges well. You don't have to break in—anyone could just walk in at any time."

"It's way off the beaten path. Or it was restored not too long ago," Jake said, but I heard the doubt in his voice again.

"Should we go in?" I asked.

"I haven't seen a No Trespassing sign, so yes, definitely."

The doors might not have been upright and working properly, but it was still difficult to get inside the building. Neither Jake nor I wanted to move the doors too much just in case we caused more damage, so we slipped ourselves through the available space, which resulted in Jake tearing his shirt and me falling ungracefully to the floor inside.

"Plenty of dust on the floor," I said after he helped me up and I wiped off my knees and hands.

"Yeah, no other footprints," Jake said as he looked inside the lobby.

He stepped forward and touched one of the benches, riding his finger along the top of its back. "Plenty more dust here, too. It's hard to tell because the place isn't sealed shut, but I don't think anyone has been here for a while, though I'm hesitant to think this is all original. It just couldn't survive—what, maybe a hundred years or more—in this condition. Could it?"

I shrugged. "You'd know more than I would."

We opened the narrow door that led to the space behind the ticket counter. Inside were an old chair and a slotted box that must have at one time held money. The items were less dusty than those in the lobby, and in just as good shape.

"I'm not touching those," Jake said.

"Me either."

We left the small room, closing the door gently.

"This way," Jake said.

On the other side of the lobby was another open space, like a foyer. At its far end was a staircase that led both up and down.

"Which way shall we go first?" I asked.

"Up, but let me lead the way."

"My hero."

"Not really. Cliff would shoot me if I let you get hurt. So would Jerome, probably, but since he could never aim well, I'm not as worried about him."

My laugh bounced off the walls and echoed slightly.

Every step that Jake took was accompanied by squeaking wood, but nothing seemed dangerously rotted.

The stairs were both narrow and steep, but there weren't many. We reached the next floor quickly and without any problems.

We were greeted by more dust and more things, though the things weren't as organized as those on the first floor. Packed together were what looked like a dentist's chair, some shelving, some old file cabinets, and more, but less impressive, chairs.

The area was open and fairly spacious, but the ceilings were sloped so that there wasn't much headroom. There were three windows on the front wall, and four windows on the back wall.

"Was this a dentist's office? I thought you said the Broken Rope station had a salon and barber shop," I said, trying to put together the idea of a train station and a dentist's office.

"I don't know, I guess. I'd say it might have been one *after* it was a train station, but that's an old dentist's chair and at the time it was used I bet trains were still running. I just don't know."

The chair was brown, looked uncomfortable and wicked.

"Any ghosts present?" Jake whispered.

"No," I said. But I was creeped out. I rubbed the goose bumps on my arms. "The ghosts aren't as creepy as the mere idea of ghosts. Well, they haven't been up to now. This place is weird, Jake. I feel like we're missing something here, but I have no idea why I feel that way."

"I know. Let's check the basement quickly and then get out of here," he said.

He led the way again as we climbed down the two flights of stairs that took us only somewhat below ground.

"This is more like it," Jake said as we stopped on the fifth step up from the basement floor. We couldn't go any farther or we'd have stepped into a dirty lake that had become the basement. The entire back wall was missing, which was a reason, I suppose, to question the integrity of the building, but we ignored that as we looked at the dilapidation.

"It's stinky down here—old, dirty water," I said.

"Look at the fish." He pointed.

A school of small fish was in the dirty water, swimming together in a nonsensical but interesting pattern.

"And," Jake continued, "look at everything else down here. The wood in the ceiling is completely rotted. The walls are barely walls. I don't understand how this foundation is holding up the rest of the building."

Jake's vocalized observations must have been some sort of cue. A snap that was louder than any tree branch breaking sounded from somewhere above us.

"What the . . . ?" Jake said.

"Let's get out of here," I said as I grabbed his hand, turned, and led us both back up the stairs.

But the way up was suddenly missing. The three top stairs had disappeared; perhaps fallen away into the murky indoor lake below. And yet, we were still able to stand on the step, but I thought that was about to change.

"What's going on?" I said.

"I don't know, Betts, but we can still get out over there." He nodded to the back of the basement where the wall was missing. "We have to swim through the water. Maybe walk—it can't be too deep."

"Jake, we'll die from some sort of bacteria in there."

One of the rotten pieces of wood that had been part of the basement ceiling fell off into the filthy water, causing it to splash up and all over us.

"Too late, and there's no other option, Betts. Come on." Jake pulled my hand the other direction.

Isabelle, stay still for a moment.

"Jerome?" I said as I stopped hard enough to pull Jake toward me again.

"Is he here?" Jake said.

"I don't see him or smell him, but I heard him. I heard his voice. He told me to stay still for a moment."

Another rotten rafter fell into the water.

"You're imagining things," Jake said. "We've got to go, Betts."

Stay still!

"Jake, seriously, don't move. I know it sounds crazy, but I know we'll be okay if we just stay still," I said. I didn't know, but I was one hundred percent sure I heard Jerome's voice.

Jake looked at me—in the flash of an instant I saw fear, confusion, and disbelief cross his face, and then I saw acceptance.

"You'd better be right," he said. He turned toward the disappearing basement. "Jerome! Get it in gear, buddy. Get us out of here."

For the longest few seconds of my life, the only thing that happened was more destruction. The ceiling fell, one piece at a time, the walls crumbled, several pieces at a time. It wasn't long before Jake and I were crouched next to each other on the remaining step, the space for us becoming smaller and smaller.

"We have only a few more seconds," Jake said. "Let's swim."

On each side of us, more cracks sounded and the stair frame started to give way.

"We're going in, Betts. Hold my hand and we'll get out of here," Jake said breathlessly.

But then the opening across the bacteria-filled-and-small-fish-riddled lake became totally blocked. The wall from the above level collapsed, closing the space.

"Oh no," I said.

"Just hold tight," Jake said as he pulled my hand close to his chest. "We'll be okay if Jerome said we'd be okay."

I remembered that Jerome hadn't visited me in person on this trip, that the ghosts actually seemed to be possessing each other as well as live people. The voice I'd heard that had sounded so much like Jerome's might have been someone else pretending to be Jerome.

"Oh, Jake," I said. "I'm sorry."

"Hold tight."

It was only about an instant before the entire building came down that invisible hands reached from above and grabbed both me and Jake and pulled us up. The storm of flying debris was even stronger on the higher level. I couldn't see much of anything or anyone.

What felt like an eternity later, we were deposited on the ground in front of the building, or where the building had been a few minutes earlier.

"You okay?" Jake said to me as he grabbed my arms. We were both on our knees.

He was windblown but he didn't look injured. I figured I looked the same.

"I'm fine, Jake. You?"

"Fine," Jake said, but I could tell he wasn't so sure.

"Betts," another voice said.

I looked up. It was so bright and sunny that the ghost was barely distinguishable.

"Robert?" I said. I turned to Jake and stood, feeling okay but a little noodle-limbed. "Robert's here. Hang on a second."

Jake nodded and sat back again on his heels, seemingly relieved to have a moment to recover.

"Robert, what's going on?" I said.

"I'm not sure. I was sent here by some cowboy. He couldn't get here, but he knew I could so he told me to come and get you two out of there."

"How'd you grab us? There's too much light out here for you to be solid." I caught a slight whiff of his old cologne-like scent, making me sure I wasn't imagining him.

He shrugged. "Cowboy told me I could. I guess I just believed him."

"Was that the Broken Rope station?"

"I do believe so."

"How'd it get here?"

"I don't know."

"Thank you."

"You're welcome."

"Why couldn't Jerome get here?"

"I don't know."

"Robert, this is going to seem terribly ungrateful, but you're here. I have to ask, did you kill Grace?"

"No!" He said the word adamantly, but then he looked back at the space where the building had been. The building wasn't there anymore. The tracks remained, but in their overgrown state. "I did not kill her, but she died here, or at the Broken Rope station, I think. That's what I'm remembering. That's why I could get here, to this building, I guess. But I did not kill her. I couldn't have."

"I don't understand. Why was the building even here? We're not in Broken Rope."

Jake stood up and walked toward where the structure had been. In its place, there was only a deep hole in the ground and the school of tiny fish swimming around.

"Why, Robert? Why here?"

"I don't know."

Jake looked at me. "The whole thing was an apparition?"

"I don't know," I said. "You saw it. You aren't supposed to see the ghost stuff."

"I more than saw it. I felt it."

"Robert said he didn't kill Grace, and that he doesn't know why the Broken Rope station was here, in the middle of nowhere."

"Huh. It's all so . . ."

"Scary?" I said.

"Interesting."

"Oh."

"Hurry up and finish with Robert. I want to get to Frankland," Jake said.

"Still? I mean . . ."

"We're going, and we're going to figure out how Justice Adams played a part in Robert and Grace's history. The sooner, the better." Jake turned and walked to his Bug. He moved directly through Robert.

"Wanna come with us?" I said to the ghost.

"No, I have to go for now. I'm a little tired of all this, Betts. I'd like to go back to where I was, even if Grace isn't there. I'm not supposed to be bothered by anything anymore. This bothers me."

"I'm sorry," I said, because I didn't know what else to say.

Robert shook his head. "Well, the cowboy will be happy that you're okay."

"It wasn't real. Could we have truly been hurt?"

Robert shrugged. "Don't know, but it wasn't worth the risk."

"Thanks, Robert. And thank Jerome, too."

"Of course," he said before he disappeared.

We drove out of the clearing that had seemed like the perfect setting for a train station, one that might not ever have really been there.

"Thank Robert and Jerome for me next time you see them," Jake said, repeating my gratitude. "If we'd swam though the water, we might have been crushed by the crumbling wall. If it was real, they saved us, Betts."

I wondered. "Well, someone did."

Chapter Fifteen

The current Frankland train station was similar to the ghostly version I'd visited. Present day, it was still simple but welcoming, still pretty and somewhat primitive. But that was just from the outside.

Inside were walls packed with posters, pictures, and placards—some things framed, some not, most everything somewhat tilted and off-center. There were no benches, but two card tables, each with four chairs, took up the waiting area. There were decks of cards and backgammon boards on each table, but no one was currently sitting around them.

"Help you?" a crackled voice said from the direction of the ticket counter, but it was located behind a floor-to-ceiling wooden beam, so we couldn't see the person attached to the voice.

"That's Mariah," Jake said before he stepped purposefully forward.

I followed behind and tried not to show my surprise when we came upon the only other person in the building.

"Jake, my love," she said as she stood from the rocking chair and stretched her arms out toward him.

I was surprised because Mariah was either in costume or she was like the building—almost authentic, in the ways of an old Missouri backwoods woman. She was short, definitely old, hunched over, and wrinkled like an apple-head doll whose apple had been left to dry for far too long. She smoked a pipe, or at least held one in her mouth; I didn't smell any smoke. She wore a long skirt with an apron and a bonnet, which only covered most of her wiry gray hair. She might have been a hundred years old. At least.

"Mariah, it's lovely to see you." Jake pulled her into a genuine and sweet hug. "I have missed you."

"Well, you don't have to miss me. Come visit me anytime; I'm here until I die. I know, I know, you've got your shows. How're they going this summer?"

"Very well."

"So many crowds there in Broken Rope. Too much of a big city for my tastes."

"I understand and I will come visit more often." He didn't make such promises unless he intended to keep them. "This is my friend Isabelle Winston. Betts. And this is Mariah," Jake said as he stepped to the side so that Mariah and I could shake hands. Jake didn't move too far away, though, probably just in case her small body wouldn't for whatever reason stay upright.

"Oh, Betts. Winston? Wait, are you related to Missouri?" she said.

"She's my grandmother," I said.

"Sweet young lady," she said.

Gram was almost eighty, but I said, "Thanks, I think so, too."

"What are the two of you doing here in Frankland? Something I can do for you?" Mariah said.

"We're here to talk about Justice, if you're up for it," Jake said.

"If I'm up for it? It's all I do anymore. It's all I really remember how to do." She laughed, her scratchy throat making a distinct but kind of adorable frog croak.

"Thanks, Mariah. We can sit while we chat." Jake guided her as she sat back down in the rocking chair. She placed her pipe on a skinny table to her side, next to a worn paperback, the title of which I couldn't see.

Jake and I took seats on barrels with tops covered in old, worn leather, the torn edges riveted into the side of the barrels. A shiny gold spittoon sat next to the rocking chair, but I didn't see any sign of chew anywhere. The floor was made of up wood planks that probably hadn't seen better days, but were put there in their ragged shape on purpose. I understood. I was from Broken Rope; I knew all about atmosphere.

"What do you want to know, Jake? You know lots about Justice already."

"I know Justice created jobs for many people, right?"

"Because of him, folks who might have gone hungry or without a roof over their heads were able to eat and have shelter. Yes, he helped a bunch of people," Mariah said.

"Other than his amazingness—and I agree, he was amazing, Mariah." He paused and his face became serious. "Do you have any idea if he had any bad traits?"

"Like what, dear?"

Jake shrugged. "I don't know. I've come across some little information that puts him in a less-than-favorable light, Mariah. I hesitate to share the details because I want to make sure the information is one hundred percent accurate before I breathe a word about it to anyone, especially you. Even Betts doesn't know. She's just here because I wanted company on the trip." Jake paused again but continued quickly. "Did Justice maybe have a quick fuse, impatience that couldn't be controlled well?"

I saw how Jake was trying to maneuver around the thing we really wanted to know. Had Justice killed Grace? It wasn't something that could be easily asked.

Mariah stopped rocking and sat forward in the chair resting her elbows on her knees. "Love, what is it that you want to know? There's no need to warm me up or beat around the bush. I will answer whatever you want me to answer to the best of my ability, which is simply my limited knowledge of my ancestor, but I know more about him than anyone. Tell me what you want to know. He's long gone. You're a friend, Jake."

Jake looked at Mariah a moment. "I don't want to hurt your feelings, Mariah, but the questions I have are about something bad, something dark. Are you really okay with that?"

"Of course I'm okay with that, Jake. I'm old enough to know that no one can be good all the time. We all have some darkness inside us."

"All right, then." Jake looked at me. He still didn't want to say anything that might offend his friend, but I nodded supportively.

"Mariah, I've found some old information about a woman named Grace. She was a black woman who was originally from Mississippi and was, allegedly, killed on her way to Broken Rope, or perhaps in or just past Broken Rope—no one knows for sure. Does the name Grace mean anything to you? In the way of being associated with Justice, I mean." Jake swallowed and looked at Mariah both apologetically and expectantly.

Mariah's mouth came together in a wrinkled pucker. She looked at Jake, blinked, looked at me, and then back at Jake. "Maybe."

Jake nodded and waited. I think I held my breath.

"As we've already discussed, love, Justice was a good man. He helped a lot of people. But he was still, from his very core to the skin over his bones, a man who loved women. He was married twice, and from the stories I've heard he never behaved monogamously. He loved women— all woman, all skin colors."

"I see," Jake said when she paused.

Mariah rubbed her chin. When she pulled her fingers away from her face they made a fan movement until they reached her lap again. It was something I might expect a hypnotist to use to focus a subject's attention on a specific spot.

"Well, there was a Grace I heard about," Mariah said. "A lovely woman. A beauty that Justice couldn't ignore, I heard. It's a story we don't tell much because it sounds made up and it ends badly."

"All right. Go on," Jake said.

"They say that he met her here, at our station. Right here. She was on her way somewhere and her beauty put him under a spell. Well, it was as good a reason as any for him to up and leave. Justice took the next train behind her, hoping to find her."

"Do you know if he did?" I said.

Mariah looked around the otherwise empty station. "Here's my secret, Jake, my family's secret. It can't be told to anyone outside this room."

"Of course," Jake said. I nodded when they both looked at me.

"He never came home."

"What? No, that's not correct, Mariah. Justice was killed by a runaway horse here in Frankland. He fell off."

"The family had to have a better excuse than that he left them to follow a beautiful woman of color that he claimed he couldn't stop thinking about even though he'd just met her. A woman of color named Grace." Mariah sat back in the chair and sighed heavily. "They had to come up with a story when they received word that he was never coming back only a few short days after he left."

"A letter?" I asked.

"A letter," Mariah said.

"Who from?"

"They say it was from Justice himself, but that part's a mystery too."

"You don't still have the letter?" Jake said.

"Wouldn't that be a treasure? No, Jake, the letter, according to the legend, was burned the same night it was received, the same night the story about Justice being thrown from the horse was concocted."

"That must have been some letter," I said. "I mean, your ancestors must not have needed much convincing if they acted that quickly."

"Perhaps the tale has transformed over time, but that is correct. Whatever the letter said, it was a convincing story."

We were all silent a moment, deep in thought, but I couldn't help myself. "Who's buried in his casket? He—well, someone—was interred, right?"

"No one. There was a funeral and a big show of him dying, but even the town doctor thought it was important that people think more highly of Justice than him running off with a woman, never to return to his loved ones again."

"Good grief, Mariah, that's a huge story and one that it might be time to tell," Jake said.

Mariah shrugged. "We'll see. I'd like for the world to know. Justice leaving his family was not an honorable way to behave, but it was for love, or so we all like to think. The family would be upset if they knew I'd told the truth, but you're a true friend, Jake."

Love or murder, or both? Jake and I looked at each other. Had Justice made it to Broken Rope, killed Grace when she didn't return his love, and then run away to avoid prosecution? Had they run off together, leaving Robert behind to visit the train station the rest of his life? Why had Grace visited me in a scene that included the Frankland station, and not the Broken Rope station?

With a great effort, Mariah rose from the rocking chair. Jake offered her his arm, which she took as she led us out to the other part of the building, the place that now held card tables but probably had been filled with hard, uncomfortable benches at one time.

"Let's look at some pictures," Mariah said.

Even before we'd made it all the way to the wall with the pictures, I could see that the man in most of them was the same jowly man that Paul had sketched based upon Gram's description.

"Here, there's Justice when he was a young man, just starting out in the world." Mariah pointed to a picture of a person standing straight and tall, looking directly at the camera and, if I wasn't mistaken, trying not to smile. No one smiled in pictures back then

"He was handsome," I said.

"Yes, for a while. Here he is with his first wife."

Justice's first wife was as pretty as he was handsome.

"He was still young when he got married the first time," I said. "He doesn't look much different from the first picture."

"Here he is with some of his friends," Mariah said.

Justice stood in the middle of a group of men. All but Justice had soot-covered faces; probably miners. None of the men in the picture seemed happy to be having the photograph taken, and Justice's expression was just as dower as everyone else's. He was older now, not old, but close to middle age, and closer in appearance to the man in the sketch.

"His second wife." Mariah pointed.

Justice had gained weight, exaggerating the already obvious jowls. His second wife was pretty, too, but just as unhappy as everyone else in the pictures. I'd often wondered when someone first smiled for a photograph. Someone must have said "Say cheese" causing the subject to laugh and everyone realized that happy expressions made for better memories.

She moved to the next picture that was of Justice only. "They told everyone that this picture was taken the day before he was thrown from the horse, but look closely. You'll see that he was actually a little younger than he was in the picture with his second wife." Mariah laughed. "They tried to think of everything, even faking the time a picture was taken. I don't understand it."

I wondered how anyone had believed this picture was taken some time after the one with his second wife. The differences were obvious. People believed what they wanted to, though, and Justice had been a hero to so many. I didn't understand the lies his family had told to protect him and the truth, but I hadn't been there. Things were different then.

"It's all over and done now. Doesn't matter, I suppose to anyone. We don't get many visitors here anymore. Justice's memory is faint but still glorious. That's what the family wants, to keep it glorious, and I'm happy to oblige because he did do a lot of good for a lot of people."

It mattered, but she was right: Nothing from the past could really be changed.

Jake bit his bottom lip and then pulled his attention away from the wall of pictures. "Mariah, are you familiar with an old train station up the highway about halfway between here and Broken Rope?"

"No, love." She inspected him. "The only train stations that used to exist on that route are this one and Broken Rope's. There were no others between the two places."

"Are you sure?" I asked.

"I'm positive. I know my train stations and I know all the stops through Missouri, at least those that were along the same route as Frankland. It's part of what people want to know about when they ask questions about Justice. Trains and their stops were very important to what he did."

Jake thought a moment and then said, "Two stories, decorative outside, dentist's office on the second floor?"

"I don't know, Jake. Doesn't sound familiar, but I know without a doubt that there has never been a station in the location you mentioned."

What had Jake and I come upon, and why? There had to be a reason, and the reason had to have something to do with the ghosts. Didn't it?

But which ghost? Grace, Robert, Jerome—or maybe even Justice or Derek, I supposed.

Mariah suddenly wilted a little, her small body hunching a bit more.

"We've taken up way too much of your day," Jake said. "Let me help you back to the chair."

Jake guided her toward the ticket booth. I followed behind, but I allowed my eyes to skim the pictures as we moved slowly through the lobby.

As I sauntered, my eyes grazed over something that seemed familiar. I had to stop and find what I thought I'd seen. I stepped closer to one picture in particular. It was Justice sitting on a high-backed chair. There was still no hint of a smile, but he was young, probably in between his two marriages.

Above a spire on the back of the chair was a whiteish pattern in the film. A swirl. A couple of swirls, that when put together looked like a cowboy hat. The pattern was something I'd seen in some pictures of Gram when she was younger. She and I had suspected the swirls had something to do with Jerome, but no one, including Jerome, could confirm or deny.

"No way," I said quietly to myself. But no matter how many times I pulled my eyes away and then looked back at the picture, the pattern didn't go away. "Why?"

But no one answered. The distinct voice I'd heard in my head earlier was silent.

Justice had lived long before Jerome had lived. But was there a connection? The last time Jerome had visited, he'd had memories that made him think he'd been haunted when he was alive. Was it possible? And was it possible that he was haunted by more than one ghost? It happened, to me and Gram at least. Were the ghosts all connected to each other? It was a big notion to ponder and one I didn't begin to have an answer to.

"She's asleep, out the second after she sat down," Jake said as he appeared behind my shoulder. "We should just let her rest."

"We know there was a connection between Justice and Grace," I said. I silently debated pointing out the swirl on the picture, but I didn't think I needed to pull Jake even further into the ghosts' grasp.

"True," he said, then sighed heavily. "I don't think we uncovered anything that will keep you safe, but I don't know what we should do next. Jerome proved he can still come to your rescue, even if it's by sending another ghost to help. Perhaps you're being watched over close enough. Let's go home, Betts. It's been a long day."

"Sounds like a good plan to me."

Chapter Sixteen

"Wow, Sis, you're either upset or you need to think super hard about something," Teddy said.

I'd been cooking. After Jake and I got back to Broken Rope, I headed straight to the school, called Teddy, and then got to work. He was right, but I was both: upset and needing to work through something. So far, I'd made spaghetti sauce, seasoned and roasted Brussels sprouts, and fried onion rings. Both the spaghetti sauce and the sprouts included onions. Yes, I needed to cook, and onions were what I'd first seen when I opened the pantry, so onions were a part of every dish I was creating.

"Want some onion rings?" I said as I slid a plate toward my brother.

"I can't think of a time I would say no to them," Teddy said as he grabbed a few and bit into them. With a full mouth he continued, "What up, Betts?"

"I have a question for you. It's a serious one, but you're going to think I'm crazy for asking."

"I think you're crazy anyway, so what difference does that make?"

Teddy and I had always gotten along, but we were, and had always been, very different. Teddy lived life like it was a party. I didn't really like to party, and according to him, I over-thought everything. Still, we liked each other and were, for the most part, willing to put up with each other's faults.

I cut into another onion with the plan to dice it into very small pieces. Corn, tomato, and onion salad would be my next creation.

Dicing was good and gave the pungent aroma a chance to water our eyes. Teddy saw what I was doing so he moved to a stool a little farther away, taking the plate of onion rings with him.

"Remember when I was shot?" I said.

"You didn't really get shot. It was just a flesh wound. Not that bad. You were fine."

"Right. But you do remember it, don't you?"

"Of course."

"Do you remember telling me that shortly before all that happened a cowboy told you to tell me to meet him in the basement of the pool hall?"

"Oh. Kind of. Yes, actually I remember that. He was some actor that I hadn't seen before and he smelled like a campfire." Teddy looked perplexed for a moment. "I don't think I ever asked. Did you meet him? What did he want?"

I wasn't as good a cook as Gram was, but I diced like a pro. Even I was impressed by my ninja skills. More than that, the activity was giving me something to do so I wouldn't over-think what I was about to tell my brother.

"Have you seen him since then?" I said.

"I'm not sure, Betts. All the cowboys look alike around here in the summer. The hats make it hard to tell one from another."

"How 'bout the wood smoke? Have you smelled it in the presence of a cowboy again?"

"Yeah, but not like that time. It was strange how strong it was, but nice, too."

"Right."

"Betts, what's up? Who was he?"

I stopped dicing a moment and looked at my brother. On the way back to Broken Rope, I'd had a silent discussion with myself. What had happened at the mystery train station (which, by the way, hadn't been there when we'd driven by again) was scary, perhaps even wrong in some sort of spiritual way, though I didn't want to give the traumatic event that much thought. I decided I was going to let Teddy in on the ghostly secrets. I thought there might be a small chance that he had some of the paranormal juju like Gram and I, and probably my dad to some extent. The thing I'd debated with myself was whether telling Teddy was a selfish or a smart thing to do.

I didn't want to talk to my dad about it. Evidently his small taste of the otherworldly had scared him. Cliff currently didn't want to know more about it, even though he had a good sense of what was going on. And I was completely certain that Cliff had zero paranormal juju, which put him in second place when it came to choosing a new confidant. I didn't *have* to talk about it with someone else, but I thought I should. As Jake had driven us back to Broken Rope I thought about Justice and what would happen if someday I or Gram or Jake, for that matter, just disappeared. One day we were there, but the next day something or someone from that weird ghostly realm pulled us into their world, without giving us the chance to escape.

I didn't want it to go that way, but if it did I certainly didn't want my world of living loved ones to think I'd just up and left them. I wanted someone to understand what might have happened and then tell the others I hadn't intentionally abandoned anyone.

As Jake had steered his Bug down the highway and past what was now only a hole in the ground with a school of small fish swimming in it, I realized that if we had truly been killed, crushed by the collapsing building, our bodies might never have been found. Or, if they were—if someone passing by noticed the Bug after it had become overgrown with vapid Missouri weeds and vines, what would they think happened when they found our remains? It wouldn't make any sense.

I didn't want Cliff to ever wonder. I didn't want my parents to wonder. I didn't want Teddy to wonder. I needed someone, and Teddy was the person I'd chosen. But I still hoped it wasn't a selfish move. I didn't want my telling him to significantly alter his life. I doubted it would. He wasn't one to think too deeply about anything, or let anything really bother him.

"Teddy, I need to tell someone something and you're the person for the job. However, you can't say a word to Opie about it."

"Uh, well, okay, you know I can keep secrets, Betts, but I'd just like to know why I can't tell Opie—not that I tell her everything anyway, but I'd just like to know."

"Because she'd dump you for me, Teddy. She'd leave your side and stick beside me all the time, and I just can't bear the thought." My eyes watered profusely now.

Teddy laughed. "I doubt she'd dump me for you, Sis, but whatever you say. Okay, it's a deal. I won't tell her a thing about what you're going to tell me."

"You can't tell anyone at all, unless something happens to me. If I disappear or something really crazy happens, something that seems to defy explanation, then you can tell Mom, Dad, and Cliff. Opie, if you're still together and you feel like you really need to."

"Betts, this is beginning to sit funny with me. Are you okay?"

"I'm fine." I wiped my hands on my apron and used the back of them to brush away a couple tears from my cheeks.

"Okay, then what's going on?"

"Teddy, Gram and I have a connection to Broken Rope's past."

"What do you mean, like Jake tells you a bunch of stuff?"

"No, I mean like we can communicate with it, talk to it."

"Okay. What are you talking about, Betts?"

"Come on." I stepped around the butcher block and grabbed his arm. I hadn't planned this part, but Teddy learned better with pictures. I pulled him out of the school and to the cemetery, stopping at Jerome's grave.

"This was the cowboy who told you to tell me to meet him, Teddy."

"You mean an actor who was portraying him."

"No, I mean him. Jerome himself. I know him."

"Oh yeah?" He didn't sound doubtful, exactly. He just sounded like he needed a minute to process the information.

"I know him, Teddy. I know this Jerome."

Teddy's eyebrows came together, and he rubbed his chin as he looked hard at Jerome's tombstone.

The humidity had been low for most of the day but it felt like it was now rising. Missouri summers could be wonderful and they could be miserable. So far this year, we'd had a little of both. Today had started off well, but the perspiration on the back of my neck made me think we were headed for some miserable.

There wasn't a cloud in the bright blue sky. I looked up, shading my eyes with my hand, and I saw a robin dart from a tree on one side of the cemetery to the other side. I glanced around the grounds. There were no ghosts that I could see, but I wondered if any were watching us, wondering, like I was, how Teddy was going to react to this news.

"Like as a ghost?" Teddy finally said.

"Exactly like a ghost. He is a ghost—as I know him. He really did die when he was shot by the sheriff, but his—spirit, or something, can come back as a ghost. There are other ghosts from our town's past too."

"Betts," he said.

It wasn't a question, and it wasn't quite a simple statement, but I knew him well enough to know what he meant.

"I'm not crazy, Teddy. It's real, and it's really weird. I'm not telling you about it so that you will be scared or worried. It's real. Gram can talk to them, too."

"Gram can do anything. She might be able to raise the dead. I'm not saying you can't do stuff, but this is a big one."

"I know, but even if you don't want to believe it, I wanted to tell you so that if something weird happens to me, or me and Gram, or even Jake, you'll know that we didn't—well, we didn't leave on our own, or get killed in a strange way because we wanted to, because we walked knowingly into something."

Teddy blinked and then became so serious that he didn't even look like himself for a minute.

"Betts, are you in danger?"

"Maybe. No. But. I don't think so, Teddy. All the stuff from the ghosts is dead stuff, but Jake and I were in a weird situation today and I suddenly thought it was important to tell someone all the things I'm telling you."

"Jake knows, then?"

"Yes. Jake is with me so often that if something ghostly happens to me, it might happen to him, too."

Teddy nodded and still looked serious, but not the least bit doubtful.

"What's Jerome like? What do you two talk about?"

Wow, how to answer that one?

"Jerome is funny. He's a cowboy from that time, but he moved here from Boston. He doesn't act at all like a city person, though. You can tell the difference."

"Sure."

"Anyway, he's a friend, if that can make any sense at all. I don't think it can—it doesn't always make sense to me."

"You're in love with him."

"What?"

"Come on, Betts, you lit up like a Christmas tree when you started to talk about him. You love him."

"Teddy."

"What can I say, I know all about love." Teddy smiled and was back to looking like Teddy. "Here's a surprise for you. I'm glad to hear it. I've been wondering what's been wrong with you when it comes to Cliff. Now I know."

"Teddy."

"Don't deny it, Betts."

I thought a long moment before I answered. "I won't—not completely. I love Cliff, Teddy. Very much. I'm working through the weirdness."

"Does Cliff know?"

"Not totally. I've given him as much of the story as he wants. I'll tell him more when he wants to know more."

"I don't think you should. I think you just need to work through it on your own."

"You do?"

"Yes. Cliff doesn't need the details. But I also think it's cool, and awesome, and kind of brilliant. It's easy to see that Broken Rope is off-kilter slightly, but I couldn't ever understand why. This helps me understand. Cool. Very cool."

"And you won't tell Opie?"

Teddy laughed. "No, Opie couldn't handle the truth on this one. You're right, she'd be all over you like bees on a picnic pudding. You'd probably kill her and then me. But we could both come back and talk to you, though."

I smiled at my younger brother. I didn't give him nearly enough credit. He was a good guy. He wasn't clueless, even if he seemed like it sometimes. And, in all honesty, he was a better cook than I would ever be; he just didn't have any interest in working at Gram's school. He couldn't help it that almost every female that he came in contact with thought he should be theirs. Well, he could temper it a little, perhaps not turn up the charm sometimes (he *had* gotten better since Opie had come into his life), but he still couldn't help who he was. None of us could.

"Thank you," I said.

"You're welcome," Teddy said.

His attention turned back to Jerome's tombstone again. "Any chance I can meet him, or any ghost?"

"I don't know. Maybe. I'll see what I can do."

"Sounds good, but, Betts . . . well, if you're really in danger, don't you think you ought to ask them to go away?"

"I've thought about it and I'm not sure there's a way to accomplish that. Gram was good about telling them to stay out of her way, but I don't feel the same. They all can use a little help to answer a question or solve a mystery or something from their lives. I can't seem to resist helping."

"Even if there's potential danger?"

I laughed. "It never really seems dangerous at first. The danger sneaks up on me."

"Huh. Well, just consider minding your own business from here on out, but whatever you do, know that I'm on your side. I'd say I've got your back, but I'm not sure I could in this case—though I would if I could."

"Just you knowing is comforting."

"I might have more questions."

"I'll do my best to answer them."

"I'd sure love some more of those onion rings," Teddy said. He'd been told the news. He'd accepted it. In his mind, at the moment there was no need to continue talking about it.

"Let's go in."

As we climbed the few front outside stairs that led up and into the school, I looked back over the cemetery again. I saw nothing unusual, smelled nothing unusual, but still I tapped down a shiver before it trailed all the way up my spine. Then I went inside and made more delicious things with onions.

Chapter Seventeen

After my cooking-a-thon and confession time with Teddy, I made my way downtown to find Cliff again. He wasn't in his fancy new crime lab this time, but camped out at the police station instead. He wasn't on duty, but had been called in to help with an active evening. Many tourists had had either a little too much to drink, a little too much fun, or had taken in a few too many skits. There was a full moon, and these sorts of evenings sometimes came along with full moons.

Both of the two holding cells inside the station were occupied. A lone young woman had made herself as comfortable as possible in one of them. I inspected her briefly as she slept on the cot, her mouth open and her makeup smeared. Though she'd probably been brought in because she was being disorderly, a police officer might have thought that placing her in a holding cell would simply help her from adding more to her list of regrets.

The other cell was occupied by what looked like a family. Parents and two teenagers. They all seemed sober and non-violent at first glance, though none of them were happy to be there and it looked as if they weren't talking to one another. The cell space was small, but somehow behind those bars no one looked at anyone else. I would ask Cliff later what they'd done.

Cliff sat at his desk, and I'd pulled a chair up to its other side. I'd only meant to make small talk, my real reason for finding him being that I *needed* to after what had happened to Jake and me. I'd needed to talk to Teddy and I needed to see Cliff. I would call Gram and my parents later. I was thinking of the important people in my life, which I recognized was probably because I'd felt so close to no longer having that life. Gratitude, reassurance, whatever it was, I was doing what I needed to do.

But since I couldn't tell Cliff why I'd tracked him down again, I'd just started the conversation with small talk. Naturally, it had morphed into me asking about details regarding Derek's murder.

"I didn't say that." He smiled. "I didn't say that we definitely thought Derek's killer was one of his ex-wives."

No, he hadn't said *that*. He'd said that Jim was spending time interviewing four of Derek's five ex-wives again, and that Cliff was going to go talk to the last one.

"But there must be something?" I said.

"We don't have much at all, Betts," Cliff said as he sat forward in his chair and put his arms on his desk. "We don't like to look incompetent, but Jim is scratching his bald head even more than usual."

Jim scratched his head often; more than usual wasn't a positive sign.

"Five wives, though? Someone's feelings were bound to get trampled," I said.

"That's what we're thinking," Cliff said far too casually.

I inspected his face, looking for and finding his serious, tight jaw and the wrinkle in between his eyes that appeared when he was hiding something. "There's something else," I said. "You've got something else. Come on, tell me."

"Can't give you details, but there truly does seem to have been an issue between Derek and Roy, as well as between Derek and Todd Rich."

I sat up straighter.

"Really? Cliff, you know they were all taking an evening vegetable cooking class from us, don't you?"

"I do."

I thought hard about the times that we'd all spent together at the cooking school and the Trigger barn. "I never saw anything that would make me think there were issues between either Derek and Roy, or Derek and Todd. In fact, I'm not even sure Todd knew Derek's name. He's been interested in a girl."

"Let me guess." He ran his finger down the page of a notebook. "April Young, new in town."

"That's right."

"Ms. Young claims that Derek had asked her out. Perhaps Todd heard about this and wasn't happy."

"Wait. Perhaps? So, this didn't come directly from April or you wouldn't be *perhaps*-ing me. Someone else told you there were issues. Who?"

"Lynn," he said with a half-smile.

"I see. And no one really believes Lynn, do they?"

"What we believe is irrelevant. Evidence is all that matters."

Cliff had shaved that morning, but his five o'clock shadow had now grown to its nine-o'clock length. I liked the layer of facial hair, but, oddly, it did make him look somewhat younger and less official.

"You think Lynn knows who killed Derek?" I said a moment later.

Cliff shrugged. "She sure is giving us lots of 'leads.' The problem with Lynn is that who can tell why she's trying to butt into the case?

237

Does she want to help or mislead, or just have something to talk about?

Hard to know."

"What have Todd and Roy said about what Lynn said?"

"We just crossed over to the part I can't tell you."

"Darnit. Can I ply the answers out of you with liquor and my body?"

Cliff laughed. "Not much of a drinker, but the other option would be appealing if I had the time."

"Too bad. As someone else who observed the players involved, though, as far as I could tell, they always got along, or at least didn't *not* get along."

Cliff bit the inside of his cheek a moment. "I can probably tell you this part. Roy is one of Derek's ex-wife's uncles. Might not mean a thing at all. It is a small town."

"Which wife?"

"Gina. She works at the post office."

"Gina, the pretty blonde at the second counter in?"

"Yes."

"I haven't talked to her yet," I said. Cliff blinked at my official tone. I cleared my throat and continued on. "What'd she say to you guys?"

"Can't tell you that either," Cliff said. "Maybe you could mail something tomorrow and ask her a couple questions. Maybe something specific like was it Derek's money that paid for her fancy car or her second home on the lake because we have nothing that gives us the legal right to subpoena her bank records, at least at this time. There's something fishy there."

"Really? You want me to do that?" I said.

"No, not exactly. You *could* maybe stop by the post office and offer her your sympathy regarding Derek's death. It would be weird and inadmissible if you got answers to any of the real questions. But I'd love to know her reaction to your offer of sympathy."

"I can do that."

"I thought you wouldn't mind."

"The money angle? I've thought about it, too, but I don't think Derek ever made much money, did he?"

"No."

"And Lynn doesn't appear to have any money either. I've thought about her bribing people to marry Derek. I mean, it's a terrible thought, but one has to wonder. Derek married some seemingly personable women and those I've talked to don't appear to have any sort of wealth other than what they've earned for themselves."

"Except Gina. Postal clerks don't make the kind of money her spending habits justify, and her family isn't wealthy."

"What do Lynn's bank records show?"

"Nothing suspicious at all. Just enough to get the bills paid and have a little expendable income. It all seems to come from legitimate places. And there's nothing to show she's giving her money away either."

"What's the supposed issue between Derek and Roy? Just the fact that Derek divorced his niece, or maybe, married her in the first place?"

"When Derek and Gina got married, Roy installed all their appliances in their new apartment—nothing like the house that Gina acquired after the marriage, by the way. Hooking things up turned out to be more tedious than normal. Roy – though not typical of him – happened to do a bad job with their dishwasher. Their place got flooded, and Derek could never forgive Roy, even after Roy paid to have everything fixed and replaced."

"That's nutty. Stuff happens." I shook my head.

"I don't think Derek had a great marriage with any of his wives," Cliff said. "But you didn't hear me say that."

I nodded. "I didn't need to. I figured that out already, but I just wish I could figure out exactly why."

"Me too. Jim, too."

"I bet."

The phone on Cliff's desk buzzed. I noticed that the station had upgraded their phone system with something that looked much more twenty-first century.

Cliff covered the mouthpiece. "Betts, I gotta get back to work. See you later?" he said, dismissing me in the most polite way possible. I got the hint and nodded agreeably before leaving the station.

The boardwalk wasn't crowded, but there were plenty people out and about. The cookie shop at the end of the street, Broken Crumbs, was still open. The Jasper Theater was also open, currently showing a movie that had premiered in St. Louis a good six months ago, but just started playing here. The theater had undergone some renovations but I hadn't visited it since the grand re-opening.

The first place I saw the ghost of Jerome was outside the theater. It had proven to be an important building when it came to our strange relationship. I wasn't sure I ever wanted to go back inside it, but I wasn't ready to go home and I was suddenly curious. I took off toward the outside ticket counter.

Once there, I sniffed deeply just in case Jerome—or another ghost for that matter—was in the vicinity, but all I smelled was buttered popcorn.

"One?" the young woman behind the ticket counter window said cheerfully.

"Actually, I'm not here to see the movie. I'd just like to look around the lobby. I haven't seen it since it was finished."

"Sure, go on in," she said.

"Thanks," I said as I looked at the wide double doors next to the booth.

"Go ahead," she said a moment later.

I didn't realize I'd frozen in place. "Thanks," I said again.

The popcorn aroma and the sound of it popping greeted me pleasantly as I went through the front doors. When I'd last been in the lobby, the space had been only a shadow of its glory days, but the renovations had brought it back to life while somehow staying true to an Old West style.

The fixtures were polished brass, the walls decorated with old-time pictures. The snack counter was modern glass, but even the machines—the soda and the popcorn—had been re-created with an antique flair. I wondered where the old items had been found, or custom made. I knew the owners were investors who lived in Springfield, but I'd never learned their names.

It was the wall around the other side of the front doors that I was most interested in inspecting. There had been a picture there of a person who turned out to be someone pretty important to Jerome. There'd been lots of things added to the wall, but that picture was still there.

I looked at it a long time and wondered about the past, about how lives changed in the blink of an eye, how everything was temporary—it was supposed to be, anyway. Ghosts weren't supposed to come back and continue on in the wake of their person's death.

"Can I help you?" a voice said over my shoulder.

"Hi," I said to the man attached to the voice. "I'm a local, Betts Winston, and I just wanted to have a look around the renovated lobby."

"It's a fine place." The man used a wooden cane that matched the style of his old-fashioned suit and top hat. I figured he was one of the owners playing a Broken Rope role.

"It is."

"This place has seen so much," he continued. "Burlesque, live theater, black and white films, the first 'talkies,' and now modern motion pictures. Well, perhaps not right up to date, but not too old."

"I know. I've heard some of the history. It's a great place."

"Yes."

The man and I looked at each other a long time. His blue eyes were almost playfully inquisitive.

"Are you one of the owners?"

"I am. Reginald Nelson."

We shook hands, his eyes remaining an intriguing focal point.

But he ended the moment. "I've got to go, dear. Time to get back to work. I'm sure something needs to be swept."

"I understand. Thanks for introducing yourself."

He turned and started to shuffle away, his cane moving in rhythm with the hitch in his left leg. When he reached the doors between the lobby and the theater, he turned.

"Isabelle," he said. "The answers are all behind the barn. Check the barn."

He went through the doors before I could react.

"Crap," I finally said as I hurried to the doors and pulled them open. Of course he wasn't anywhere that I could see, and he hadn't been transparent at all. He hadn't brought a special scent with him, unless it had been buttered popcorn. I hadn't picked up on the fact that he'd been a ghost. I wished I'd tried to touch him.

"Miss, you need a ticket if you're going in to see the movie," a kid behind the snack counter said.

I closed the doors. "Sorry. Hey, is one of the owners of the theater named Reginald Nelson?"

The kid laughed. "No, I've never met someone named Reginald."

"Yeah," I said. Reginald Nelson. I filed the name away as one I'd ask Jake about. I would have bet some of Teddy's onion rings on the fact that Reginald Nelson was, in fact, an owner of the theater, but one before my time, long before.

I hurried out of the theater and down the boardwalk. When I reached the other end, I crossed to the street and hurried even faster to the barn.

The doors were open and the lights were blazing brightly.

"Roy?" I said as I peered in.

"I'm back here," he said. "Come on back or I'll be up in a minute."

I threaded my way around the Triggers and all the tools, glancing only briefly at the spot where I'd found Derek. Roy was on the ground but still all in one piece and breathing—a sight that was surprisingly a relief. He was halfway under an elevated motor—though I didn't think it was a motor for a Trigger.

"Hey, Betts, how are you?" he asked as he peered up with a grease-dotted face.

"I'm fine, Roy. You?"

He shrugged. "Okay, I suppose."

"Hey, do you mind if I look around out back?"

"Suit yourself. Nothing back there but an open yard. And I'm sure the police scoured it for evidence."

"Thanks."

I stepped around him and tiptoed through the organized scatter of tools that was also on the ground next to him. I pushed open the slim back door—which was as Roy had said, more a slat than a door—and stepped out onto the grass.

And didn't find much of anything. The field was too small to truly be called a field, but too big and overgrown to be called a yard. It was long, extending back a good distance. It was as wide as the barn, but for some reason, probably because it extended back so far, it didn't feel as wide. I had the urge to crouch down and inspect it, almost like I was inspecting a green before executing a perfect putt. From the low position, I could see a swerve in the land. It veered mostly to the left.

I stood, and confirmed that I didn't quite see the curve from a higher vantage point. I crouched once more and saw the curve again, realizing that it was simply a subtle roll that was better seen from a lower view. There was nothing magical or paranormal going on. And there was no reason to think I needed to inspect the spot on the inside of the curve.

Except, the niggling in my gut told me that was exactly what I should do.

I stepped forward, glancing at my feet as I moved. It was dark, but there was enough light coming from the open back door of the barn and a street light just past the field that the ground was murky but not black.

The ground was also uneven but not dangerously so. As I walked, I wondered how in the world the answers—to whichever questions—could possibly be here. I must be missing something, or perhaps something was supposed to show itself to me. A ghost? I sniffed, but there was nothing unusual in the air.

"Doesn't make sense," I muttered quietly.

I put my hands on my hips and stood silently for a moment. Maybe I was just being impatient.

Nothing happened. I literally threw up my hands and turned to go back into the barn. And my big right toe hit something hard. I bent down and ran my fingers over the ground, finding the hard object that was also cold and shiny upon further inspection.

It took only another moment to know what I'd found. A railroad rail. I stood, found the rail with my toe, gently this time, and followed it. It stopped about twenty feet later. Just stopped. Where there was one rail, there should be two, right? I scooted my foot across the ground and at about three to four feet away, I found the other rail. After a little more exploration, I decided that the two rails were both about thirty feet long, neither of them extending any farther.

I hurried into the barn.

"Roy, do you know anything about what used to be back there?" I asked him.

He scooted himself out from under the motor and stood, wiping his hands on his jeans.

"Can't say that I really do," he said.

"Anything to do with trains?" I said hopefully.

"Maybe. I know this barn was a train station at one time."

"What? No, I thought the station was down the street from my house. In a different field."

Roy's eyebrows came together as he looked at me. "Well, I'm not sure, Betts. But I know that when I went to lease this place, I talked to

Bunny. She's owns everything around here. She told me that this barn was once a train station. You should ask her, or better yet, ask Jake. He knows everything about this town."

"I will," I said as I fell into thought. I was sure that Jake told me that the station had been at the end of my street, was sure he'd confirmed as much when I told him about my recent ghostly visits. He'd never said one word about this barn being a station.

"You okay, Betts?" Roy said.

"I'm fine. Sorry to bug you."

"No bother at all," he said. "Hey, has Cliff given you any indication that they might be close to knowing what happened to Derek?"

"Not really, Roy. He wouldn't tell me anyway," I said.

Roy's face fell as he nodded slowly.

"I'm sorry, Roy," I said.

"I know. Me too. I just hope they figure it out."

"They will."

Roy nodded again, still without much confidence.

"I need to go, Roy. We'll talk later?"

"Sure. Tell Miz hi for me."

I hurried out of the barn. I wanted to talk to Bunny and Jake. Bunny was closer, and I was sure she was working; she was always working. But I stopped outside in front of the barn. I turned and inspected it. It was a barn, nothing more, but its shape was familiar in that it could have at one time been a two-story building with a wide porch on the bottom level, though there was no evidence of that porch now. The building was a similar size even if all the inside walls weren't there. I didn't know how a building could be hollowed out while the exterior walls remained the same, but it could happen, I guessed.

I hurried to Bunny's and then inside, eyeing Bunny and her ever-present pot of coffee zipping across the far side of the seating area.

"One?" the young girl behind the cash register said as she grabbed a menu off the stack in front of her.

"No, thanks. I'm just going to go ask Bunny a question," I said.

"I don't think she likes to be bothered when she's working."

"I know she doesn't, but I'll apologize." I kept walking, hoping the girl wouldn't chase after me.

"Bunny," I said as she turned from the counter, presumably after grabbing a new pot.

"Betts, what can I do for you?" she said as she stepped around me and took off for another empty cup. The pot was like a divining rod.

I followed at her heel.

"You own the barn where Roy puts the Triggers, right?"

"Yes."

"What was it before it was a barn?"

"It's been a barn as long as I've owned it. Long before, too." She poured. I smiled over Bunny's shoulder at the couple sitting in the booth.

"But do you know what it was originally?"

She stopped moving a moment and twitched her faint but visible and always surprising mustache as she looked at me. "Yes, I think it was the town's original train station."

"Original?"

"Yes, I think I heard something about the train tracks once going right through town, but that had proved to be poor planning, so the townspeople themselves moved the tracks."

"So that building, the barn, was the station building?"

Bunny shrugged. "Probably. Maybe. That's what I assumed."

"Do you know if there was a dentist's office inside it?"

Bunny shrugged. "I would have no idea, Betts. Ask Jake. He knows all about everything like that."

"I will. Thanks."

I realized I forgot to apologize to Bunny as I left the restaurant. However, I smiled and nodded my thanks to the girl at the cash register on my way out. I found my cell phone the second I stepped onto the boardwalk.

Chapter Eighteen

"Oh, Betts, I can't believe I forgot all about that story," Jake said as he opened a file on his computer. "That's exactly what happened. The train running over there was a big bother. The town got together and changed the tracks. In fact, what they did was illegal, but I can't remember the specifics of the law or laws they broke. They rerouted the tracks themselves."

I'd called Jake and asked him to meet me at his archive room. He hadn't even asked why, but was there to unlock the door a short fifteen minutes later.

"I would think that people who hadn't been properly been trained on laying train tracks would be in trouble for doing so."

"Right. They were, but I think the government sent out inspectors . . . Yes, it's right here. Let me print this article."

Another moment later I had a printed version of the article in my hands. It repeated what Jake had summarized, explaining that the townspeople took on the project without regard to the law, but it wasn't the way of Broken Rope citizens to pay much attention to the law anyway. They did a good job, too; all inspections passed muster. They re-created the old station and then pulled up most of the old tracks only moments after the new route was approved. It must have been a monstrous project.

"There are no pictures," I said.

"I know. I'm working on it," Jake said, his finger clicking the button on the mouse. "Yep, here it is. Printing."

Another moment later, I held a picture of the station. It was the same one that had almost crushed us on the way to Frankland, the one that looked *almost* like the Broken Rope station.

"This is really crazy, Betts," Jake said as we both looked at the picture.

"I know. And guess what, Jake. I just now see the difference. This station, the one that's now a barn, apparently, had a bell hanging from the roof of its front porch. The one where I met Robert didn't, I'm sure of it. The one that almost killed us did, or there was one lying on the front porch, probably fallen from its spot."

"But you met Robert at the one without the bell. Maybe that's why we had to come upon the one with the bell, so you—or we—would know that the location was important. But back when he was alive, he must have been at the original one, the one with the bell. Maybe. Hang on."

Jake went back to his computer. "Oh! This explains it, Betts. The reason you saw Robert at the new station was because it was completed in November of 1888, a few months after Grace and Robert were supposed to meet at the original station. He spent the rest of his life waiting for her, but it was mostly at the new station."

"That makes a little more sense. I guess." I sat on a stool and thought. "Come back to the barn with me, Jake. Nothing happened other than the fact that I found remnants of train tracks. Bring your camera. Maybe something will happen now. For the first time ever, I kind of have a sense that it will. The ghosts and their antics have mostly been surprises, but I think something might happen tonight."

"You do? Why?"

"I . . . Reginald Nelson," I said. "Do you know who he is, how he might be associated with the Jasper Theater?"

He worked the computer keys again. "He was one of the original owners of the Jasper Theater. What in the world does he have to do with this?"

"I think he was the only conduit available at the moment," I said, mostly to myself. I suspected that Reginald spent a lot of time at the Jasper, even if I—and maybe Gram, I'd have to ask—had never seen him before.

"What do you mean?"

"Come on and I'll explain on the way."

"Let's go." Jake hesitated but then grabbed the camera bag from the back of his desk. "I doubt it will work, but why not."

Roy was gone by the time we arrived at the barn. All the doors were locked so we had to walk around the building, both of us wishing for a machete to chop down the tall grasses in our way.

"You think it was Jerome in Reginald's ghostly form?" Jake asked.

"Yes. No one else calls me Isabelle."

"Of course."

The full moon now shone brightly on the field and the wind had picked up enough to cast dancing shadows everywhere.

"Oh, this is a perfect spot for a ghostly encounter," Jake said as he pulled his camera out of the bag and held it at the ready. "Tell me where to point if something happens."

"Will do."

We stood silently for a moment as unseen crickets and frogs chirped and croaked loudly. The barn was dark and silent, looming. I heard car doors close from the direction of Bunny's parking lot, bubbles of laughter and conversation from Main Street.

"Am I seeing lightning bugs, Betts, or are those something else?" Jake asked.

I looked around. "Plain old lightning bugs. No need to record."

"Too bad."

"Let's just give it a few more minutes. We'll call it a night if something doesn't happen soon."

"I didn't have time to see if Reginald was the one to give the credit to, but I know that one of the original owners of the Jasper was responsible in a big way for the town becoming a tourist stop. He was on the first town council that voted for Old West skits, if I remember the history correctly. The skits started off on the Jasper's stage, that I'm sure of," Jake said, adding conversation to our wait.

"The idea clicked."

"Even if they could never have known how well or for how long."

After a few more minutes of a noisy, critter-filled Missouri summer night, Jake cleared his throat. "Maybe Jerome's calendar was off? He doesn't really have to keep any sort of schedule."

"No, but . . . well, I just thought. It's not looking good."

"Another night?" Jake said as he put his hand on my arm.

I plopped my hands on my hips and looked up at the sky. There were no answers there either.

"All right, come on," I said.

But as we turned to leave, something did happen. Out of the corner of my eye, I saw the glow from the appearing station. It didn't take the place of the barn, but was farther back on the field. I looked at it and at the barn. I didn't understand why the apparition came into view where it did.

"Hang on." I grabbed Jake's arm. "See it?"

"I see nothing," he said.

"Point the camera over there and wait for me." I pointed. But before I could take a step, Robert appeared in between us and the station.

"Robert's here, Jake." With my fingertip I angled the camera more toward Robert.

"Betts, hello," Robert said with surprise.

"You didn't expect to be here?" I said.

"I don't know what I expect anymore," he said. "I'd like to just go . . . back."

"I'm sorry. Your trip here won't last forever. They never do."

Robert was the first ghost I'd met who wasn't okay with being in Broken Rope for a short time.

"I hope not."

"Robert, I'm sorry but I need to ask some more questions. Is that all right?"

"Sure," he said resignedly.

"Did you know someone named Justice Adams?"

Robert blinked and frowned. "I'm not sure. When you said his name, I knew immediately who you meant, but I didn't have any inkling of him before that moment. I don't understand."

"He was somehow involved with you and Grace. He . . . loved Grace, too." It had been more obsession than love, but I figured this version would get us where we needed to go.

"He did? Is he her killer?"

I swallowed. "We think that either he or you killed her."

"I didn't kill Grace, Betts. Why do you keep saying that?

"Are you sure, Robert? I mean, really sure. Remember, it doesn't matter all that much except to get at the truth. You're both good and dead right now. Nothing can change that. You can't be arrested, or hanged, for that matter."

"I did not kill Grace," Robert said. He was almost solid—at least to me—in the dark. I could see the anger and adamancy in the fine lines at the corners of his eyes.

"Do you remember who did, then?" I said.

"You know I don't. I would have told you."

"That might not be true, Robert. It's been my experience that you ghosts remember more the longer you're here. Maybe you haven't remembered it yet."

Robert frowned again and then turned to look at the station. "I know this, but like I said, it's as if I wasn't aware of it a moment ago but am now: something terrible happened here." He looked at me again. "Betts, I didn't kill Grace. I couldn't have. Nothing, absolutely nothing, could have driven me to hurt her in any way."

"Okay. Let's go with something happening here. Let's try to get more of *that* story."

Instead of merely glancing at the building, Robert turned all the way around and faced it.

"Justice Adams. When you said his name, a picture of him formed in my head. When I look at the building and think about him, I get a bad feeling in my gut. Was he a bad man?"

"Actually, he was thought of as a very good man."

"But you think he might have killed Grace?"

"It's a possibility."

"Oh no," Robert said a moment later. "Betts. I remember."

"What?"

"I did not kill Grace. I loved her with all my heart."

"Okay."

"But I know who Justice Adams was. He wasn't a good man. Not at all." Robert faced me again. "And I *did* kill him."

"Oh, dear. Why? Because he loved Grace?"

"Must have been the reason, or something like it. I must have been so angry. I was a gentle man, not a murderer. I can only think that he must have done something to hurt Grace. That would be the only way I could have killed him, or anyone."

Perhaps there was a noble reason in there somewhere, but we still didn't have the answers.

Robert continued, "I'm tired of being here, or having the urge to be here as the case may be. I'd just like to go back to . . . wherever I'm supposed to be."

"Maybe you're supposed to be here? Do you think?"

"No, I don't think that at all. Nothing can change. You said it yourself."

"True, but if Grace understands what happened to her, or if you understand how you could have possibly been so angry as to have killed Justice, maybe you'll . . . rest better."

He looked directly at me and for an instant I thought he was going to tell me something important, something about that place where he had been before he came back to Broken Rope. But it was as if a shield suddenly came down over his thoughts, as if he knew that admitting to being a killer was okay, but telling me any of the secrets about that other place was taking it too far. I'd seen the same sort of thing happen with other ghosts.

"I guess I just don't know," he said.

"You want to look inside the station? It's still here." I swallowed, hoping that it wouldn't collapse again. "Jake, do you see the station?"

"No. I'm not seeing anything except you and the camera. But, Betts, do I understand correctly? Did Robert kill Justice?"

"I think so."

"Get more about that if you can."

"I'll work on it. Come on, Robert. Let's have a look around. Jake, point the camera over there. I'm going to see if we can find anything inside the station. It's right ahead of us."

Once Jake held the camera in what I thought was the right direction, I led the way with Robert in tow.

I carefully placed one foot up onto the platform. Then I stepped solidly with both feet.

"What do you see?" I asked Jake.

"You standing there."

"Did you see me step higher up?"

"No, but I saw you take a step. You're still on the ground."

"Interesting." I walked toward the doors, Robert still at my side. My footfalls made noise, but his didn't. I was used to that.

The lobby was much as I'd already seen it on the way to Frankland, but there was one new addition. There was someone sitting in the ticket booth.

"I do believe we should have a chat with that man. There must be a reason he's here," I said as I moved quickly in that direction.

"Hello, miss, how can I help you today? Ticket to St. Louis, perhaps, or Springfield? We've got trains going both those places today, with stops along the way."

The young man might have needed a meal or two, or he was just wearing a uniform that was a couple sizes too big. His long, skinny face and pointed chin exaggerated the small space between his eyes and the hat upon his head reminded me of an old-time train conductor's hat: straight sides and a narrow brim. Tufts of black hair shot up around the hat, and his smile and voice were pleasant and friendly.

"Hi," I said. "I'm Isabelle Winston. You can call me Betts. May I ask your name?"

"Frederick Elvis Rothington," he said. "People call me Elvis."

I memorized the full name so I could tell Jake later. From inside the station, I couldn't see him on the outside. I had no idea if he could see me.

"Elvis," I said with a smile. If only he knew the future *that* name would bring. "We don't have a lot of time, but I need to explain something to you. It will seem strange."

Elvis blinked. "I feel a little strange, miss, so go on."

There was no real *Reader's Digest* version of the ghosts' travels back to Broken Rope, but I'd explained it a few times by now and was getting a little better at hitting only the high points. Gram didn't much care how clear she was with the ghosts, but I did and at this moment even more than usual. Elvis was here for an important reason, I was sure. He had an answer or some important part of the puzzle, or why else would he have appeared? I needed him to trust me quickly and enough to offer his contribution willingly.

"I'll be," he said when I'd finished. "How'd I die?"

"I don't know. I don't know much about any of the ghosts until I meet them the first time. I can research it and let you know just in case we meet again."

"I'd like that," he said. "Well, I think I'd like that."

"You probably would," I said.

"Alrighty, then. What can I do for you and Mr. Robert there?"

"I don't know. Let's start with this: Do you remember him?"

Elvis looked at Robert. Robert grimaced at us both. He wasn't having a good day. Elvis blinked and thought and recognition briefly skipped over his narrow face, but it disappeared again quickly.

"I can't be sure. He looks like so many of the passengers. After a while and unless they ride the trains lots and lots, everyone begins to look alike."

"His girlfriend was a black woman who was murdered," I said. Again, no reason for sensitivity. We needed answers.

"Oh, well, gracious, that does change things a bit. I might have seen him come in here with her a time or two."

"Not possible," Robert said. "Remember, Grace and I never met up here at the station."

"Grace? Your girl's name was Grace?" he said.

"Yes," both Robert and I said hopefully.

"A negro woman named Grace?"

I cringed, though from his perspective Elvis hadn't said anything wrong.

"Yes," Robert said. I nodded.

"Grace was a beauty. She was here, I remember her. She came back for two days, claiming to be here to meet someone. Was that you?"

"Yes."

"Why weren't you here?" Elvis said. He didn't vocalize the words "you fool" but I heard them in my head. Robert probably did, too.

"I was ill."

"She didn't know where you were. She didn't know what to do."

"I'm sorry," Robert said with a sigh, reaffirming that he was truly tired of reliving this whole mess.

"Well, another man came along and took her right on out of here. He was a well-known man, but I can't remember his name."

"Justice Adams?" I said.

"That's it! Yes, he came and took her away."

"Did she go willingly?" I asked.

Robert looked at me briefly before he turned his attention back to Elvis.

"Let me . . . I don't know. Gosh, she was the prettiest lady I'd ever seen, even if she was black and all," Elvis said.

Again, I cringed and wanted a way to somehow reach into their long-gone and decayed brains, shake them up a little, and take these ghosts out of their racist and old-fashioned ways of thinking, but that wasn't possible.

"Okay. Can you remember any specifics of what she was doing when you saw her, or her with Justice?" I asked. "Think about it, Elvis, please. We really need to know."

Elvis pondered a moment. He cocked his head and squinted at

Robert. He looked at me and then back at Robert again.

And then he said, "Ha! I believe I do remember."

"Okay," I said again.

"Yes, it was an ugly scene. The man named Justice sat with Grace for a day. Sat beside her, right over there." He nodded. Robert and I turned and the benches in the lobby appeared. And then so did Justice and Grace.

"Grace!" Robert said as he ran to her. He went to his knees and reached for her hands.

But she behaved as though she didn't see or hear him.

"Grace?" I said as I moved behind Robert.

No response. I reached for Grace's shoulder, but my hand when through it, as if we weren't surrounded by darkness.

"I think we're just supposed to watch," I said to Robert. I put my hand on his shoulder, and it landed, didn't go through. "Right, Elvis?" I said as I turned. But he was gone. The ticket booth was empty. "Come on, Robert. Step back a little with me and let's see what happens."

Robert stood and we moved back just a little.

Grace and Justice unfroze and began talking.

"Grace, dear, the man isn't coming. He's not at his home. He's abandoned you," Justice said.

"No, I don't believe that. It's just not possible. Perhaps something happened to him. Perhaps he's ill. I should ask around town for him. Someone is bound to know him."

Grace made a move to stand, but Justice grabbed her arm and pulled her back to the bench.

Justice had a focused concentration to his gaze. It was something I hadn't seen in the pictures of him, but I could tell that he never gave up; he always got what he wanted. He was intense, and depending upon who you were in his life, his intensity could have been a curse or a blessing.

It had probably served him well, but his glare at Grace, full of desire and determination, was disturbing.

I looked at Robert. He was watching the two on the bench closely, and I knew he saw it, too.

"Please release my arm," Grace said.

Surprising me, he did release her. "I'm so sorry. I'm just scared for you, worried about you. Forgive me. I am not a violent man."

His statement seemed like a pretty bad sign to me. He protesteth too loudly.

"I realize that, Justice," Grace said, appeasing him with her own practiced tone. "And I'm ever so grateful. But I need to look for Robert. I need to make sure I have explored every possible corner before I leave Broken Rope. If he doesn't want me, if I have been duped, then perhaps you and I shall meet again. The circumstances will be different, and we can discuss that at that time."

"That's my girl," Robert said quietly.

"Fine," Justice said, but it clearly wasn't. Nevertheless, he continued, "Look for him. You won't find him, I'm sure. I have business to attend to in town myself. Let's meet back here tonight—if you don't find him. If you find him, I won't expect to see you."

"All right."

"Do you have any money, Grace?"

"Well . . ."

"I'll tell you what, I will pay for your ticket home if you don't find your Robert. Tonight, I will give you the money."

"That's how he got her to come back to the train station," I muttered to myself.

She'd had no choice. It was truly a different time. There were no credit cards that she could have used to buy an emergency train ticket. She'd probably saved for the ticket that got her to Broken Rope, and she'd probably thought she wouldn't need the safety net of enough money to buy a return ticket.

She was a woman alone. She was a black woman alone. At that time those hadn't been easy circumstances.

"Thank you, Justice," she said, but I was sure Robert heard her determination as much as I did. She did not want to come back to that station. She didn't want to take money from Justice Adams. She probably didn't want to take money from anyone. She'd had no choice.

"Oh, Grace," Robert said. "I'm so desperately sorry."

"You are welcome," Justice said. "Now go. I will see you tonight. Right here. At this bench."

Grace stood and stepped surely out of the station. As she moved by Robert and me, I missed the movement of air that should come with a person walking by.

"Isabelle."

Elvis had reappeared over my shoulder.

"Yes?" I said.

"You made it here, Isabelle. This is where you will find all the answers," he said. And then he surprised me even more by reaching for my face. He held it and kissed me softly, quickly, as if it was just his normal way of greeting me. Even still, I recognized that though they weren't Jerome's lips, it was unmistakably Jerome's kiss.

"Are you okay?" I said.

"Yes. I'd like to see you as myself, but I'm not sure that will happen. I have to go again," Elvis said with a smile that was as close to the crooked one that belonged to Jerome as it could be.

"You know Elvis?" Robert said when the ticket taker had disappeared.

"No."

"That kiss sure looked like you knew him."

"It's a really long story."

"Oh, don't tell me. I've got my own long story going to deal with. What do we do now?"

"I wish I knew. Did we learn much of anything?" I said.

"Justice and Grace really did meet."

"And she really hadn't found you," I said.

"I am positive she *never* found me, Betts. Positive."

"I'm going to go back with Jake to his archives and have him pull up the old newspapers from the days after they were to meet."

"Why?"

"If there was a body, even an unidentified one, there might have been a story. Maybe that will give us more," I said.

"How?"

"I have no idea, Robert, but it's the only plan I can come up with at the moment."

"All right. I'll come with you."

But he didn't come with me. Suddenly, he and the rest of the station disappeared, poofed away. Since I had stepped up to get onto the station platform, my body braced itself as if I was going to fall to the ground. I didn't. I was already on the ground. I looked over to see Jake still standing there with the camera held up and pointing this direction.

"Hi!" I called and waved.

"Hi. Did something happen?"

"What did you see?" I said as I hurried toward him.

"You walking around a little, talking to the air."

"Hope the camera got more."

"Me too."

"We need to go back to the archives. Right now if possible," I said.

"Sure. Let's go." Jake clicked off the camera and folded the screen in.

The barn doors, both front and back, had been locked when we'd taken the side path to the field behind the building. The back one still was, but as we came around the front corner of the building, I heard a voice coming from inside the barn.

"Hang on. Did you just hear something?" I asked Jake.

"I did."

We tiptoed to the front doors. They were no longer locked. One was pushed in so that it created an opening of a few inches. Light from a flashlight beam danced around inside the barn.

And the people inside were definitely talking about murder.

Chapter Nineteen

"This is where he was killed?" a familiar voice said.

"This is the spot. Right here, I was told," another voice said. This one was even more familiar.

"Call Cliff," I whispered to Jake. "At least a couple of Derek's ex-wives are in there. I'll stay here and listen, but get Cliff over here."

I thought the two voices I heard belonged to Ridley and Wendy, but I couldn't be completely sure.

Jake stepped far enough away from the barn so they wouldn't hear him but made sure he could still see me and pulled out his phone.

"He was hit on the head?" Wendy, I think, said.

"With a wrench," Ridley, I think, said.

I wondered whether the murder weapon was common knowledge, but I couldn't remember what had been shared with the public and what hadn't.

"That's awful," Wendy said. "He was a boring idiot, but he didn't deserve to die so violently."

"I know. I actually spent a moment feeling sad about it," Ridley said.

And then they did something that both surprised and scared me. They laughed. Both of them, with a cackle that was almost evil.

When they stopped laughing, as if they had to work to gather themselves, Wendy continued, "Do you think she did it?"

"Gosh, I don't know. Anything's possible. He put her through hell. He put lots of people through hell. It was his way."

"Who? Which she?" I whispered.

"Right, well, despite the benefits, the whole thing was hellish. Still is, if you ask me," Wendy said.

"It is."

Jake came up behind me and tugged on my sleeve. He pointed toward the police station. The door was still closing, but Cliff was jogging this direction. I didn't want to stop eavesdropping, but I didn't want Cliff's appearance to let the women know I was listening in on their conversation. I reluctantly stepped away from the barn and met Cliff in the street, just before he was about to step over the curb.

"You okay?" he asked me, but he looked at Jake, too.

"We're fine. At least two of Derek's ex-wives are in the barn. I don't think they're doing much of anything and I probably jumped the gun by having Jake call you, but it just seemed weird. I feel kind of dumb now. They might have been talking about the killer, using a 'she' pronoun. I can't be sure."

"You shouldn't feel dumb. They're trespassing. Roy and Bunny are the only ones with keys. I'll see what I can get out of them and what they're up to."

I did regret having Jake call Cliff so quickly. Maybe I could have learned more if I'd just given it a little longer.

Jake and I watched Cliff disappear through the slot.

"What were they doing?" Jake asked.

"Just talking, wondering about Derek, acting a little too gleeful about his death. Come on, let's have a seat over there and wait for Cliff. Maybe he'll tell us more."

Jake and I took a seat on a bench at the end of the boardwalk. We probably wouldn't be noticed by the women as they exited the barn, but if they did happen to look our direction our attempt to be casual and blend in with the scenery had a fifty-fifty chance of being convincing.

"They were talking about Derek?" Jake asked as we sat. "As in, they or 'she' killed him and they were reliving their evil deed?"

"Not really their evil deed. Someone elsc's. Maybe."

"So, listening for another minute would have been better than calling Cliff right away?" Jake said.

"Probably, but I got spooked."

"I see. That spooked you? Not the ghosts or anything?" Jake said.

"So what did your camera capture?" I smiled.

"Oh." He opened the side screen and hit the power button. A second later and after hitting some more buttons, he said, "Not one thing."

"Really?"

"I don't think so." He continued to push and scroll through things.

"That's disappointing."

"Very."

When he'd had enough, he closed the screen and sct the camera on the bench.

"I think I'm done with it. It's a good thing it captured you and Jerome at the bakery. At least I know all this stuff is real, not a figment of your imagination."

"You saw Sally briefly."

"I did, but if that was all I had to go on, I'd wonder if we were both loopy."

"I told Teddy," I said.

"You did? How did that go?"

"Fine. He's not doubtful, but that's only because he wants to be supportive. I told him after our incident outside Frankland. If something had happened to us and someone had come upon our bodies, it would have been unexplainable and beyond bizarre. I wanted Teddy to understand that there are forces at work that might make things hard to understand but that neither you nor I, nor Gram for that matter, are interested in hurting ourselves on purpose."

"Huh. I guess I never thought about that much. Telling Teddy was the right thing to do. Want to tell me what happened behind the barn?"

"Sure."

I told Jake about Robert and Elvis, and Justice and Grace. I told him that Robert was sure that he killed Justice, but he still wasn't sure what happened to Grace. Jake concurred that Justice must have somehow hurt Grace, or worse, which was the reason Robert killed him. It wasn't a difficult conclusion to make, but the small pieces that were missing still left too many questions.

"And Elvis kissed me," I said.

"He was possessed by Jerome at the time?"

"Yes."

"Gracious, Betts, if we're ever sexist enough to have a kissing booth attraction on the boardwalk, I know who should do the work."

"I'm more popular than I could have ever predicted."

Jake laughed. "You've always been popular. You just mostly ignored it."

Turning our attention back to the barn, Cliff, Ridley, and Wendy exited one at a time through the slot. From our vantage point, we couldn't hear their conversation but the women's demeanor was uncomfortable and apologetic. Cliff extended his hand, and Wendy placed a key in it. He locked the padlock and then put the key in his pocket. Wendy and Ridley exchanged a look and then Wendy said something to Cliff. He listened patiently but then shook his head. The women seemed disappointed, but they took their leave together, crossing the street and moving toward Ridley's Explorer, which was parked right around the corner. They didn't even look our direction.

Cliff walked over and joined us on the bench, sitting at the end, keeping Jake in between the two of us.

"How'd it go?" I asked.

"They claim they don't know who the killer is and weren't speculating, but I could tell they were lying about that. They stole the key from Bunny," Cliff said.. "It was sitting on the counter by the cash register. It has a tag on it." Cliff took out the key and showed it to us. It did have a tag with one handwritten word on it. *Barn.*

"They just took it?" Jake asked.

"Yep. They didn't have plans to steal it, but they saw it sitting there and took it. They planned to return it after they had a look around."

"Let me guess. You're going to return it and tell Bunny what happened," Jake said.

"That's probably what I'll do. The women didn't mean any harm, I don't think. They were trespassing, but they weren't causing any damage to anything that I could see. I might just go put it back on the counter and tell Bunny I found it. We'll see."

"You don't think one of them killed Derek?" I said. I knew this because if he did he would have arrested them for something or taken them to the station for more questioning.

"No, not at all, but, honestly, that's just instinct at this moment."

I replayed the brief few moments I'd overheard, and then I leaned forward and inspected Cliff around Jake. He was looking at the barn, but his forehead was creased in concentration.

"What's up, Cliff?" I said when he fell silent.

He blinked and looked at me. "I think we've gone the wrong direction when it comes to Derek's murder. We've missed something big that might be coming clearer."

"From what I just told you?"

"Care to share what that is?" Jake said.

"No," Cliff said with a smile.

"Didn't think so. Betts and I have some research to do. Come along when you can," he said to me as he stood and headed down the boardwalk, allowing Cliff and I to scoot a little closer together. "I'll get the archive room warmed up."

"I'll be right there," I said.

Jake wasn't leaving us alone so we could have a romantic moment. We'd had plenty of romantic moments with Jake in the vicinity. I knew he was hoping that Cliff would share something with me that he wouldn't with Jake. I didn't think it would work, but I understood and appreciated the effort.

"Jake wants me to tell you a secret that he thinks you'll tell him when you join him in the archives," Cliff said.

"He tried to be subtle," I said.

Cliff laughed. "We've known each other a long time. It would have been difficult not to catch that one."

"So, what'd'ya say? Got something you want to tell me?"

"Yeah. I love you," he said, catching me so totally off guard that I about fell off the bench.

We'd expressed those sentiments when we were teenagers, and many times during our relationship revival, even though we were both more about actions than words. But neither of us had said it much lately, and it suddenly felt kind of new. I liked it.

"I love you, too," I said. Honestly, I was surprised at how there was not one tiny note of hesitation in my voice. And then I was somewhat horrified that I'd been surprised.

"Good. I knew you did, but it was nice to hear it again," Cliff said. "Now, as for Derek's ex-wives, more specifically the two who were in the barn, they know something they aren't telling. I have no doubt, but I also don't know how to get more information out of them."

"I know they're scared of Lynn," I said.

"Yes, they're all scared of Lynn, so she knows something that could make their lives miserable. Neither Jim nor I have any idea what that could be, or, frankly, why they're so genuinely scared. Lynn can be an annoying person, but I don't think she's truly capable of causing harm. She's cried wolf too often."

"There must something she's holding over them, like something emotional or financial," I said.

"Yes, but . . ." Cliff sat up straighter on the bench.

"What?"

He looked at me.

"Just talking to you has made me think of everything differently, from another angle. That one missing piece, maybe," he said.

"I have no idea what I did to get you this excited, but I like it." I smiled.

Cliff lifted an eyebrow. "Why can't it be something *both* emotional and financial?"

"I bet it can be."

"Maybe it is. I need to go talk to Jim."

Cliff leaned toward me. I thought it would be a quick kiss, but after a few seconds I thought about asking if we should maybe just call it an evening and get a room somewhere.

Unfortunately, he pulled back. "Gotta go, but I will see you soon. Be at your house later?"

"I will. I hope you will, too."

Cliff jogged back to the police station. I watched and enjoyed the view of his retreat.

"Jake was right, these lips are popular lately," I said to myself.

I did my own quick jog to Jake's place, let myself inside the open front doors, and then through the doors that led to the back.

"Did he tell you anything?" Jake said. "I left so he'd tell you a secret."

"No, but thanks for leaving. He kissed me like I haven't been kissed in a long time."

"That's really not something I need to hear about, but considering you're locking lips with every man you're meeting these days, kisses are old news."

"Okay, Jake, we need to look at some editions of the *Noose* in 1888. Let's go August fifteenth through August twentieth just to get a good span. I want to see if there was any news about Justice Adams or Grace. Maybe their murders made the news, or their bodies, I mean. If they'd been identified, I think you'd know the stories."

"That's one of our easier searches." Jake rolled his chair to his computer and started typing.

The *Noose* was never a big enough paper to microfiche all its old copies, but Jake had tediously taken the time to archive as many as possible by taking pictures of the original copies that were currently held together by giant hard bindings and some string in the *Noose's* back office. He'd gotten as far back as 1858. It was impressive, and I'd heard that a software company had contacted him for help in creating a program that would aid other papers in similar situations. He wouldn't talk about the details.

"Here we go. Let me just print out the first few pages and we'll see where that takes us."

Another moment later, the printer came to a gentle stop and Jake grabbed the papers from its tray. He spread them out on the table.

"Let's see. We had a hanging," he said as he peered at the page. "It probably only made the news because it was successful. The rope did not break."

"That would have been news," I said.

"Three cows got loose from a local farm. Apparently, they caused quite the commotion downtown."

"Okay," I said. I was looking at the second sheet, but the news was similar to what Jake had mentioned. There'd been a bar brawl and a gunfight. Typical day in Broken Rope.

But on the third page in an article dated August eighteenth, I found something.

The small headline said: *Potential Disturbance Reported Behind the Train Depot. Police Seek Answers.*

"Jake, here." I pointed at the small article.

Jake read the rest of it aloud: "Mrs. Truman Oliphant reported that she thought she heard screams last night coming from the field behind the train depot. She sent Mr. Truman out to investigate, but he did not find a disturbance. Police followed up with a search of the scene and reported that they discovered what might be blood. They are asking for the public's help in determining if someone was hurt."

"That's it?" I said when he didn't say more.

"That's it for that day," Jake said. "More might have happened later. I can look." He went back to the computer.

"Another 'almost there,'" I said.

"Well, yes, but we're a little closer than we were a few minutes ago."

"My ever-optimistic friend."

"A quick scan at the next few days isn't showing me anything, but we can look closely at the weeks following the incident. Hang on." He stifled a yawn.

He would work at this all night if I asked him to. It wasn't fair. "Not tonight, Jake. I've taken up more of your time than I should have. Maybe tomorrow if you have time."

"Sure? Okay. Hey, Betts, are you all right?" He looked at me like he might check my forehead for fever again.

"I'm great. Why?"

"Lots going on."

"No more than what's becoming usual."

"Still."

I looked at my concerned friend. "You know what, I'm great, Jake. Maybe better than I have been for a long time. There was something about telling Teddy about the ghosts that really helped. It was like I shrugged some of the burden off on him, even though I know I truly didn't. He can't see or communicate with them. I get why Gram was pleased to have me aboard the ghost train, so to speak."

"So to speak." Jake smiled patiently. He didn't need to tell me that I was speaking a little too quickly or with too high a pitch.

I cleared my throat. "I think I'm going to go home and get some rest."

"Good plan. Me too." Jake pushed the power button on his computer.

Chapter Twenty

The good news was that Cliff was on his way over at some point. The bad news, it turned out, was that Cliff was on his way over at some point. He wouldn't be too bothered by the person sitting on my front porch, but since he'd witnessed us kissing recently, it might put a crimp in the evening.

"Paul. Hi," I said as I got out of the Nova. I parked on the street in front of my house more often than in the narrow driveway.

"Hey, Betts. Don't worry, I'm not going to attack," he said. He tried to sound humorous, but it was easy to hear his embarrassment.

"I'm not worried. What's up? Have you been here long?"

"Not too long," he said. "When you didn't answer the door, I wasn't sure if I should call you or not. I decided to just wait and see if you showed up. And here you are."

"Here I am." The last time I'd checked the clock on my phone, it had been after ten. I didn't want to be rude and check it in front of Paul.

Surely he realized how late it was.

I climbed the stairs and sat down next to him on the porch. I didn't want to invite him in and it didn't seem like something he expected. He smiled, not totally uncomfortably, in my direction and then scooted over a little to give me more room.

"I'm not here to throw myself at you, though I'd like to apologize one more time for the way I behaved. I'm sorry."

"No need. All is well. What's up?" I asked again.

"I was wondering if you heard something the day before Derek was killed. We were all in the barn, and I wasn't sure if I heard it correctly. I wanted to talk to someone else to confirm before I went to the police. I trust you the most."

"What do you think you heard?"

Paul nodded. "I have to set the stage a little. We were all there. It was Sunday but remember that Roy wanted to show us how he tightened the brakes. We needed to get a quick feel for them before we took out any tourists."

"Yes, I remember," I said, noting silently to myself that this was something I'd been thinking about earlier but hadn't been able to pinpoint. I knew that Roy had recently done *something* with the brakes, but I hadn't been able to remember exactly when. I was suddenly pretty sure these moments were what my mind had been searching for. Also, hadn't he dropped a wrench or two at the morning meeting at the cooking school? I was pretty sure he had, and then he'd seemed puzzled as he put them away. I decided I should mention those moments to Cliff. "In fact, I've thought about that day in case something happened that might be important, but I didn't remember anything."

"I didn't at first either, and what I remember is pretty small but it keeps coming back to me now."

"What?"

"Roy climbed up onto the first Trigger and was about to demonstrate for us, right?"

"Got it. I remember that now."

"Just as he got up there, remember the clanging noise behind the Trigger? We all turned and Roy asked if everything was okay?"

"Sure, but it was all pretty quick."

"Exactly. Well, then Todd stood up straight and said that he'd knocked a tool off the back end of the Trigger, but that he'd put it away in the toolbox when Roy was done with the demonstration."

Honestly, I didn't remember that part well. I'd been next to Lynn and April and they were chatting about something; my focus was on them, though currently I couldn't remember what they'd been talking about either. And, really, Roy hadn't turned to see if everything was okay so much as just asked the question over his shoulder quickly and then moved on to the next step of the demonstration without waiting for an answer. There'd been no figurative spotlight on Todd as he stood back up and proclaimed that he had the tool. It had all just been a part of the moment, a small, blended part.

"That's a little murky to me," I said.

"I know; me too. The other women were on your one side and I was on your other side. I was . . . well, my thoughts were distracted from the demonstration. But now that a few days have passed, that moment keeps coming back to me. Was that a wrench?"

"Even if it was, so what?" I said.

"What if Todd didn't put it back? What if it was the wrench that killed Derek and hurt you?"

"Even if it was, Todd probably did exactly what he said he did, and put it back later. Anyone could have grabbed it."

"I know, but something else occurred to me, and I know it's as weak as the other parts of all this. But I wonder if Todd dropped the wrench instead of knocking it off the Trigger. Roy doesn't typically leave his tools lying around. There would have been no place for the wrench to be resting. I mean, Roy would never in a million years leave a tool just sitting out on a Trigger. He might leave one on a back work table, but chances are that he would put it away in his toolbox no matter when he thought he might need it again."

Paul made some interesting points, but he was right; they were weak. Or, they were terribly insightful. I didn't for one minute think that Todd had killed anyone. Murder wasn't on his mind, love was. Unless he thought Derek was some sort of threat in the love department. Had Derek actually been on a date with April, not just asked her out? Stranger things had happened, five times, to be specific.

"I think you should tell Cliff. Or Jim," I said.

"You do?"

"Absolutely."

"Okay. Good. Yeah, I just needed another opinion."

"Sure." I thought about telling him that Cliff would be over eventually, but I decided he could handle it on his own and not at my house.

If that was somehow rude, I was about to make myself look even ruder.

The smell of flowers was suddenly overwhelming. I liked flowers, but the scent this time was so strong that I was immediately nauseated and the first ping of a headache slammed at my temple.

It took only another few seconds to locate Grace. She was in the middle of the street, facedown and not moving.

"Well, gotta go, Paul. I'll talk to you later," I said as I stood and then hurried inside the house.

I would apologize later maybe but for now I really needed him to go away.

I plopped my knees on the chair by the front window and peered out. Fortunately, Paul made a quick exit without any indication that he'd just been run from.

Once his car was out of sight, I ran back outside and to Grace. As I'd done so many times since the ghosts came into my life, I told myself: She's dead. There's nothing you can to for her.

Nevertheless, when you see someone face down in the middle of the street, your first instinct is to try to help them, ghost or not.

"Grace," I said as I crouched next to her, reached for her shoulder, and gently rolled her over. Even with the streetlights, it was dark enough that she was solid under my touch.

At first she didn't respond, but lay there, unmoving with her eyes closed.

"Grace," I said as I shook her gently. I wished I knew what I was supposed to do. Leave her be, keep trying to get a response? Watch as unknowing drivers propelled their cars through the ghost they couldn't see?

"Grace, come on, wake up," I said.

Finally, her eyelids started to flutter and a moan escaped her throat.

"Grace," I said as I helped her sit up.

"Betts. That's your name, right? Betts?" she said.

"Yes," I said. "We're in the middle of a road, which won't hurt you, but it might be better to go somewhere where people can't see me out here talking to the air."

"Yes," she said after she blinked and seemed to remember that she was a ghost.

I helped her stand. After we both decided she wasn't too wobbly, we moved toward my house, climbed the stairs, and went inside. I hoped Cliff wouldn't show up right away.

"What's going on? Are you . . . do you feel pain?" I said as I sat her on the couch.

"No, not at all," she said.

In tandem, both of us looked down at her dress. A huge circle of blood filled the area over her stomach.

Without even thinking, I reached forward and touched the spot. It felt nothing like blood. It wasn't wet or sticky or warm, it was part of the mostly solid figure that was Grace. I turned on a light in the kitchen, but kept the front room dark so I could still see her.

"It looks like something must have happened there." She laughed.

"Maybe you were stabbed. That could have been how you were killed," I said, my tone and words oddly clinical.

"Maybe," she said. "It's difficult for me to consider that idea. Gruesome."

"Do you remember anything from tonight, before you saw me?" I thought back to the article that Jake had found that mentioned the discovery of blood behind the depot. Was the wound on Grace's stomach representative of where it had come from?

Grace bit her lip. I was struck again by her beauty. I was surprised that every man that met her hadn't followed her to the ends of the earth.

Perhaps they had.

"Grace," I interrupted her thoughts. "We've been focusing on Robert and another man named Justice Adams."

She gasped. "I know that name. He was a very bad man. He hurt me." She looked at the blood on her dress.

"Was he your killer?"

"It's very possible. He was . . . oh, dear, he was a scary man. He found me at the station, I believe, and wouldn't leave me alone. Yes, there's a good possibility that he killed me."

"But you don't know for sure?"

"I'm afraid not. But tonight, Betts, I remember running from someone tonight. I was scared, but I don't think anything happened to me that could have caused this." She pointed to the blood.

"Robert, then. Maybe he was your killer?" I said.

"I refuse to believe that. I loved him so much. He loved me; I'm certain of it."

"Did you have a lot of men fall in love with you?" I asked.

For a moment she was caught off guard by the question, perhaps embarrassed.

"Grace, you were—are—absolutely gorgeous. I'm not just saying that. Why would I? But I can't imagine any man—and most women, frankly—not staring at you as you passed by. You are a classic beauty. And you are kind and gentle and sweet and intelligent. You seem like the whole package."

"Goodness, well, thank you."

"I'm not saying that to compliment you. I'm stating it as a fact that might help us solve your murder."

"I see. Well, I suppose people noticed me. It was uncomfortable sometimes, but at other times, it was just what it was. I was told many times that I was beautiful, I think, but white men weren't supposed to find me beautiful. White men weren't supposed to even look at me that way."

There was no bitterness in her voice, and I was aware that she was doing what I'd done, stating a fact.

"This won't be easy because it would be hard to remember this stuff anyway, but think back to before you were killed. We've got Robert and Justice." I didn't tell her that Gram had dreamt about them and that those dreams were violent and awful. I didn't want to plant the seeds if they ultimately weren't real. "Who else, Grace, who else?"

"My husband, perhaps, but I know I got out of town without him knowing. He would never have been able to find me."

"He was cruel to you?"

"Yes. He was also a drinker, a big drinker, Betts. I filled him full of moonshine before I left town. I knew how he'd react. He'd pass out for a couple days, wake up mad as a bear that I was gone, get over it in a day or two, and find another woman to pester."

I laughed even though she hadn't meant to be funny. "Grace, I'm sorry, but I expect that once a man found you, his standards might never be met again."

"Trust me, Betts, my husband wasn't picky. Any woman would do. I can't believe I stayed with him as long as I did."

"Nevertheless, I'll have Jake check him out."

She nodded. I'd missed when the hole in her middle had filled in and the blood disappeared, but she was now back to the whole version of herself.

"Okay, you went to look for Robert. And I know Justice said he would meet you later that evening. Think about your search. You must not have found Robert, but what did you find?"

"I don't remember."

I glanced out the window as a car pulled up behind the Nova.

"It's Cliff, my boyfriend," I said to Grace.

"Yes. I'll be on my way. I'll work on remembering more, Betts. I'll try," she said.

"All right," I said. "Tomorrow. Let's try again tomorrow."

I didn't want to interrupt our conversation but there was no way we could continue with Cliff in the house. And, truthfully, I was really happy to see him and looked forward to a night with just the two of us humans.

Thankfully, that's exactly what I got.

Chapter Twenty-One

I woke the next morning refreshed and with an idea re-blossoming in my mind. It was as if a night of not focusing on anything but Cliff helped settle everything else in my mind, and suddenly I wanted to see someone about my idea. Anyone who might substantiate it would do, but I knew where I wanted to begin.

Cliff left early, but I took my time, making a few notes and drinking a few cups of strong coffee. I'd told him I would stop by the post office and check on Gina, another of Derek's ex-wives, but something else gnawed at me. Gina got moved to second place, but another ex-wife took first.

When I felt ready I hopped in the Nova and steered it past downtown, pulling into an empty parking spot in front of Doc's office. It looked like Ridley was already there; her Explorer was next to the building. There were a couple other cars in the street that might have belonged to patients inside, but it didn't look like the office would be too busy.

"Hi," I said over the counter. "I don't have an appointment, but Ridley has been helping me with my pain meds. Any chance she has a minute or two?"

"Oh, well, I'll see. We're busy this morning."

I glanced back at the empty waiting room.

"The patients are all in the back."

"I understand," I said.

"Give me a minute."

She got my name, not acting as though she remembered me, and disappeared down the short hallway that led to the examination rooms. I took a seat and tried to look like I was interested in a magazine.

I didn't think Ridley would want to see me, but since I was here (falsely, of course) in a patient capacity and she couldn't risk letting anyone know that we'd spoken about Lynn during my last visit, she would probably see me and play along, even if she didn't want to.

I imagined the thoughts turning over in her head as she tried to figure out a way to ignore me, but ultimately couldn't come up with one.

A long moment later, she stepped through the doorway.

"Betts, what can I do for you?" she asked.

"Have a minute? I'd like to talk to you about these headaches," I said as I put my fingertips to my left temple.

Ridley looked around and then said, "Sure, come on back."

Silently, she led the way back to the same cowboy examination room we'd been in before. She shut the door after I followed her inside and took a seat on the exam table.

"I take it you're not really here for your headaches," she said.

"Nope," I said.

My idea had come to me somewhere in the middle of the night, though I wasn't sure exactly when it had sprouted; I'd been too busy with Cliff. It had blossomed with the rising sun, though, and then mellowed with some strong coffee. It was a relatively weak theory, sparked by Grace's visit and the coffee consciousness made that very clear. However, it still made sense. Kind of.

"So," I began, "did it really take five wives for Derek to realize he was the problem? He was the one who couldn't father a child, right? It had absolutely nothing to do with the women he'd married."

I hoped I was dropping a bomb, exposing a big secret, that she'd think I was extra clever. But that wasn't how she reacted. Instead, she steeled her stare and her stance.

"Yes, it took five," she said plainly, as if she wasn't surprised in the least that someone might have figured out this part of the mystery. But, then again, as she confirmed my suspicion I realized how obvious it had been.

I'd been asking how in the world Derek had chosen to marry five times. That was now clear, but there was still a big piece missing from the puzzle. Why had these women agreed to marry him? That was going to be more difficult to draw out of her, out of anyone, apparently.

"Ridley, I've only met a few of Derek's ex-wives, but every single one of you seems, intelligent, and savvy. Forgive me for asking this because there is no way to phrase it without being insulting, but why in the world would you all marry him, a sour, unfriendly man? I'm missing something. It makes no sense."

The corner of her mouth twitched twice. "So, you don't have it all figured out?"

"That's why I'm asking. I think the answer will lead everyone directly to his killer. Am I right?"

"You are one hundred percent correct, but you're still thinking about it the wrong way."

"Point me the right way."

This time she laughed out loud. "No, Betts, I'm not going to do that. You might assume that my reasoning for not doing so is because I killed Derek. Here, let me add another glitch to your thinking. I did not kill him, but I did not like him. I never did. Why haven't the police asked me that question—did I even like him? They've asked me where I was that night, and if I thought anyone wanted him dead. No one has asked if I liked him. I'm sure they all assume that we divorced because we 'fell out of love' or something, but that's not true. I was never in love in the first place."

"That brings me right back to the question—why did you marry him, then?"

She shrugged, crossed her arms in front of herself, and looked at me.

I forged on. "You got something out of the marriage. Security? No, you're a nurse and you live in Broken Rope. Your living expenses aren't high. Companionship? No, evidently not that. Money? But Derek didn't have money."

"Still on the wrong track. But we could go round and round all day. I need to get back to work. There are real patients scheduled to come in, you know."

"Sure," I said as I scooted off the exam table, hiding my

disappointment.

Ridley held the door open and signaled that I should walk through first.

"I'm going to tell Cliff about our conversation," I said.

"I didn't expect you not to. He's a good guy and a smart police officer, but he hasn't asked about my feelings for Derek either. Again, too many people assumed too many things. Marriage isn't always about love."

"Did any of Derek's wives marry him for love?"

"You'll have to ask them. Or tell Cliff to ask them."

"I will."

"Good luck with the headaches," she said as a final dismissal.

"Uh-huh," I said.

I looked at her a long moment, but she was clearly done with our conversation. I walked past her and then past the receptionist out front. There was one patient in the waiting room, but he didn't look all that sick so I didn't feel too guilty. I left the building and walked toward the boardwalk.

I wasn't ready yet to let go of my idea, but first I needed to talk to Cliff.

"Really? We didn't ask her about her feelings for Derek?" Cliff said, truly puzzled.

"She said everyone assumed that she just fell out of love and they got divorced. No one asked if she ever liked him."

Cliff blinked. "That's either some wordplay on her part, or some less-than-stellar police work on our part," he said. "We'll take another close look."

I'd managed to catch Cliff outside the station, just as he was coming back from an official visit with Lynn, the details of which he couldn't share. Jim left as Cliff and I walked into the station together, but Jim didn't tell either of us where he was going. I got the impression that Cliff already knew.

"Cliff," I said as I repositioned myself in the chair across his desk. "Have you found out any more about Derek's or Lynn's financial situation?"

"Nothing new since yesterday, Betts."

"I can't let go of it. I can't let go of the idea that the women who married Derek could not have possibly done so without some sort of financial benefit. It's a horrible, rotten thing to say, but I've become obsessed, I think. Nothing else fits."

Cliff nodded. "We've thought about that too, Betts, but we keep running into dead ends. Lynn doesn't really have any bills; her house is paid for, so she must have spent her money wisely. Nothing looks fishy."

"What money, Cliff?" I said. "She worked as a retail clerk for many years. How did she have enough money to pay off that house? How deeply have you looked?"

"She inherited the house from her parents."

"Oh, that makes sense." I was disappointed in the lack of mystery in that answer. "All right, how about under her mattress?"

Cliff smiled. "We searched the house after Derek was killed. I think we checked the mattress—underneath it at least, maybe not inside it. But, still, if she or Derek had money, Betts, how did they get it? We know for a fact that Derek's bank account was always very low."

"I'm not surprised."

Cliff cocked his head and looked at me with his eyebrows tight together. "You really can't let go of the money angle, can you?"

"What else could it possibly be? What's that Sherlock Holmes saying—when you've eliminated the impossible . . ."

"What remains, no matter how improbable, it must be true. Or something like that," Cliff said. "Yes, Mr. Holmes is unquestionably an excellent detective, even in his fictional form."

"It seems impossible that any of the women who married Derek actually liked him," I said.

Cliff laughed. "Let us dig a little deeper to make sure, but you might be right."

"Thanks," I said. "I'm still going to the post office later this morning. I promise."

My next stop, however, was Lynn's house, but I didn't tell Cliff. After talking to him, I'd become more doubtful about my idea, embarrassed, maybe. What had seemed so possible when I woke up was fading to silliness. However, I still wasn't quite ready to give up on it all the way yet either.

As I turned the corner that led to Lynn's street, I saw another car I thought I recognized parked in front of her house. I pulled in the same semi-hiding spot Gram and I had used and waited only a few minutes for someone to exit the house. It was Bonnie. She didn't hide her furtive glances in every direction as she stood on the front stoop. Was she hiding from someone, hoping no one, or someone in particular, didn't see her?

Or was it something worse? I'd been thinking so hard that perhaps my imagination got shifted up to overdrive, but I wondered about Lynn's safety. I reached for my phone with the idea that I'd ask Cliff to come out and check on her, but then she appeared. She stepped out of the doorway and she and Bonnie had a brief conversation, Lynn from the porch, Bonnie from halfway down the walkway. The moment wasn't contentious and a second later Lynn went inside and Bonnie hurried to her car.

I put the phone back in my pocket and ducked lower than the dashboard, just like any proper spy, as Bonnie drove by. The Nova was a pretty distinct car, and if she hadn't known it was mine before she'd stopped by my house the other day, she'd probably put the pieces together well enough by now, but I hoped her mind was occupied with whatever she and Lynn had been discussing.

Once the noise from her engine faded away, I scootched back up and stared at the house. It was a nice house, and though property in Broken Rope wasn't too expensive, it wasn't cheap. She'd been fortunate to inherit it from her parents. But there had to be more. There *had* to be.

"Show me the money, Lynn," I muttered quietly to myself.

My plan had been to talk to Lynn, just casually to see if she could say anything to substantiate my obsession, but Bonnie being there and the mere idea that she might have recognized the Nova made me think again. Maybe I'd come back later.

A trip to the post office and a discussion with Gina might be more fruitful anyway. I turned the car around and headed back to town.

As I waited to turn into the post office parking lot, a truly fortuitous event occurred—there was no other way to describe it. A horse came out of nowhere and ran down the middle of Main Street. Though there had never been any formal training or any sort of declaration that we as citizens of Broken Rope, Missouri, were to stop every runaway horse we saw, we all did, nonetheless. It was probably written somewhere in some ancient bylaw, but it was most definitely an unspoken code that the tourists and their safety were our number one priorities.

I jumped out of my still-running car and ran toward the street and the horse with the hope I'd get to it before it hurt someone.

But someone beat me to the punch. By the time I made it to the middle of the street, Grant, the barber, had stopped the animal and was holding tight to its reins. A second later, a man dressed as an old-time cowboy ran past me in a bow-legged trot that was befitting of his getup.

"He's mine. Sorry!" the running cowboy said.

No one had gotten hurt.

This time.

Thanks to the runaway horse, the idea I'd had that had all but disappeared sprung wings and legs again. As sure as I could see and talk to ghosts, I was sure the runaway horse had been a sign, telling me not to give up quite yet. And with the sign came new inspiration. I didn't need to talk to Lynn or any of Derek's ex-wives to get answers. They wouldn't give them to me anyway. I hurried back to the Nova, and I couldn't get to the courthouse fast enough.

Chapter Twenty-Two

We had two—courthouses, that is. One that was built back in our violent

Old West days and where we now performed courtroom skits like the one

featuring the trial of Sally Swarthmore. The other one was built in the

1970s and was where we conducted our present-day legal business. It was

also where all the town's records were stored. Additionally, sometime in

the 1980s, it had become the storage facility for the *entire* county's

government records. Even a country county in Missouri could produce

large amounts of government paperwork. The courthouse wasn't large; it

was made up of two cramped stories. The bottom level housed our small

courtroom on one side and our DMV on the other side. If someone in

Broken Rope wanted to obtain a driver's license or renew their current

license or had other legal motor vehicle issues, this is where they went.

There were days when the line stretched out the front door and halfway

down the block, almost to the other courthouse. In fact, sometimes people

made the choice to drive to either Springfield or St. Louis just to avoid the wait.

Today, there was no line—no one even standing at the help desk. I didn't know the person sitting there waiting to assist customers, and they didn't look up from the book they were reading as I sped past them and then took the stairs, two at a time, up to the second floor.

The second floor was where the good stuff was anyway. It was divided into four different rooms, each of which held their own varieties of files and paperwork. This place was packed with papers that had, for one reason or another, needed or been the result of legal attention or intervention. Jake loved it here, but he was also intimidated. He'd mentioned once or twice that he didn't understand Danni Heather's filing system and he didn't like to rely on anyone to help him find anything. And she'd never let him run free through *her* files without supervision.

Danni did her have own filing methods. Of course, the stories of her ability to pinpoint that one piece of paper in what sometimes looked like a gigantic, disorganized mess were legendary. I didn't point out to Jake that he had his own methods, too, and though he wasn't messy, he could be just as mysterious.

Danni Heather was a fireball; an odd, old, wrinkled fireball who happened to be one of Gram's biggest fans. I didn't understand their friendship because Gram never seemed all that excited at the prospect of a dinner with the ever-energetic Danni, but they always had a great time together. Danni loved Gram's food, all of it. I'd watched her eat three helpings and not only remain skinny but look around for more. And Gram would smile and laugh at Danni's jokes and observations about the old legal documents she found and thought were humorous.

Danni had a few part-time employees working for her, but most of the time it was just Danni and her papers. As I stepped onto the landing of the second floor, I saw her carrying a box toward the back room. As she leaned the box against the wall so she could free a hand to open the door, I took off toward her.

"Danni, hang on. Let me help."

She turned and peered at me through the top of her bifocals. Her short, gray hair was a complete mess, but that was probably because she never brushed it.

"Betts, hi. You have good timing." She pulled the box back and waited until I got the door open.

"Can I carry that in for you?"

"What? Why would you do that? I'm perfectly capable."

"I know. Just asking."

"I'm fine, but thanks for the door," she said as she heaved the box up to the counter inside the room. She turned and faced me and wiped her hands on her jeans. "Do you need something?"

"I do," I said, knowing the direct approach was always the best with Danni. "I was wondering about lawsuits against the city, or township, or whatever. Do you have those sorts of records?"

"Of course. What are you looking for?"

"When Lynn Rowlett was young, she was knocked over by a performance horse. She actually ended up saving others from getting hurt, but I think she was hurt. I was curious if she sued anyone and if she won."

"Well," Danni said as she pushed up the glasses and put her hands on her hips. "I might have those types of records, Betts, but some of them are closed, particularly if cases were settled."

"Is that what happened?"

"Now, I'm not saying that."

Danni walked past me and back out the door and toward hallway. I didn't see any other option but to follow her.

"Can you look?" I said.

"Where is it you think I'm going?" she said over her shoulder.

"Oh. Good. Thank you."

"No promises. I might not be able to find what you need."

I squelched a laugh. "Okay."

We went to the front west-side room. It was warmer than the rest of the building. Stuffy, even. I didn't know where Danni spent most of her time, but I thought it probably wasn't in this room. It wasn't a big space, maybe only about ten by fifteen feet with windows that were shut tight and covered in closed blinds.

"Stay on this side," Danni said to me before she walked around the partial front counter and toward some file drawers. She didn't hesitate a second before she pulled open the second drawer on the first cabinet and reached inside. She read something from a file and then put it back before making her way back to the counter.

"Well?" I said.

"All I can tell you is that there is a filed lawsuit on the records that is titled Lynn Stevens v. the township of Broken Rope, Missouri. Stevens is Lynn's maiden name."

"And?"

"That's all I've got."

"I can't see the details?"

"No, I don't have them."

I looked around her toward the file cabinet. "What was in the file?"

"Something that told me very specifically that I can't tell you anymore."

"So a settlement was reached?"

Danni shrugged and made a small *hmm* noise.

"If I promise you that Gram will make you dinner in the next two weeks, could I convince you to tell me more?" It was low, I knew, but at that point I didn't care.

"What kind of dinner?"

"What's your favorite?" Gram was not going to be happy, but I'd help her.

"Something with beef and mashed potatoes, and her green bean casserole, of course."

"Consider it done."

"Well, I cannot tell you the details, but the file and the settlement . . . oops, I mean the *file* was sealed. That happens sometimes when settlements are reached, but I'm not saying that's what happened."

I leaned a little closer to her. "Was it big?" I whispered. When she didn't answer, I added, "Apple crisp for dessert." I *knew* it was her favorite.

She looked at me with wide expectant eyes behind her bifocals, but then she squinted. She didn't like being manipulated, but I smiled innocently and waited.

It worked. "It was huge," she whispered before she pushed past me again, this time with a slight shove thrown in, and then headed toward the door. She stood in the doorway, waiting for me to leave the room, too. She wasn't going to risk tempting me to look at the records on my own. Smart move.

"Thanks, Danni," I said as I passed by her. I hurried out of the building and then back to the police station.

And no one was there. Well, one person was there but he wasn't a police officer. In fact, I hadn't even met him yet. He introduced himself as Frank Stanley and he was from Chicago. He'd moved to Broken Rope and was planning on becoming a police officer, but he wasn't one yet. The only people I wanted to talk to at the moment were Jim and Cliff, but Frank wasn't sure where they'd gone.

I stepped outside the police station and called Cliff's mobile. I checked the area for curious listeners, but no one seemed to care what I was doing or saying, so I left a simple message saying that Lynn does or did have money and it came from a lawsuit settlement from when she was younger. Who knows where she put it.

After I ended the call, I tried to bring the pieces together in my head, but they weren't fitting. I didn't understand the specifics, but, of course, I was aware that people could hide their money in offshore or overseas accounts. If I'd stayed in law school I might have learned how to do such things. As it was I really had no idea how to even begin. But there was money there somewhere, and the fact that it existed seemed to make a few things clear—okay, maybe not clear, but probable.

Lynn or Derek, using Lynn's money, paid five women to marry Derek. I couldn't quite pinpoint the exact reason but it undoubtedly had something to do with bribing them to be with Derek. Had I really been so close to the truth during my last conversation with Ridley? Had it been about a child? Had five women attempted to have a child with Derek Rowlett?

Why? Money?

I looked up and down Main Street. Jake's building was clear, which meant he wasn't performing. If he had been, the crowd would have been so big that some people would be watching from the open doorway—they always did. He was available, at least short term.

I stuck my head back into the real police station and asked Frank if he would tell Cliff to come find me at Jake's. He didn't ask who Jake was, but he seemed to get the idea.

I trotted across the street and peered into Jake's, only to find it empty except for the stick pony, Patches. I was always surprised that no one stole the prop that had been part of Jake's act for years. I knocked on the door that led to the archive room and opened it a little bit.

"Jake," I said as I went through and then shut the door behind me.

He was standing on the other side of the room, looking at something on the table that was apparently much more interesting than me.

"What do you have?" I said as I joined him and looked at the items, too.

I'd seen them before. They were the historical items that Jake had gathered on Jerome, but he'd added one thing. On his paranormal camera that seemed to have worked only one time, he filmed Jerome and I together in the middle of a kiss. He'd taken that film and made a still of that moment in time. I reached for the picture.

"When did you add this?" I said.

Jake looked up at me with his handsome face and bright blue eyes and said, "Hello, Isabelle."

I put the picture down. "Jerome? You're . . . you're in Jake?"

"For the moment."

"Oh, wow, he's going to flip when I tell him about this. Don't kiss me, though. We'd never be able to get past that one."

He laughed and smiled—it was Jake's face, but unquestionably Jerome's smile.

"All right, I'll try to contain myself," he said.

"What are you doing here—in Jake?"

"I'm not sure. It's just where I needed to be. I thought as long as I was here, I'd take a look at Jake's papers again. I wasn't the bad guy they made me out to be, you know."

"I know that. I've known that since your first visit."

"Good," he said.

"What's with all the strange possession stuff? It's new, that's for sure."

"I know, and I don't understand it at all, except I know that things are off-kilter over in the place I am when I'm not here, and I know that whatever caused them to be off-kilter occurred over by the barn where those wagon contraptions are located."

"You saw those?"

"I did, and I was going to get Jake to walk us over there now so we could have another look. In fact, seeing through his eyes might be the most intelligent view I've had. Jake knows Broken Rope."

"Do you think the thing that happened to put everything off-kilter happened recently or is it something from the past?" I said.

"I don't know, Isabelle."

I smiled at hearing Jake's voice say my name the way Jerome always did.

"Will Jake remember this? I mean it didn't seem like Paul remembered his possession very clearly and Elvis was a ghost so he doesn't matter. I have no idea what Reginald thought."

He laughed. "I don't have any idea, but if I can control it, do you want me to make sure he remembers or doesn't?"

"Remembers."

"I'll certainly try."

"Thanks. Let's take a walk."

I put a sign on the front of Jake's door announcing that his next show was canceled. Though that would not go over well with the tourists, a note was better than just not showing up. As we made our way down the boardwalk, I was surprised that we didn't see anyone who wanted to chat with us. It would have been interesting to see how Jerome handled such a meeting, but it was better not to have to worry about it.

I'd gone to find Jake to tell him what Danni Heather had told me and how there was now money somewhere. I couldn't have the same conversation with Jerome.

Surprisingly, the barn doors were locked. I tried the lock and the doors a few times just to be sure.

"Do you remember—does Jake remember he and I being here last night?"

"I remember seeing through the ticket seller's eyes, but nothing more than that really."

"We'll have to take the path down the side," I said.

He stretched his neck and peered down the pathway. It was daytime, tourists still filled the boardwalk and surrounding areas, but the path between the barn and the end of the boardwalk buildings was clear except for all the tall grasses.

"All right. Follow me, Isabelle." He stepped around me and forged down the path.

Once on the other side of the building, we stood side by side, both of us with our hands on our hips. I'd seen Jake put his hands on his hips plenty times, but there was something different about his posture this time, something about the way his hip turned outward slightly. He stood just like Jerome would stand.

"Anything?" I asked as we looked out over the field.

"A little," he said. "Something terrible happened back here, I know that."

"I'd love more details."

"Don't have them at the moment."

I realized that the only time Jerome's wood smoke scent had been present with his recent visits was when he'd jumped into Paul. I hadn't smelled anything with Elvis, Reginald, or with Jake. But another scent suddenly filled the air. The distinct smell of onions, pungent and aggressive, rode a small breeze through the field.

"I think we're about to see the train station again. It was originally where the barn is, but it materialized back here behind it last night. Do you see it?" It was faint, but definitely coming into view.

"I do. This is the one that collapsed on you and Jake?"

"I think so. Yep, there's the bell." I squinted toward the porch and saw the bell, its brass glimmering.

"I see. Stay close by, Isabelle. We'll get through whatever this is."

"Whatever you say."

The strong smell was unsettling. I liked the smell of onions, even in their rawest, most powerful form, but there was an extra edge to this smell, something that didn't make my eyes water, but made the back of my throat burn.

When the building was completely there though very transparent, a person appeared on the steps the led into the front door. He was a ghost I hadn't yet met, but the first one I'd known back when they were a live person.

"Derek?" I said as I hurried toward the station and the man who I'd apparently almost died with.

"Isabelle, wait," Jake/Jerome said.

But I didn't listen.

"Derek," I said as I stood on the platform below and looked up at him, the onion smell even stronger. "Derek?"

He didn't seem confused. He seemed angry and bothered, but not at all confused.

"Betts, Jake, what are you two doing here?"

I looked around. "I was about to ask you the same question. I was also going to ask if you knew where you were and what happened to you."

"Of course. I was killed right over there." He nodded toward the barn. "I'm a ghost."

That was easy. "Yes. You were killed. Who killed you?"

As Derek looked up quickly, day turned into night, the field stepped back in time. We were there, at the original station, at night. Everything and everyone became solid. I looked at Jake/Jerome who nodded, confirming that he was also seeing the changes.

"Where's the train?" Derek asked.

I turned and looked where it seemed a train would be.

"I don't know," I said. "Are you expecting one?"

"Yes. It was my only option, as far as I could figure. There it is," Derek said.

We turned and looked back toward the direction of the barn. It was now gone and a faraway light was beginning to come into view.

Derek stepped around both Jake and me, off the stairs and onto the platform. He looked toward the train.

Jerome/Jake and I looked at each other.

"Derek, please tell me. Do you know who killed you? Do you know what happened?"

"Of course."

"Tell me!"

"I won't have to. I'll show you. When the train arrives. I hope it's on time."

I sighed, but I realized that this was Derek's show and he was going to reveal what he wanted to reveal in his own time frame. Before I could contemplate what more I could say, the other ghosts came into view.

Robert, Grace, and Justice appeared on the platform, right in front of us. They looked at us and at one another. For a moment, we all took in what was happening.

Finally, I said, "Grace, Robert, you two okay? Justice, do you know what's going on?"

"I'm fine. Grace is here," Robert said as the two of them took each other's hands.

But if there was about to be a romantic moment, it was thwarted.

"You killed me!" Justice said as he looked at Robert. "It was right here. You killed me right here."

As though the words didn't quite make sense even to himself, Justice pulled back his anger and put his hands on his hips. "What's this? What's going on?"

Robert nodded at Grace, kissed her on the forehead, and then stepped around her.

"I did kill you. You killed my Grace. I killed you."

Were those answers, or speculation? Jake/Jerome and I shared a hopeful glance.

For a long moment the only sound was the faraway but approaching train. Derek ignored the rest of us as he looked out toward where it seemed the train was coming from. Grace observed the two men who'd loved her so much that somehow she and one of them had ended up dead. Justice and Robert looked at each other with fierce hatred and surprised confusion. They communicated with their eyes. A stare down. Playing chicken.

And then Justice spoke. "I did not kill her. I fell in love with her. I would never have killed her."

I stepped forward and decided that some clarification might be needed.

"Justice, I need to explain a little of where you are and why." I gave him the spiel. He didn't argue or protest his circumstances, but listened thoughtfully. Then I added, "We think you were angry when Grace left the station to search for Robert. We think it's possible you became jealous and killed her so Robert couldn't have her either."

"No! That's not what happened."

"Okay. What happened?" I said.

"I'm not exactly sure," Justice said after another long moment.

The train was still very far away, the light not seeming to grow brighter and the sound remaining at a constant low level. We stalled, like the film in the projector was stuck and would break momentarily if someone didn't do something. I had only one idea.

"Should we go inside?" I asked Jake/Jerome.

"It's probably okay."

"Derek, come in, too. I might need your help." I had no idea how I might need his help, but I wanted him with us, or at least I didn't want him to disappear when he was out of my sight. He looked at me with disdain but then grudgingly followed the rest of us in.

The inside was just as real as the outside and like the station had been the night before.

Derek brought his onion stink in with him, but I thought Jake/Jerome and I were the only ones to notice it. He took a seat on one of the benches and looked around without curiosity. He'd come in, but he looked like he was going to wait his turn for something, without needing to know what else was going on. I was okay with that—for now.

Elvis, the ticket salesperson, was in his spot behind the window, ready to exchange money and tickets with customers, but there were no customers, just the mixed up group of ghosts, Jake/Jerome, and me.

"Okay," I said as I moved to a bench and pointed. "The night we think everything happened, Justice and Grace were sitting here, on this bench. Sit."

They did.

"Now, do you remember your conversation?"

They blinked and looked at each other.

"Yes," Grace said. "I was going to go search for Robert."

"And I made plans to meet her back here if she couldn't find him. I wanted to take care of her."

"That never happened. What happened? Remember," I said.

"I left. I left the station," Grace said.

"And I watched her go. Watched until she turned a corner," Justice said.

"Watched her? You didn't follow her?" I said.

"No, I watched her just from the platform out there." Justice stood up and walked to the doorway. "Right in that spot. I stood there and watched her go."

"You met her later?" I said.

"I don't think so. No, I know I didn't! I went to find Robert—I went to find Robert and I found him." Justice moved back to Robert's side. "And you killed me."

"Whoa, we need some of the other details," I said. "Why would he just kill you? Did you just kill him, Robert?"

"I killed him, yes," he said as his ghostly eyes looked to the past. "But I think I had a good reason."

I looked at Grace. "Try extra hard to remember, Grace. What happened to you after you left to search for Robert?"

Grace stepped away from the crowd and to the door that Justice had explored.

"I know I didn't find Robert. I know I came back here, but I was earlier than Justice and I had talked about. I gave up. I become desolate after only a few more dead ends. I began to believe that Robert had abandoned me."

"Oh, Grace," Robert said. "I'm so sorry."

"All right." I sighed and then became distracted by a commotion at the ticket counter. More people from the past had appeared and were upset about something.

I approached the small crowd.

"Hang on. No one move," I said to the ghosts. They all nodded absently.

"How are we supposed to get our tickets now?" said one of the potential ticket buyers.

"He just up and left!" said another.

They were talking about Elvis. The ticket seller's chair and booth were empty.

"Where did he go?" I asked them.

A sour looking old woman turned to me with what looked like a painful neck bend. "He was watching all of you over there, and he suddenly got up and left. What did you do to him?"

I nodded and then looked back toward the other ghosts. I'd known that Elvis must have had something to do with the answers we were searching for. Why else would he have appeared?

I walked back to Jake/Jerome. "Still you, Jerome?"

"Yes, Isabelle."

"When you hopped into that Elvis guy—the one selling tickets—did you sense that he knew anything about what was going on here?"

"No, not really. He was just the easiest to jump into."

"Grace, do you remember anything about the ticket seller?" I said.

She looked up at me, first in confusion and then only a small moment later, with complete understanding.

"Of course!" she said. "He was angry with me for—what was the word he used? Loitering. There were no other people here. He wanted to lock the doors, or so he said. He told me I needed to buy a ticket or leave."

Suddenly, Elvis appeared by her side and grabbed her arm.

"If you aren't going to buy a ticket, you need to leave," he said, his grip on her arm clearly tight and probably painful.

And his voice was vicious. A thread of fear danced up my spine. I was fully aware that Elvis could do nothing to me—how must Grace have felt when he'd done that to her all those years ago?

"I'm sorry," Grace said. "I won't be long. I really am meeting someone soon. Look, I'll leave. Just let go of my arm and I'll leave."

Elvis looked around and seemed not to see anyone else. I presumed that we were viewing what had happened, not a revival, but the moments of what really occurred. Grace also seemed to suddenly not notice the rest of us.

"Grace!" Robert and Justice said as they both moved toward her.

"Stop," I said as I grabbed Robert's arm and the sleeve of Justice's jacket. "This has to happen. There's no bringing her back, but you want the truth, right? Then I think we just have to watch."

They both looked at me like I'd lost my mind.

"Isabelle is right," Jake/Jerome said. "This will give you the answers you were looking for."

It was awful. In fact, it might have been one of the worst times of my life, watching what happened to Grace. What Elvis, out of anger, desire, hatred, and loathing, had done to her. Gram's nightmares would now be mine, too.

Grace had been extraordinarily beautiful. And she'd had black skin. Elvis had found Grace as beautiful as everyone else had. But he'd been wired wrong. Something had been horribly off about him, something that made him think it was his place to take what he wanted, particularly from someone he deemed "lesser" than himself. No one else had been around. Robert was ill, Justice wasn't supposed to be there yet. When Grace fought Elvis, he took what he wanted from her, and then became so angry with her obvious disgust and hatred of him that he killed her. What happened to Grace made the loathing I had for prejudice and small minds grow to a vile, choking size. But if I allowed it to truly take a place in my heart, I knew I would have been as awful as those people with small minds had been, and some still were. I couldn't allow myself to be like them.

When it was done, we learned that Justice had found Robert and brought him back to a darkened, empty station, and they'd found Grace's body behind the station. Robert had made an illness-induced and horror-filled assumption. He'd thought Justice had killed Grace. He was so sick, dangerously fevered and teetering on the brink of death. His muddled mind couldn't grasp that Justice was innocent of everything except falling in love with Grace. And no matter his love for Grace, Justice had been trying to help her and Robert. He believed in doing the right thing. Robert *had* killed Justice and made his way back to his sickbed, waking up only the next day, realizing what he'd done. He hid their bodies in the Missouri woods, and sent a letter to Justice's family in Frankland. Then he proceeded to enact his own punishment.

Answers. Did they help?

Actually, they did. After the dreadfulness, Elvis disappeared, and so did the others who'd been in line to purchase tickets.

But Grace, Robert, Justice, Jake/Jerome, and I remained. So did Derek, but he didn't count at the moment.

"How does a man apologize for murdering another man, particularly a good one?" Robert said as he looked at Justice.

"How does a man apologize for leaving a beautiful woman to a killer?" Justice said.

"Gentlemen, apologies are no longer necessary," Grace said. "We have the truth."

In fact, Grace was practically giddy, the weight of the past gone from her pretty shoulders.

"What happens now?" I said.

It seemed they were about to tell me, but Jake/Jerome jumped in. "No matter. Friends, I think you can be on your way now."

Grace, Robert, and Justice looked at Jake/Jerome and smiled and nodded.

"Thank you, Betts," Grace said as she moved toward me and hugged me tightly. She said into my ear, "Love is strange and doesn't understand time. You know that, don't you?"

"I'm working on it." I looked at Jake/Jerome. I loved them both, and in such different ways. And I loved Cliff.

"Thank you, Betts," Robert said with a smile and a nod. "This was all terribly exhausting, but it has ended well."

"Thank you, miss. Thank you," Justice said.

"You're all very welcome. Is this good-bye?"

But they didn't answer. They disappeared, back to wherever. I hoped it was a good place.

I turned to Jake/Jerome. As he reached for my arm, perhaps to guide me someplace, a wind rushed through the station, and blew the building away. I had a sense again that I should be falling to the ground, so I braced myself, but there was no fall, just a transition from the station to the field. It was still a nighttime version so I knew we weren't home yet.

"The bad thing that happened here, the thing I sensed was dangerous to you?" Jake/Jerome said above the wind and as he looked over my shoulder.

"Yeah?"

"It had nothing to do with Grace, Robert, Elvis, or Justice. It was about Derek. I know that now. The viciousness of his murder made him strong, Isabelle, almost too strong. His anger is overwhelming and partially directed at you because you didn't die too."

I nodded even though I wasn't sure exactly what he meant and then turned. Derek was standing and looking down at the train tracks—at a body on the train tracks.

"Oh no," I said. "Who is that?" I stepped toward Derek and the body as Jake/Jerome followed close behind.

The body on the tracks was Lynn. In fact, she was still alive and tied to the tracks just like Nell Fenwick of the *Dudley Do-Right* cartoon that had been a favorite of my dad's. She'd played a damsel in distress in a Broken Rope skit when she was younger. Now she really was one.

I pushed past Derek and crouched next to Lynn.

"Oh, Betts, thank heavens you're here. Untie me, please!"

"Of course," I said as I reached for the knots on the ropes around her arms. "What's going on?"

I didn't know if she could see her son as he hovered above us, the tips of his shoes at the edge of my peripheral vision.

"He," she looked up at Derek, "tied me here."

I paused and looked at Jake/Jerome.

"Derek is dead," he said to Lynn.

"Oh, I know he's dead. He's haunting me, and trying to kill me."

Derek laughed and said, "Because she killed me."

"What? Lynn?" I said.

"I had no choice," she said. "Please untie me."

It wasn't necessary to let her know right away that all of this was a ghostly illusion, that the train whistle we just heard wasn't real. I thought she was in a pretty good spot to answer some questions.

"Why did you kill your own son?" I said, my heart hurting at the question, the idea of it.

"He was going to expose me, expose us, and I didn't want to face it. Everyone in Broken Rope would have been appalled. We would have had to leave."

"I wouldn't have left. I would have stayed and hoped you left. You paid them, Mom. You paid them to marry me. Why didn't you just tell me?" Derek said.

Why didn't you just tell me? Just as Gram and I had suspected, it had been Derek inside Grace that day at Lynn's. Way too much crossover for my tastes.

"Technically, I was just trying to have a grandchild or two. You were pathetic, Derek. You were never going to get a wife on your own. I had to do something. I wanted more family. I deserved to have more family."

Derek's fists balled and anger pulled at his features. I couldn't imagine how awful it was to hear your parent call you pathetic. These two were a mess, a horrible, scary mess.

"How dare you?" he said to his mom. "How could you interfere like that?" And then he laughed, maniacally, of course. He threw his head back and the wind carried his ironic cackle. "And, it took you five wives to realize that maybe I was the one who couldn't have children? Those women took advantage of you, you fool. They took advantage of my future and the fortune I was supposed to inherit from you. You gave it to some useless women who wouldn't have known how to be good wives even if they'd wanted to."

Words of protest rumbled in my throat, but now wasn't the time to point out how they all thought he was a pretty awful husband.

"If you'd just accepted my help," Lynn said, "I wouldn't have hurt you." She looked at me. "I'm sorry I had to hit you, too, Betts. I didn't really want to hurt you either, but I had to get out of there. I'm glad you're okay. Would you please untie me now?"

"Uhm. Right," I said.

The ghost train was closer, close enough that the glow of the light was coming into clearer focus in the distance.

I reached forward, but not hurriedly, and then something hit my back hard. I went down, face first on the ground next to the tracks. If I'd hit the tracks, I would have surely fractured bones in my face. As it was, the maneuver hurt badly enough. And I realized something. The tracks—they were no longer short and incomplete; they were whole and continuous. The ropes around Lynn's limbs were real. How had Derek done that? There was no way the train could be somehow "real," too, was there? Jerome had said that the viciousness of his murder had made him strong. I must have been seeing evidence of just how strong.

My mind worked through this information along with the pain in my back, shoulder, and face, and Jake/Jerome's yells of protest all at once.

I saw stars for a second or two as I tried to turn my head toward Derek and Jake/Jerome. Jerome, even as a ghost, was strong, a big man who'd lived his life outdoors, doing things that required lots of physicality. Jake wasn't weak, but he was more a lover than a fighter. Derek was pushing him around easily.

I needed to get Lynn off the tracks. Maybe Jake/Jerome could distract Derek long enough.

I pulled my woozy head up and crawled the couple feet back toward Lynn.

"Hurry, Betts," she said.

I nodded, looked toward the train light, and then did the best I could. The knots were tight. Behind me, I could hear the scuffle between Derek and Jake/Jerome. It didn't sound like one was doing better than the other, but I couldn't move my fingers quickly enough. I hoped the train wasn't real.

"Leave her alone, Betts," I heard Derek say. "She deserves to die."

While continuing to work the knot, I turned to see Derek being held back by his arms by Jake/Jerome. I was impressed by my friend's strength.

"I can't, Derek. I'm sorry for what happened to you, really I am, but I can't risk someone else dying. I'll tell the police what she did."

"Hurry up, Isabelle," Jake/Jerome said.

I turned my full attention back to Lynn and the approaching train light. A huge surge of adrenaline shot through me, and my fingers suddenly became stronger and faster. I pulled and yanked, and the ropes came loose. Lynn was finally free. She sat up and looked me directly in the eye.

"Thank you, Betts, you saved me. Thank you."

"You're . . ." I began.

Before I could finish, though, Lynn had shoved me down onto the tracks and pinned my body with her bigger one straddling over mine, her hands pushing on my shoulders. She looked back at the train light and then at me.

"Sorry, Betts, but you just can't turn me in. I'm sorry."

"What?" I said. I couldn't believe two things—one, that she was so ungrateful. And two, that I hadn't seen this coming.

I hoped that the train wasn't real. Lynn was real. The tracks were real. What were the chances that the train would do me harm, though?

I didn't want to find out. I squirmed and tried to move myself enough that I could get Lynn off me. I wished for more adrenaline, but fear seemed to be the overriding thing inside me now.

"Isabelle," I heard Jake/Jerome yell. He was now being held back by Derek.

Why would Derek hold him back from helping me? I thought I understood, and decided I might be able to use the idea to my advantage. I grabbed Lynn's arms and squeezed them tightly.

"If I go, you go," I said.

Lynn's eyes opened wide. She looked toward the train and then tried to pull herself away, but I held on with a viselike grip, hoping that we'd both get off the tracks because she didn't want to die.

The train whistle blew and I realized that I could feel its vibrations underneath my back. I could smell the steam, the burning coal. It all seemed real. And I realized with a deep and sad regret that the ghosts were always dimensional in the dark when I was in the area, even, apparently, if the dark was an apparition. So the trains were probably fully dimensional, too.

This wasn't going to end well.

At least I'd talked to Teddy.

Chapter Twenty-Three

In the next instant and when the train seemed only inches away, Lynn was propelled off me and over to the other side of the tracks, and I was lifted and pulled back in time to feel the train brush my flying ponytail but nothing else.

I landed on the ground next to Jake/Jerome, who'd somehow gotten away from Derek and had enough strength—or could ghostly possessed bodies have adrenaline, too?—to push Lynn away and pull me off.

The train passed and then disappeared and so had Derek, leaving only me, Lynn, Jake/Jerome, and the ancient moonlight to cast a glow over the empty field. I would never know if the train really would have killed me. I figured that was a good thing. I looked at Jake/Jerome.

"Good job," I said. "Thank you. Are you still Jerome?"

"I am, Isabelle."

There was no mistaking his tone and the way he looked at me. I could see his gentle eyes as part of Jake's pretty blue ones. Jake loved me, but not like this.

I looked across the tracks at Lynn. She was sitting up, but it looked like she was woozy and trying to gather her senses. She'd need a doctor, but I needed a minute.

"Derek's gone?"

"Yes, he is. He made sure this trip was hard on everyone."

"Are you going to leave Jake now?"

"Yes."

"Any chance I'll get to see you as you?"

"There's no reason for me to stay right now, but I suppose I'll be back someday. Just don't know when or how. I would never have thought I'd jump inside other people's skin, dead or not. I sure wish I could have sensed what that Elvis fellow had done when I was in him. Sorry about that."

I waved away the apology. "But you'll be back?"

He laughed. "I'm pretty sure. You seem to keep finding ways to get into trouble."

I smiled. "Well, I can't miss my chance, then. Don't tell Jake."

I leaned over and kissed him. Jake would never have kissed back on his own, but I was pleased to see that Jake was pretty good at kissing when he had some motivation, even if said motivation was an old cowboy ghost under his skin.

When I pulled back, he was still looking at me in that way.

"I'll see you later, Isabelle. I'd say to stay out of trouble, but I think I'm going to have to give up on pretending I want that. Get into a little trouble, and let me come save the day again."

"I'll work on it."

And then, Jake transformed back into Jake. The changes were subtle but obvious. Jake held his own shoulders a little differently than Jerome had held them. His head wasn't quite as cocked to one side.

"You okay, Jake?" I said as I put my hand on his arm.

He looked at me a long minute. "I'm fine. I was here, too, Betts, and I want you to know that I probably have cooties now."

I laughed—feeling the fear and knot of tension in my stomach relax. "Sorry about that."

Jake wanted to tease me, but he only smiled, too. "Well, I suppose it's fine. I'm not telling Cliff, though. No way."

I laughed. I thought that someday I might tell Cliff, but not today. "We should help Lynn."

"Sure. You're probably right."

The night turned back into day—our present day. We gathered Lynn, who was fine but confused and shaken up just enough that she didn't mind that we each held one of her arms as we took her directly to Cliff at the police station.

On the way, I explained that her very angry son would haunt her for the rest of her life if she didn't just confess to her crime. I had no idea if this was true or not, but she'd seen enough (though I would never be exactly sure what she saw because I never asked) to know that she didn't want to deal with Derek forever. Sadly, I got the impression that she hadn't ever wanted to deal with him when he was alive either.

It was good that she listened to me and confessed, because the explanation for how Jake and I knew she was guilty would have been impossible to share. As it was, Cliff wondered why Jake and I both looked so disheveled. I just shrugged, and Jake told Cliff he'd been busy fighting off my amorous advances. Cliff and I laughed. Jake just gave me one of his ever-patient eye rolls.

Chapter Twenty-Four

"That is a beautiful mirror," Cliff said from over my shoulder.

I wasn't sure why my dad had decided to put it up in the house, but it looked great in the spot he'd chosen—on the wall, right between some sliding glass doors that separated the dining room and the outside back patio.

"It is," I said.

"It's got an antique feel about. Mysterious. I like it," he said as he put his arms around me.

I nodded and leaned into his chest. "I agree."

"Teddy sent me in with the specific question as to whether you want a hamburger or two hot dogs. He said you never eat just one. I did not know that about you," Cliff said.

"He's right. I always thought that two hotdogs were equal to one hamburger. However, I'm really hungry. I'd like one hamburger and one hot dog."

"Sounds perfect."

The mysteries had been solved for a week now, and my parents had invited us all over for a barbecue, which meant that Teddy would man the grill. He was the best at it. Jake had joined us. So had Opie, and, so far, she and I had gotten along fairly well.

Lynn had, in fact, paid Derek's wives to marry him and try to have a child with him. The five of the ex-wives had gotten together not too long ago and concocted a blackmail scheme. They'd gone to Lynn and told her that she needed to keep paying them or they'd tell Derek what she'd done, and they knew she couldn't bear for Derek to know. She paid the blackmail for some time, but one of the ex-wives, Gina, the one I'd never talked to at the post office, told Derek about his mother's involvement when he confronted her about her lavish post-marriage lifestyle. Derek had been devastated and was going to expose his mother—for her wife-paying scheme as well as the amount of money she'd received from Broken Rope from her lawsuit. She had moved the money to somewhere other than the United States, an offshore account, I'd heard, though I still didn't quite understand what that meant, so the people of Broken Rope wouldn't ever know what she took from them.

I remembered the strong onion scent as I left the school the day I was hit in the head. At the time I was in a hurry so I didn't pay it any attention, but looking back I realized that I smelled it at probably the exact time Derek was killed. It might not have meant much, but it was interesting to me, and made me realize that I could never just ignore a strong, insistent smell.

The big piece that everyone had been missing had simply been Lynn's personality. She'd lived in Broken Rope all her life and had made it her business to complain about almost everyone and everything. She knew that if everyone knew the amount of money she'd received from the city's coffers, they'd think she didn't have a right to complain about anything. She would have had to change her ways—and potentially share the money to help fix the objects of her complaints. Not her style. And, then when she so desperately wanted a grandchild and she knew that no one would marry Derek on their own, she used her money—and somehow found five women to take the bait. Even with the facts out in the open, the story was still hard to believe.

The ex-wives actually weren't afraid of Lynn. They were afraid of their scheme being exposed. They almost had me. Almost. They were in for some legal trouble, but blackmail wasn't as bad as murder, and attempted murder. Though I didn't think Lynn meant to kill me by hitting me with the wrench, she sure had wanted me dead on the train tracks. I couldn't tell anyone about that, but I didn't argue the attempted-murder charge. It wouldn't have mattered anyway. Cliff was going to make sure Lynn paid for her crimes.

Lynn had stolen the wrench from Roy's toolbox, during the Monday-morning meeting at the cooking school. I'd seen Roy looking at the toolbox. Apparently he'd been looking for the wrench he was sure was inside it.

By stealing the wrench and killing Derek in the barn, Lynn thought Roy would be the main suspect. She'd never known that though Cliff and Jim were actually considering him, he'd never really made it high on the suspect list.

But neither had Lynn. Mothers aren't supposed to kill their sons.

The last week had been pretty terrific for Cliff and me. He'd had some time off and our previous conversations about the weird thing that was the third party in our relationship had changed his mood substantially. He was no longer wary or suspicious. He still wasn't ready for the details, but he had completely accepted the fact that I wasn't cheating on him. Well, not really. He was at least okay with the otherworldly cheating, thinking it could never be a real threat.

I still didn't completely understand why Jerome could only visit via others this time around. It must have had something to do with Derek, but I had nothing to substantiate that, and I really hoped I never would. I didn't need to ever see Derek again. I wondered if I'd ever really see Jerome again, or perhaps he'd transitioned to only visiting via other bodies now.

Jake and I had talked about how we were going to tell Mariah the truth about her ancestor. We couldn't *not* tell her, but we hadn't formulated a plan yet. Another trip to Frankland was in our future. I wanted to check the pictures of Justice again, too. I wondered if the cowboy-hat swirls would still be there. And, of course, Jake and I both wondered if the accidental pond with the small fish was still there, but we weren't sure we'd exit the freeway to take a close look.

As we stood together a moment, looking at my dad's mirror, Cliff kissed the top of my ear and pulled me closer.

"Oh, please, must you two always be so in love?" Jake came in through the sliding glass doors.

"Yes," Cliff and I answered together.

"All right. If you insist."

Jake smiled at me and squeezed my arm before walking around us and toward the kitchen. If Cliff thought his behavior was odd, he didn't say anything.

Jake and I had had many conversations about me kissing everyone, about me kissing him. Mostly, we laughed, but he made sure I knew that he knew who those kisses had been meant for and that I probably still had some issues to work through. I didn't argue.

Gram was at the barbecue, too. Her nightmares were totally gone, and she was extremely grateful that the mysteries and murders had been solved.

I'd invited Roy, Todd, April, and even Paul. Paul had declined. So had Todd and April. Apparently, they had a date—with each other. I almost applauded when April told me as much on the phone. Apparently there had been nothing strange at all about Todd retrieving a tool that had fallen off the back of a Trigger. It hadn't been a wrench, though, it had been a screwdriver. Derek and April had never gone out, and Lynn had never tried to arrange anything with her.

Roy had joined us, too, and was in the back, working on an idea to make the umbrella over my parents' patio table go up and down easier. I was sure he'd figure it out. I was excited to hear that he and the woman he'd met online were going to meet in person in one week. We were all thrilled for him and Gram was giving him extra private cooking lessons. He was turning into quite the foodie. I'd already bought him some new clothes, but I hadn't told him about them yet. I was still working on the best way to approach the subject of his lacking wardrobe.

"Hey," Cliff said softly.

"Yes?" I said just as softly.

"I want you to think about something."

"Okay."

"Start putting a little thought into us getting married. You'll need some time to let the idea soak in so I'm bringing it up now. But there just might be a proposal in your near future. Maybe."

I pulled away, turned around, and looked at Cliff. This was not a huge surprise. He and I had been destined to marry since we were in high school, or so everyone thought.

But it was still a shocking moment. "Really?" I said, not able to keep from smiling.

"Well, this isn't official yet. Just think about it. I want you to be sure."

I nodded, but I couldn't find the words to go with the swell in my chest.

Cliff laughed and then kissed my forehead. "You seem agreeable, but your eyes tell me you are scared to death. We'll go slow, Isabelle, I promise. I'll go tell Teddy what you want to eat."

Isabelle? He never called me Isabelle.

I watched him exit back out the sliding glass doors and tried to figure out what I was feeling.

Happiness? Fear? Anxiety at the idea of commitment? Loving the idea of starting my own family? Worried about what Jerome would feel and think? Yep, all that, but other than the Jerome part, the rest of my emotions were probably pretty normal.

I looked in the mirror. I inspected it. I bored my eyes into it.

"You there?" I whispered.

No one answered.

"What's up?" Jake said, as he emerged from the kitchen.

"Nothing," I said.

"Beautiful mirror," he said. "Help me get this stuff out to the patio. You take the ketchup and mustard. I'll get the rest."

I grabbed the bottles and glanced into the glass one more time before I followed Jake out to the patio.

All that was there was me, and I was smiling.

Recipes

Onion, Corn, and Tomato Salad

33 ounces whole-kernel corn, either thawed or fresh

2 large tomatoes, diced

1 large sweet onion, cut into thin strips

4 green onions, chopped

1 bunch cilantro, minced

Juice of 2 limes

1/3 cup rice vinegar

salt, to taste

Mix all of the ingredients together, adding the vinegar and salt last. Cover and chill for an hour. Serve.

Serves 8 to 12

Cauliflower Au Gratin

1 medium head of cauliflower

4 cups water

1 cup sour cream, halved

1 cup sharp cheddar cheese, grated and halved

1 teaspoon toasted sesame seeds, halved

Salt and pepper, to taste

Preheat oven to 350°F. Separate the cauliflower into flowerets. Heat the water to boiling, then add a pinch of salt and the cauliflower. Cook for ten to twelve minutes until tender. Drain. Place half of cauliflower in a 1-½ quart casserole dish. Season with salt and pepper. Spread half of the sour cream, half of the cheese, and half of the sesame seeds over the cauliflower. Repeat layers. Bake 15 minutes or until cheese melts.

Serves 6

Broccoli Rice Casserole

2 cups cooked white rice

3 packages (10 ounces each) frozen chopped broccoli, cooked and drained

1 can (10-¾ ounces) cream of mushroom soup

1 can (8 ounces) sliced water chestnuts, drained

1 can (8 ounces) bamboo shoots, drained

1 jar (8 ounces) Cheez Whiz (yep, Cheez Whiz)

½ cup butter, melted

8 ounces cheddar cheese, grated

1 jar (2 ounces) pimientos, drained

Preheat oven to 325°F. Combine all ingredients except cheddar cheese and pimientos. Pour into a greased three-quart casserole dish. Sprinkle cheddar cheese and pimientos over the top. Bake 30 to 40 minutes.

Serves 8-10

Sweet and Sour Asparagus

2/3 cup white vinegar

½ cup sugar

½ teaspoon salt

1 teaspoon whole cloves

3 sticks cinnamon

1 tablespoon celery seed

½ cup water

3 or 4 cans (fifteen ounces each) asparagus spears, drained

In a saucepan, combine all ingredients except asparagus spears, and bring to a boil. Place asparagus in a shallow casserole dish and pour marinade over them. Cover and refrigerate 24 to 48 hours. Drain and discard marinade, and serve asparagus.

Serves 8 to 10

Onion Rings

1 large onion, cut into ¼ inch rings

1 ½ cups flour

1 teaspoon baking powder

1 teaspoon Lawry's Seasoned Salt

1 egg

1 cup or so milk

¾ cup dry breadcrumbs

Salt to taste

1 quart or so vegetable oil for frying

Heat the oil in a deep-fryer to 350°F.

In a small bowl, mix together the flour, baking powder, and Lawry's salt.

Dip the onion rings into the flour mixture and set aside.

Whisk the egg and milk and then add to the flour mixture.

Dip the rings into the mixture again and set on a wire rack so the excess drips off the rings.

Place the breadcrumbs on a plate or flat surface. Place the dipped rings in the crumbs, coating as thoroughly as possible, and then shake off excess.

Deep fry the rings a few at a time for 2 to 3 minutes. Place on paper towels to drain. Salt to taste. Serve.

Serves 3

Made in the USA
Columbia, SC
16 July 2021